Alexander Leighton

Mysterious Legends of Edinburgh

Alexander Leighton

Mysterious Legends of Edinburgh

ISBN/EAN: 9783337393311

Printed in Europe, USA, Canada, Australia, Japan

Cover: Foto ©Andreas Hilbeck / pixelio.de

More available books at **www.hansebooks.com**

MYSTERIOUS LEGENDS

OF

EDINBURGH.

NOW FOR THE FIRST TIME TOLD IN PRINT.

BY

ALEXANDER LEIGHTON,

AUTHOR OF "CURIOUS STORIED TRADITIONS," ETC., ETC.

EDINBURGH:
WILLIAM P. NIMMO.
1864.

PREFACE.

IN presenting to those readers who are fond of a story, this book,—in the preparation of which, happily, there has been small expense of either the oil of Demosthenes, the wine of Anacreon, or the opium of Coleridge,—the author has a few words to say as to the class to which it belongs; and these have been suggested by a descriptive epithet bestowed by an influential journal on his prior work of "Storied Traditions." These have been baptized "annalistic fiction,"—a term not altogether happy, insomuch as, according to the authority of Sir Walter Scott's euphuistic knight of the sheers, it may, and, if sound, ought to stand the test of being reversed, so that we would have, as the characteristic of the book, "feigned annals." This would certainly be untrue, for the annals, however meagre, and, so far as regards quantity, like another knight's ration of bread, are, nevertheless, not fiction, any more than the said bread was spiced sack.

If it were to be objected, that while he has generally indicated his sources, he has not stated the amount of matter derived from them, it may be a very good answer to say, that his object was merely to tell a story which might be invested with so much more of that verisimilitude derived from an imitation of nature as would result from truth being at the bottom of the superstructure. Belief is still the enigma of

the metaphysician. Without going into nominalistic subtleties, we are all aware, at least we ought to be, that belief in a
narrative of bygone events is influenced by the words being
taken for the things they represent, much in the same way as
retinal images are taken for the objects that impress them.
We neither hear the past events, nor do we see the present
objects, and hence it is that our affections are called up by a
good imitation, as well as by the reality. Even where there is
nothing in nature for the words to represent, they still work
their effect by something we might call "verbal perception;"
the truth being, as Malebranche has shewn us long ago, that
what we call our beliefs—often nothing more than verbal impressions sealed by authority—are intended primarily to prompt
our affections, and instigate us to action ; any other use of
them being apparently destined to lead us by exhaustive definitions into doubts and perplexities. It may, indeed, be questioned whether the stanchest belief entertained by an adult
could be stronger than the child's conviction of the truth of
" Goody Two-shoes." Yet withal there are *degrees* in this
working : there must be in words so much, at least, of a
representative power as to recommend them to the reason ;
and the author hopes the reader will find this much in these
Mysterious Legends.

YORK LODGE, TRINITY, *May* 1864.

CONTENTS.

	PAGE
LORD KAMES'S PUZZLE,	I
MRS CORBET'S AMPUTATED TOE,	30
THE BROWNIE OF THE WEST BOW,	57
THE ANCIENT BUREAU,	83
A LEGEND OF HALKERSTON'S WYND,	119
LANG SANDY WOOD'S WATCH,	145
DEACON MACGILLIVRAY'S DISAPPEARANCE,	168
LORD BRAXFIELD'S CASE OF THE RED NIGHTCAP,	191
THE STRANGE STORY OF SARAH GOWANLOCK,	216
JOHN CAMERON'S LIFE POLICY,	242

MYSTERIOUS LEGENDS

OF

EDINBURGH.

————⊹❦⊹————

Lord Kames's Puzzle.

N looking over some Session papers which had
belonged to Lord Kames, with the object, I con-
fess, of getting hold of some facts—those entities
called by Quintilian the bones of truth, the more
by token, I fancy, that they so often stick in the throat—
which might contribute to my legends, I came to some sheets
whereon his lordship had written some hasty remarks, to the
effect that the case Napier *versus* Napier was the most curious
puzzle that ever he had witnessed since he had taken his seat
on the bench. The papers were fragmentary, consisting of
parts of a Reclaiming Petition and some portion of a Proof
that had been led in support of a brieve of service; but I got
enough to enable me to give the story, which I shall do in
such a connected manner as to take the reader along with
me, I hope pleasantly, and without any inclination to choke
upon the foresaid bones.

Without being very particular about the year, which really I
do not know with further precision than that it was within the
first five years of Lord Kames's senatorship, I request the

A

reader to fancy himself in a small domicile in Toddrick's Wynd, in the old city of Edinburgh ; and I request this the more readily that, as we all know, nature does not exclude very humble places from the regions of romance, neither does she deny to very humble personages the characters of heroes and heroines. Not that I have much to say in the first instance either of the place or the persons, the former being no more than a solitary room and a bed-closet,—where yet the throb of life was as strong and quick as in the mansions of the great,—and the latter composed of two persons: one, a decent, hard-working woman called Mrs Hislop, whose duty in this world was to keep her employers clean in their clothes; wherein she stood next to the minister, insomuch as cleanliness is next to godliness—in other words, she was a washerwoman ; the other being a young girl, verging upon sixteen, called Henrietta, whose qualities, both of mind and body, might be comprised in the homely eulogy, " as blithe as bonny." So it may be that if you are alarmed at the humility of the occupation of the one—even with your remembrance that Sir Isaac Newton experimented upon soap-bubbles—as being so intractable in the plastic-work of romance, you may be appeased by the qualities of the other ; for has it not been our delight to sing for a thousand years, yea, in a thousand songs too, the praises of young damsels, whether under the names of Jenny or Peggy, or those of Clarinda or Florabella, or whether engaged in herding flocks by Logan Waters, or dispensing knights' favours under the peacock? But we cannot afford to dispose of our young heroine in this curt way, for her looks formed parts of the lines of a strange history, and so we must be permitted the privilege of narrating that, while Mrs Hislop's *protégée* did not come within that charmed circle which contains—according to the poets—so many angels without wings, she was probably as fair every whit as Dowsabell. Yet, after all, we are not here concerned with beauty, which, as a specialty in one to one, and

as a universality in all to all, is beyond the power of written description. We have here to do simply with some traits which, being hereditary—not derived from Mrs Hislop —have a bearing upon our strange legend: the very slightest cast in the eyes, which in its piquancy belied a fine genial nature in the said Henney; and a classic nose, which, partaking of the old Roman type, and indicating pride, was equally untrue to a generosity of feeling which made friends of all who saw her—*except one.* A strange exception this *one;* for who, even in this bad world, could be an enemy to a creature who conciliated sympathy as a love, and defied antipathy as an impossibility? Who could *he* be? or rather who could *she* be? for man seems to be excluded by the very instincts of his nature. The question may be answered by the evolution of facts; than which what other have we even amidst the dark gropings into the mystery of our wonderful being?

Mrs Hislop's head was over the skeil, wherein lay one of the linen sheets of Mr Dallas, the writer to the signet; which, with her broad hands, she was busy twisting into the form of a serpent, and no doubt there were indications of her efforts in the drops of perspiration which stood upon her good-humoured, gaucy face, so suggestive of dewdrops ('bating the poetry) on the leaves of a big blush peony. In this work she was interrupted by the entrance of Henney, who came rushing in as if under the influence of some emotion which had taken her young heart by surprise.

"What think ye, minny?" she cried, as she held up her hands.

"The deil has risen again from the grave where **he was** buried in Kirkcaldy," was the reply, with a laugh.

" No, that's no it," continued the girl.

" Then what is it?" was the question.

" He's dead," replied Henney

" Who is dead?" again asked Mrs Hislop.

"The strange man," replied the girl.

And a reply, too, which brought the busy worker to a pause in her work, for she understood who the *he* was, and the information went direct through the ear to the heart; but Henney, supposing that she was not understood, added—

"The man who used to look at me with yon terrible eyes."

"Yes, yes, dear, I understand you," said the woman, as she let the coil fall, and sat down upon a chair, under the influence of strong emotion. "But who told you?"

"Jean Graham," replied the girl.

An answer which seemed, for certain reasons known to herself, to satisfy the woman, for the never another word she said, any more than if her tongue had been paralysed by the increased action of her heart; but, as we usually find that when that organ in woman is quiet more useful powers come into action, so the sensible dame began to exercise her judgment. A few minutes sufficed for forming a resolution, nor was it sooner formed than it was begun to be put into action, yet not before the excited girl was away, no doubt to tell some of her companions of her relief from the bugbear of the man with the terrible eyes. The formation of a purpose might have been observed in her puckered lips and the speculation in her gray eyes. The spirit of romance had visited the small house in Toddrick's Wynd, where for fifteen years the domestic *lares* had sat quietly surveying the economy of poverty. She rose composedly from the chair into which the effect of Henney's exclamation had thrown her, went to the blue chest which contained her holiday suit, took out, one after another, the chintz gown, the mankie petticoat, the curch, the red plaid; and, after washing from her face the perspiration-drops, she began to put on her humble finery—all the operation having been gone through with that quiet action which belongs to strong minds where resolution has settled the quivering chords of doubt.

Following the dressed dame up the High Street, we next find her in the writing-booth of Mr James Dallas, writer to Her Majesty's signet. The gentleman was, after the manner of his tribe, minutely scanning some papers—that is, he was looking into them so sharply that you would have inferred that he was engaged in hunting for "flaws;" a species of game that is both a prey and a reward—*et præda et premium*, as an old proverb says. Nor shall we say he was altogether pleased when he found his inquiry, whatever it might be, interrupted by the entrance of Mrs Margaret Hislop of Toddrick's Wynd ; notwithstanding that to this personage he and Mrs Dallas, and all the Dallases, were indebted for the whiteness of their linen. No doubt she would be wanting payment of her account ; yet why apply to him, and not to Mrs Dallas? And, besides, it needed only one glance of the writer's eye to shew that his visitor had something more of the look of a client than a cleaner of linen—a conclusion which was destined to be confirmed, when the woman, taking up one of the high-backed chairs in the room, placed it right opposite to the man of law, and, hitching her round body into something like stiff dignity, seated herself. Nor was this change from her usual deportment the only one she underwent ; for, as soon appeared, her style of speech was to pass from broad Scotch, not altogether into the " Inglis " of the upper ranks, but into a mixture of the two tongues—a feat which she performed very well, and for which she had been qualified by having lived in the service of the great.

"And so Mr Napier of Eastleys is dead ?" she began.

"Yes," answered the writer, perhaps with a portion of cheerfulness, seeing he was that gentleman's agent, or "doer," as it was then called—a word far more expressive, as many clients can testify, at least after they are " done ;" and seeing also that a dead client is not finally "done" until his affairs are wound-up and consigned to the green box.

" And wha is his heir, think ye ?" continued his questioner.

" Why, Charles Napier, his nephew," answered the writer, somewhat carelessly.

" I 'm no just a'thegither sure of that, Mr Dallas," said she, with another effort at dignity, which was unfortunately qualified by a knowing wink.

" The deil 's in the woman," was the sharp retort, as the writer opened his eyes wider than he had done since he laid down his parchments.

" The deil 's in me or no in me," said she ; " but this I 'm sure of, that Henrietta Hislop,—that 's our Henney, ye ken,— the brawest and bonniest lass in Toddrick's Wynd, (and that 's no saying little,) is the lawful heiress of Mr John Napier of Eastleys, and was called Henrietta after her mother."

" The honest woman 's red wud," said the writer, laughing. "Why, Mrs Hislop, I always took you for a shrewd, sensible woman. Do you really think that, because you bore a child to Mr John Napier, that therefore Henney Hislop is the heiress of her reputed father ?"

" *Me* bear a bairn to Mr Napier!" cried the offended client. " Wha ever said I was the mother of Henney Hislop ?"

" Everybody," replied he. " We never doubted it, though I admit she has none of your features."

" Everybody is a leear then," rejoined the woman, tartly. " There 's no a drap of blood in the lassie's body can claim kindred with me or mine ; though, if it were so, it would be no dishonour, for the Hislops were lairds of Highslaps in Ayrshire at the time of Malcolm Mucklehead."

" And whose daughter, by the mother's side, is she then ?" asked he, as his curiosity began to wax stronger.

" Ay, you have now your hand on the cocked egg," replied she, with a look of mystery. " The other was a wind ane, and you 've just to sit a little and you 'll see the chick."

The writer settled himself into attention, and the good dame thought it proper, like some preachers who pause two or three minutes (the best part of their discourse) after they have given out the text, to raise a wonder how long they intend to hold their tongue, and thereby produce attention, retained her speech until she had attained the due solemnity.

"It is now," she began, in a low mysterious voice, "just sixteen years come June,—and if ye want the day, it will be the 15th,—and if ye want the hour, we may say eleven o'clock at night, when I was making ready for my bed,—I heard a knock at my door, and the words of a woman, 'Oh, Mrs Hislop, Mrs Hislop!' So I ran and opened the door; and wha think ye I saw but Jean Graham, Mr Napier's cook, with een like twa candles, and her mouth as wide as if she had been to swallow the biggest sup of porridge that ever crossed ploughman's craig?"

"'What's ado, woman?' said I, for I thought something fearful had happened.

"'Oh,' cried she, 'my lady's lighter, and ye're to come to Meggat's Land, even noo, this minute, and bide nae man's hindrance.'

"'And so I will,' said I, as I threw my red plaid ower my head; then I blew out my cruse, and out we came, jol ing each other in the dark passage through sheer hurry and confusion— down the Canongate, till we came to Meggat's Land, in at the kitchen door, ben a dark passage, up a stair, then ben another passage, till we came to a back-room, the door of which was opened by somebody inside. I was bewildered, the light in the room made my een reel; but I soon came to myself, when I saw a man and Mrs Kemp, the howdie, busy rowing something in flannel.

"'Get along,' said the man to Jean; 'you're not wanted here.'

"And as Jean made off, Mrs Kemp turned to me—

"'Come here, Mrs Hislop,' said she.

" So I slipt forward ; but the never a word more was said for ten minutes, they were so intent on getting the bairn all right, —for, ye ken, sir, it was a new-born babe they were busy with, —they were as silent as the grave, and, indeed, everything was so still that I heard their breathing like a rushing of wind, though they breathed just as they were wont to do. And when they had finished—

" ' Mrs Hislop,' said the man, as he turned to me, ' you 're to take this child and bring it up as your own, or anybody else's you like, except Mr Napier's, and you 're never to say when or how you got it, for it is a banned creature, with the curse upon it of a malison for the sins of him who begot it and of her who bore it. Swear to it,' and he held up his hand.

" And I swore ; but I thought I would just take the advice of the Lord how far my words would bind me to do evil, or leave me to do guid when the time came. So I took the bairn into my arms.

" ' And wha will pay for the wet nurse ?' said I ; ' for ye ken I am as dry as a yeld crummie ; but there is a woman in Toddrick's Wynd wha lost her bairn yestreen—she is threatened with a milk-fever, and by my troth this little stranger will cure her—but, besides the nourice-fee, there is my trouble.'

" ' I was coming to that,' said he, ' if your supple tongue had left you power to hear mine. In this leathern purse there are twenty gowden guineas — a goodly sum — but, whether goodly or no, you must be content ; yea, the never a penny more you may expect, for all connexion between this child and this house, or its master, is to be from this moment finished for ever.'

" And a guid quittance it was I thought, with a bonny bairn and twenty guineas on my side, and nothing on the other but maybe a father's anger and salt tears, besides the wrath of God against those who forsake their children. So with thankfulness enough I carried away my bundle ; and ye'll guess that Henney Hislop is now the young woman of fifteen who was then that child of a day."

"And is this all the evidence," said the writer, "you have to prove that Henrietta Hislop is the daughter of Mr and Mrs Napier ?"

" Maybe no," replied she ; " if ye weren't so like the English stranger wha curst the Scotch kail because he did not see on the table the beef that was coming from the kitchen, besides the haggis and the bread-pudding. You've only as yet got the broth, and, for the rest, I will give you Mrs Kemp, wha told me, as a secret, that the child was brought into the world by her own hands from the living body of Mrs Napier. Will that satisfy you ?"

"No," replied Mr Dallas, who had got deeper and deeper into a study. " Mr Napier, I know, was at home that evening when his wife bore a child ; that child never could have been given away without his consent ; and as for the consent itself, it is a still greater improbability, seeing that he was always anxious for an heir to Eastleys."

"And so maybe he was," replied she ; " but I see you are only at the beef yet, and you may be better pleased when you have got the haggis, let alone the pudding. Yea, it is even likely Mr Napier wanted an heir ; and, what is more, he got one, at least an heiress ; but sometimes God gives and the devil misgives, and so it was here, for Mr Napier took it into his head that the child was not his, and, in place of being pleased with an heir, he thought himself cursed with a bastard, begotten on his wife by no other than Captain Preston, his lady's cousin. And where did the devil find that poison growing but in the heart of Isabel Napier, the sister of that very Charles who is now thinking he will heir Eastleys by pushing aside poor Henney? And then the poison, like the old apple, was so fair and tempting; for Mr Napier had been married ten years, and enjoyed the love that is so bonny 'a little while when it is new,' and yet had no children, till this one came so exactly nine months after the captain's visit to Scotland that Satan had little more to do than hold up the temptation. You see, sir, how things come round; but still, according to the old fashion, after a long weary, dreary turn. Mrs Napier died next day after the birth; Mr Napier lived a miserable man; Henney was brought up in poverty and sometimes distress, but now I hope she has come to her kingdom."

Here Mrs Hislop stopt, and as there could be no better winding-up of a romance than by bringing her heroine to her kingdom at last, she felt so well pleased with her conclusion that she could afford to wait longer for her expected applause than the fair story-tellers in the *brigata* under Queen Pampinea; and it was as well that she was thus fortified, for the writer, in place of declaring his satisfaction with her proofs, seemed, as he lay back in his chair in a deep reverie, to be occupied once more in hunting for flaws. At length raising himself on his chair, and fixing his eyes upon her with that look of scepticism which a writer assumes when he addresses a would-be new client who wants to push out an old one with a better right :—

"Mrs Hislop," said he, "if it had not been that I have always taken you for an honest woman, I would say that you are art and part in fabricating a story without a particle of foundation. There may possibly be some mystery about the birth and parentage of the young girl. You may have got her out of the house of Meggat's Land in the Canongate from a man,—not Mr Napier, you admit,—who may have been the father of it by some mother residing in the house; and Mrs Kemp may have been actuated by some unknown means to remove the paternity from the right to the wrong person. All this is possible; but that the child could be that one which Mrs Napier bore is impossible, for this reason, and I beg of you to listen to it, that Mrs Napier's child *was dead-born, and was, according to good evidence, buried in the same coffin with the mother.*"

A statement this which, delivered in the solemn manner of an attorney who was really honest, and who knew much of this history, appeared to Mrs Hislop so strange that her tongue was paralysed—an effect which had never before been produced by any one of all the five causes of the metaphysicians. Even her eyes seemed to have lost their power of movement, and as for her wits, they had, like those of the renowned Astolpho, surely left her and taken refuge in the moon.

"If you are not satisfied with my words," continued the writer, (no doubt ironically, for where could he have found better evidence of the effect of his statement?) "I will give you writing for the truth of what I have said to you."

And rising and going towards a green tin box, he opened the same, and taking therefrom a piece of paper, he resumed his seat.

"Now listen," said he, as he unfolded an old yellow-coloured sheet of paper, and then he read these words :—"'Your presence is requested at the funeral of Henrietta Preston, my wife, and of a child still-born, from my house, Meggat's Land, Canongate, to the burying-ground at St Cuthbert's, on Friday the 19th of this month June, at one o'clock ;' and the name at this letter," continued Mr Dallas, "is that of 'John Napier of Eastleys.' Will that satisfy you?"

And the "doer" for Mr Charles Napier, conceiving that he had at last effectually "done" his client's opponent, seemed well pleased to sit and witness the further effect of his evidence on the bewildered woman ; but we are to remember that a second stroke sometimes only takes away the pain of the former, and a repetition of blows will quicken the reaction which slumbered under the first. Whether this was so or not in our present instance, or whether Mrs Hislop had recovered her wits by a process far shorter than that followed by the foresaid Astolpho, we know not, but certain it is that she recovered the powers of both her eyes and her tongue in much less time than the writer expected, and in a manner, too, very different from that for which he was probably prepared.

"Weel," replied she, smiling, "it would just seem that even the haggis has not pleased you, Mr Dallas;" and, putting her hand into a big side-pocket, that might have served a gaberlunzie for a wallet, she extracted a small piece of paper. She continued : " But ye see a guid, honest Scotchwoman's no to be suspected of being shabby at her own table; so read ye that, which you may take for the bread-pudding."

And the writer, having taken the paper and held it before his face for so long a time that it might have suggested the suspicion that the words therein written stuck in his eyes and would not submit to that strange process whereby, unknown to ourselves, we transfer written vocables to the ear before we can understand them, turned a look upon the woman of dark suspicion :—

"Where, in God's name, got you this?" he said.

"Just read it out first," replied she. "Ye read yer ain paper, and why no mine?"

And the writer read, perhaps more easily than he could understand, the strange words :—

" This child, born of my wife, and yet neither of my blood nor my lineage, I repudiate, and, unable to push it back into the dark world of nothing from which it came, I leave it with a scowl to the mercy which countervaileth the terrible decree whereby the sins of the parent shall be visited on the child. This I do on the 15th of June 17—. JOHN NAPIER, of East-leys, in the county of Mid Lothian."

After reading this extraordinary denunciation, Mr Dallas sat and considered, as if at a loss what to say ; but whether it was that scepticism was at the root of his thoughts, or that he assumed it as a mask to conceal misgivings to which he did not like to confess, he put a question :—

" Where got you this notable piece of evidence ? "

" Ay," replied Mrs Hislop, " you are getting reasonable on the last dish. That bit of paper, which to me and my dear Henney is worth the haill estate of Eastleys, was found by me carefully pinned to the flannel in which the child was wrapt."

" Wonderful enough surely," repeated he, "*if true* "—the latter words being pronounced with emphasis which made the rough liquid letter sound like a hurling stone ; " but," he continued, "the whole document, in its terms of crimination and exposure, and not less the wild manner of its application, is so unlike the act of a man not absolutely frantic, that I cannot believe it to be genuine."

" But you know, Mr Dallas," replied she, " that Mr John Napier was a man who, if he threw a stone, cared little whether it struck the kirk window or the mill door."

" That is so far true ; but, passionate and unforgiving as he was, he was not so reckless as to be regardless whether the stone did not come back on his own head."

" And it 's no genuine," she resumed, as, disregarding his latter words, she relapsed into her more familiar dialect. " The Lord help ye ! canna ye look at first the ae paper and then the ither ? and if they 're no alike, mustna the ither be the forgery ? "

An example of the conditional syllogism which might have amused even a writer to the signet, if he had not been at the very moment busy in the examination of the handwriting of the funeral letter and that of the paper of repudiation and malison—the resemblance, or rather the identity, of which was so striking as to reduce all his theories to confusion.

" By all that 's good in heaven, the same," he muttered to himself ; and then, addressing his visitor, " I confess, Mrs Hislop," said he, " that this paper has driven me somewhat off

my point of confidence; but I suppose you will see that, if the
child was actually, as the letter indicates, buried with its mother,
Henrietta's rights are at an end. It is just possible, however,
I fairly admit, that Mr Napier, who was a very eccentric man,
may have so worded the letter as to induce the world to believe
that the so-considered illegitimate child had been dead-born,
while he gratified—privately he might verily think—his vengeance by writing this terrible curse. Still, I think you are
wrong; but as this wonderful paper gives you a plausible plea,
I would recommend you to Mr White, in Mill's Court, who
will see to the young woman's rights. He will be the flint
and I the steel; and between our friendly opposition, we will
produce a spark which will light up the candle of truth."

" Ay," replied she; "only, as the spark of fire comes from the
steel, we 'll just suppose you are the flint: and, by my troth,
you 're hard enough ; but, come as it may, it will light the
lantern that will shew Henney Napier to the bonny haughs of
Eastleys."

Mrs Hislop, having got back her paper from Mr Dallas,
left the writer's chambers, and directed her steps to Mill's
Court, where she found Mr White, even as she had Mr
Dallas, busy poring over law papers. She was, as we have
seen, one of those people who can make their own intro-
duction acceptable, and, moreover, one of those women, few
as they are, who can tell a story with the continuity and
fitting emphasis necessary to secure the attention of a busy
listener. So Mr White heard her narrative not only with
interest, but even a touch of the pervading sympathy of the
spirit of romance ; and so he might, for who doesn't see
that the charm of mystery can be enhanced by the hope of
turning it to account of money? Then he was so much of a
practical man as to know that while every string has two ends,
the true way to get hold of both is to make sure in the first
place of one. Wherefore he began to interrogate his client

as to who could speak to the doings in the house in Meggat's Land on that eventful night when the child was born; and having taken notes of the answers to his questions, he paused a little, as if to consider what was the first step he ought to take into the region of doubt, and perhaps of intrigue, where at least there must be lies floating about like films in the clear atmosphere of truth. Nor had he meditated many minutes till he rose, and taking up his square hat and his gold-headed cane, he said—

" Come, we will try what we can discover in a quarter where an end of the ravelled string ought to be found, whether complicated into a knot by the twisting power of self-interest or no."

And, leading the way, he proceeded with his client down the High Street, where, along under the glimmering lamps, were the usual crowds of loungers, composed of canny Saxon and fiery Celt, which have always made this picturesque thoroughfare so remarkable. Not one of all these had any interest for our two searchers; but it was otherwise when they came toward the Canongate Tolbooth, where, out from a dark entry sprang a young woman, and bounding forward seized our good dame round the neck. This was no other than Henney Hislop herself, who, having been alarmed at the long absence of her " mother," as she called her, and of course believed her to be, was so delighted to find her that she sobbed out her joy in such an artless way, that even the writer owned it was interesting to behold. Nor was the picture without other traits calculated to engage attention; for the girl whose fortunes had been so strange, and were perhaps destined to be still more strange, was dressed in the humblest garb,—the short gown and the skirt peculiar to the time,—but then, every tint was so bright with pure cleanliness, the ear-rings set off so fine a skin, the indispensable strip of purple round the head imparted so much of the grace of the old classic wreath ; and, beyond all this,

which might be said to be extraneous, her features—if you
abated the foresaid cast or slight squint in the eyes, which imparted a piquancy—were so regular, if not handsome, that you
could not have denied that she deserved to be a Napier, if she
was not a very Napier in reality.   A few words whispered in
Mrs Hislop's ear, and the girl was off, leaving our couple
to proceed on their way.   Even this incident had its use; for
Mr White, who had known Mr Napier, and had faith (as
who has not?) in the hereditary descent of bodily aspects,
could not restrain himself from the remark, however much it
might inflame the hopes of his client:—

"The curse has left no blight there," said he.   "That is the
very face of Mr Napier,—the high nose especially,—and as
for the eyes, with that unmistakeable cast, why, I have seen
their foretypes in the head of John Napier a hundred
times."

An observation so congenial to Mrs Hislop, that she could
not help being a little humorous, even in the depth of an
anxiety which had kept her silent for the full space of ten
minutes:—

"Nose, sir! there wasn't a man frae the Castle yett to
Holyrood wha could have produced that nose except John
Napier."

And without further interruption than her own laugh, they
proceeded till they came to the entry called Big Lochend
Close, up which they went some forty or fifty steps, till they
came to an outer door, which led by a short dark passage to
two or three inner doors in succession, all leading to separate
rooms occupied by separate people.   No sooner had they
turned into this passage than they encountered a woman in
a plaid and with a lantern in her hand, who had just left the
third or innermost room, and whose face, as it peered through
the thick folds of her head-covering, was illuminated by a gleam
from the light she carried.   She gave them little opportunity

for examination, having hurried away as if she had been afraid
of being searched for stolen property.

"Isbel Napier," whispered Mrs Hislop: "she wha first
brought evil into the house of the Napiers, with all its woe."

"And who bodes us small hope here," said he, "if she has
been with the nurse."

And entering the room from which the ill-omening woman
had issued, they found another, even her of whom they were
in search, sitting by the fire, torpid and corpulent, to a degree
which indicated that as it had been her trade to nurse others,
she had not forgotten herself in her ministrations.

"Mrs Temple," said Mr White, who saw the policy of
speaking fair the woman who had been so recently in the
company of an evil genius, "I am glad to find you so stout
and hearty."

"Neither o' the twa, sir," replied she; "for I am rather
weak and heartless. Many ane I hae nursed into health and
strength, but a' nursing comes hame in the end."

"And some, no doubt, have died under your care," continued the writer, with a view to introduce his subject; "and
therefore you should be grateful for the life that is still spared
to you. You could not save the life of Mrs Napier."

"That's an auld story and a waefu' ane," she replied, with
a side look at Mrs Hislop; "and I hae nae heart to mind it.
Some said the lady wasna innocent, and doubtless Mr Napier
thought sae, for he took high dealings wi' her, and looked at
her wi' a scorn that would have scathed whinstanes. Sae it
was better she was taen awa; ay, and her baby wi' her, for if
it had lived it would have dree'd the revenge o' that stern
man."

"The child!" said Mr White, "did it die too?"

"Dee! ye may rather ask if it ever lived; for it never drew
breath, in this world at least."

A statement so strange that it brought the eyes of the two

B

visitors to each other, and no doubt both of them recurred in memory to the statement in the funeral letter, which, whatever may have been the case with the assertion now made by the nurse, never could have been dictated by her they had met in the passage; and no doubt, also, they both remembered the statement made by Mr Dallas, to the effect that both the mother and child were buried together.

"Never drew breath, you say, nurse!" resumed Mr White, with an air of astonishment; "why, I have been given to understand, not only that the child was born alive, but that it is actually living now."

"Weel," replied the nurse, "maybe St Cuthbert has wrought a miracle, and brought the child out o' the grave by the West Church; but he has wrought nae miracle on me to mak' me forget what my een saw, and my hands did, that day when I helped to place the dead body o' the innocent on the breast o' its dead mother; ay, and bent her stiff arms sae as to bring them ower her bairn, just as if she had been faulding it to her bosom. And sae in this fashion were they buried."

"And you would swear to that, Mrs Temple?" said the writer.

"Ay, upon fifty Bibles, ane after anither," was the reply, in something like a tone of triumph.

Nor could the woman be induced to swerve from these assertions, notwithstanding repeated interrogations; and the writer was left to the conclusion—which he preferred, rather than place any confidence in the funeral letter—that the nurse's statement was in some mysterious way connected with the visit of Isobel Napier; and yet, not so very mysterious after all, when we are to consider that her brother was preparing to claim Eastleys, as well as the valuable furniture of the house in Meggat's Land, as the nearest lawful heir of his deceased uncle. The salvo was at least comfortable to both Mr White and his client, and no doubt it helped to lighten their steps as, bidding adieu to the "hard witness," they left her to the nursing which comes "aye hame in the end."

But their inquiries were not finished; and, retracing their steps up the Canongate, they landed in the Fountain Close, where, under the leading of Mrs Hislop, the writer was procured another witness, with a name already familiar to him through the communication of his client, and this was no other than that same Jean Graham, who was sent to Toddrick's Wynd on that eventful night fifteen years before, to bring Mrs Hislop to the house in Meggat's Land; one of those simple souls—we wish there were more of them in the world—who look upon a lie as rather an operose affair, and who seem to be truthful from sheer laziness. There was, accordingly, no difficulty here; for the woman rolled off her story just as if it had been coiled up in her mind for all that length of time.

"There was a terrible stir in the house that night," she began. "The nurse, wha is yet living in Lochend Close, and Mrs Kemp, the howdie, wha is dead, were wi' my lady; and John Cowie, the butler, was busy attending our master, who had been the haill day in ane o' his dark fits, for we heard him calling for Cowie in a fierce voice ever and again; and his step sounded ower our heads upon the floor as he walked back and fore in his wrath. Then I was sent for you, and brought you, and you'll mind how Cowie bade me go along; but I had mair sense, for I listened at the door and heard what the butler said to ye when he gae ye the bairn; and think ye I didna see ye carry it along the passage as ye left? Sae far I could understand ; but when I heard nurse say the bairn was dead, Mrs Kemp say the bairn was still-born, and Cowie declare it was better it was dead and awa, I couldna comprehend this ava: nor do I weel yet, but we just thought that as there was something wrang between master and my lady, he wanted us to believe that the bairn was dead, for very shame o' being thought the father, when maybe he wasna. And then he was so guid to me and my neighbour Anne Dickson,—ye mind o' her—puir soul, she's dead too,—that we couldna, for the very heart o' us, say a word o' what we knew. But now when Mr Napier is dead, and the brother o' that wicked Jezebel, Isbel Napier, may try to take the property frae Henney, wha I aye kenned as a Napier, with the very nose and een o' the father, I have spoken out; and may the Lord gie the right to whom the right is due!"

"It's all right," said the writer, after he had jotted with a pencil the evidence of Jean, as well as that of the nurse, "and if we could find this John Cowie we might so fortify the orphan's rights, as to defy Miss Napier and her brother, and Mr Dallas, and all the witnesses they can bring."

"Ay," continued the woman, "but I doubt if you'll catch him. He left Mr Napier's service about ten years ago, and I never heard mair o' him."

"Nor I either," said Mrs Hislop.

"Well, we must search for him," added Mr White; "for that man alone, so far as I can see, is he who will unravel this strange business."

And thus the day's work finished. The writer parted for Mill's Court, and Mrs Hislop, filled with doubts, hopes, and anxieties, sought her humble dwelling in Toddrick's Wynd, where Henney waited for her with all the solicitude of a daughter; but a word did not escape her lips that might carry to the girl's mind a suspicion that the golden cord of their supposed relationship ran a risk of being severed, even with the eventual condition that one, if not both of the divisions, would be transmuted into a string of diamonds.

Meanwhile the agent was in his own house revolving all the points of a puzzle more curious than any that had yet come within the scope of his experience. Sometimes he felt confidence, and at other times despair ; and of course he had the consolation which belongs to all litigants, that the opposite party was undergoing the same process of oscillation. It was clear enough that Cowie was the required Œdipus ; and if it should turn out that he was dead, or could not be found, the advantage was, with a slight declination, on the part of Charles Napier ; insomuch as, while he was indisputably the nephew of the deceased, the orphan, Henrietta, was under the necessity of proving her birth and pedigree. And so, as it appeared, Mr Dallas was of that opinion, for the very next day he applied to Chancery for a brieve to get Charles Napier served nearest and lawful heir to his uncle; and as in legal warfare, where the judges are cognisant only of patent claims, there is small room for retiring tactics, Mr White felt himself obliged, however anxious he was to gain time, to follow his opponent's example by taking out a competing brieve in favour of Henrietta.

The parties were now face to face in court, and the battle behoved to be fought out ; but as in all legal cases, where the circumstances are strange or peculiar, the story soon gets wind, so here the Meggat's Land romance was by and by all over the city. Nor did it take less fantastic forms than usual, where sympathies and antipathies are strong in proportion to the paucity of the facts on which they are fed. It was a favourite opinion of some, that the case could only be cleared by supposing that a dead stranger child had been surreptitiously passed off, and even coffined, as the true one; while others, equally skilled in the art of divining, maintained that the child given to Mrs Hislop by Cowie was a bastard of his own, by the terrible woman, Isobel Napier, who was thus, according to the ordinary working of public prejudice, raised to a height of crime sufficient to justify the hatred of the people : on which presumption, it behoved to be assumed that the paper containing the curse was a forgery by Cowie and his associate in crime, and that the money paid to Mrs

Hislop was furnished by the lady—all which suppositions, and others not less incredible, were greedily accepted, for the very reason that it required something prodigious to explain an enigma which exhausted the ordinary sources of man's ingenuity ; just as we find in many religions, where miracles— the more absurd, the more acceptable—are resorted to to explain the mystery of man's relation to God, a secret which no natural light can illuminate.

But all these suppositions were destined to undergo refractions through the medium of a new fact. The case, by technical processes, came before the Court of Session, where the diversity of opinion was, proportionably to the number of the judges, as great as among the quidnuncs outside. The only clear idea in the heads of the robed and wigged wiseacres was, that the case, Napier *versus* Napier, was a puzzle which no man could read or solve. It seemed fated to be as famous as the old Sphinx, the insoluble Mœnander, or the tortuous labyrinth, or the intricate key of Hercules—*ne Ap llo quidem intelligat;* and, if it had not happened that Lord Kames suggested the possibility of getting an additional piece of evidence through the examination of the coffin wherein Mrs Napier was buried, the court might have been sitting over the famous case even in this year of the nineteenth century. The notion was worthy of his lordship's ingenuity, and accordingly a commission was issued to one of the Faculty to proceed to the West Church burying-ground, and there cause to be laid open and examined the coffin of the said Mrs Henrietta Preston or Napier, with the view to ascertain whether or not the body of a child had been placed therein along with the corpse of the mother.

This commission was accordingly executed, and the report bore, that "he, the commissioner, had proceeded to the burying-ground of the parish of St Cuthbert's, and there caused David Scott, the sexton, to lay open the grave of the said Henrietta Preston or Napier, and to open the coffin therein contained ; which having accordingly been done by the said David Scott and his assistants, the commissioner, upon a faithful examination, aided by the experience of the said David Scott, did find the skeletons of two bodies in the said coffin identified as that of the said lady, one whereof was that of a woman apparently of middle age, and the other that of a babe, which lay upon the chest of the larger skeleton in such a way or manner as to be retained or held in that position by the arms of the same being laid across it. That having satisfied himself of these facts, the commissioner caused the coffin to be again closed and the grave covered with all decency and care, and he accordingly made this report to their lordships."

The fact thus ascertained, in opposition to the expectation of those who favoured the orphan, was viewed by the court as depriving, to a great extent, the case of that aspect of a riddle by which it had been so unfortunately distinguished ; and, as the case had been hung up even beyond the time generally occupied by cases at that period, when, as it was sometimes remarked, lawsuits were as often settled by the old rule, *Romanus sedendo vincit*—by the death of one or other of the parties— as by a judgment, the case was again put to the roll for a hearing on the effect of the new evidence. It was contended for the nephew by Mr Wight that the question was now virtually settled, insomuch that the court was not bound to solve riddles, but to find to whom pertained a certain right of inheritance. The birth of the child had been sworn to by the nurse, as well as its death, and the final placing of it in the coffin ; and now the court had as it were ocular demonstration of these facts by the body having been seen by their own commissioner, placed on the breast of the mother in that very peculiar way described by Mrs Temple. All claim on the part of the girl was thus virtually excluded, for the proceedings which took place that evening in another room, under circumstances of suspicion, were sworn to only by Mrs Hislop herself, an inter-

ested witness, and were only partially confirmed by an eavesdropper, who, as eavesdroppers generally do, (except when
their own characters are concerned,) perhaps heard according
as foregone prejudices induced her to wish. These suspicious
proceedings might be explained by as many hypotheses as
had been devised by the wise judges of the taverns, among
which was the theory of the living child being Cowie's own by
Isobel Napier, and palmed off as Mrs Napier's to hide the
shame of the true mother—all unlikely enough, no doubt, but
not so impossible as that the coffined child should now be
alive and awaiting the issue of this case, in the expectation of
being Lady of Eastleys.

On the other side, Mr Andrews, counsel for Henrietta, maintained that while his learned brother assumed the one half of
the case as proved, and repudiated the other as a lie or a
myth, he had a right to embrace the other half, and pronounce the first a stratagem or trick. The proceedings in
the back-room into which Jean Graham introduced Mrs Hislop
were more completely substantiated than those in the bedroom
where Mrs Napier lay ; for while the one were sworn to by Mrs
Hislop herself, a soothfast witness, and confirmed in all points
by the woman Graham, the other were attempted to be proven
by the solitary testimony of the nurse Temple. The paper containing the curse was as indisputably in the handwriting of Mr
Napier as was the funeral letter. The money paid was proved
by the fact that the orphan had been kept and educated for
fifteen years. The name Henrietta was not likely to have
been a mere coincidence, and it was still more unlikely that
a respectable woman such as Mrs Hislop would invent a story
of affiliation so strangely in harmony with the secrets of the
house in Meggat's Land, and fortify it by a forged document.
Then Mrs Hislop was unable to write, and no attempt had
been made on the other side to prove that Henrietta had a
father other than he who was pointed out by the paper of the

curse. So he (the counsel) might follow the example of his brother, and hold the other half of the case to be unexplainable by hypotheses, however ridiculous. The child having been disposed of to Mrs Hislop—a fact thus proved—what was to prevent him (the counsel) from going also to the haunts of the *tabernian* Solons, or anywhere else in the regions of fancy, for the theory that Mr Napier, or some plotter for him in the shape of Mrs Kemp or John Cowie, substituted the dead child of a stranger for the living one of his wife, and bribed the nurse Temple to tell the tale she had told? to which she would be the more ready by the golden promptings of the woman Isobel Napier, the niece, whose brother would, in the event of the stratagem being concealed, succeed to the estate of Eastleys.

At the conclusion of these pleadings, the judges were inclined to be even more humorous than they had been previous to the issuing of the commission, for they had thought they saw their way to a judgment against the orphan. The president, (Braxfield,) it is said, indulged in a joke, to the effect that he had read s*mewhere*—it was not for so religious a man to say where—of a child having been claimed by two mothers; he would like to see two fathers at that work, at least he would not be one; but here the claim was set up by Death on the one side, and Life (if a personification could be allowed) on the other, and they could not follow the old precedent, because he suspected none of their lordships would like to see the grim claimant at the bar to receive his half. And so they chuckled, as judges sometimes do, at their own jokes —generally very bad—altogether oblivious of the fable of the frogs who could see no fun in a game which was death to them; for, as we have indicated, the opinion of a great majority was against the claim of the young woman, nor would the decision have been suspended that day had not Mr Andrews risen and made a statement—perhaps *as* fictitious as a coun-

sel's conscience would permit—to the effect that the agent (Mr
White) had procured some trace of the butler Cowie, who
could throw more light on the case than Death had done, and
that if some time were accorded to complete the inquiry, something might turn up which would alter the complexion even of
this Protean mystery. The request was granted.

But, in truth, Mr Andrews's suggestion was simply a bit of
ingenuity, intended to ward off an unfavourable judgment, and
allow a development of the chapter of accidents ;—a wise
policy, for, as the womb of Time is never empty, so Fate
writes in the morning a chapter of every man's life of a day,
at which in the evening he is sometimes a little surprised. No
trace had yet been got of Cowie — it was not even known
whether he was alive. But if we throw some fourteen days
into the wallet-bag of Saturn, we may come to a day whereupon
a certain person, in an inn far down in a valley of Westmore-
land, and in the little town called Kirby Lonsdale, was busy
reading the *Caledonian Mercury*—for it was not more easy to
say where the winged *Mercury* of that time would not go, than
it is to tell where a certain insect without wings, "which aye
travels south," might not be found in England as an immi-
grant. It was at least no wonder that that paper should contain an account of the romance wrapped up in the case Napier
versus Napier ; and certainly, if we could have judged from
the face of the individual, we would have set him down as one
given to the reading of riddles ; for, after he had perused the
paragraph, he looked as if he knew more about that case than
all the fifteen, with the m..cers to boot. Nor was he contented with an indication of a mere look of wisdom, he
actually burst out into a laugh — an expression wondrously
unsuited to the gravity of the subject. You who read this will
no doubt suspect that we are merely shading this man for
the sake of effect ; and this is true, but you are to remember
that, while we are chroniclers of things mysterious, we **work**

for the advantage to you of putting into your power to
venture a shrewd guess : in making which you are only working in the destined vocation of man, for the world is only
guesswork all over, and you yourself are only guesswork as
a part of it. The reader of the *Mercury* was verily Mr John
Cowie, whilom butler to Mr John Napier, and now waiter
in the Lonsdale Arms of the obscure Kirby,—a place like
Peebles, where, if you wanted to deposit a secret, you could do
so by crying it out at the market-cross,—and, moreover, he was
verily in possession of the key to the Napier mystery.

Accordingly, Mr White of Mill's Court in two days afterwards received a letter, informing him that John Cowie was
the writer of the same, and that, if a reasonable consideration
were held out to him, he would proceed to the northern
metropolis, and there settle for ever a case which apparently
had kept the newsmongers of Edinburgh in aliment for a length
of time much exceeding the normal nine days. Opportune
and happily come in the very nick of time as the latter was—
for the delay allowed by the court had all but expired—Mr
White saw the danger of promising anything which could be
construed into a reward ; but he could use other means of
decoying the shy bird into his meshes, and these he used in
his answer with such effect, that the man who could solve the
mystery was in Edinburgh at the end of a week. Nor was
Mr White unprepared to receive him, for he had previously
got a commission to examine him and take his deposition ;
but then an agent likes to know what a witness will say before he cites him, and the canny Scotchman, of all men in the
world, is the most uncanny if brought to swear without some
hope of being benefited by his oath. There was therefore
need of tact as well as delicacy ; and Mr White contrived in
the first place to get his man to take up his quarters in the
house in Mill's Court. A good supper and chambers formed
the first demulcent—we do not say bribe, because, by a legal

fiction, all eating and drinking is set down to the score of hospitality. A Scotch breakfast followed in the morning, at which were present Mrs White and Mrs Hislop, and our favourite Henney—the last of whom, spite of all the efforts of her putative mother to keep from her the secret of her birth and prospects, had caught the infection of the general topic of the city, and wondered at her strange fortune, much as the paladin in the "Orlando" did when he got into the moon. No man can precognosce like a woman, and here were three; but perhaps they might have all failed, had it not been for the natural art of Henney, who, out of pure goodness and grati-tude, was so delighted with the man who had rolled her in a blanket and sent her to her beloved mother, as she still called her, that she promised to make him butler at Eastleys, and keep him comfortable all his days.

"Now," said the cautious agent, "this promise of Henney's is not made in consideration of your giving evidence for her before the commissioner."

"I'm thinking of nothing but her face," said John. "I could swear to it out of a thousand; and Heaven bless her! for I think I am again in the once happy house in Meggat's Land."

And John pretended he was wiping a morsel of egg from his mouth, while the handkerchief was extended as far as the eye.

"A terrible night that was," he continued. "Mrs Napier had been in labour all day; and when Mrs Kemp told me to tell my master that my lady had been delivered of TWINS——"

"*Twins!*" cried they all, as if moved by some sympathetic chord which ran from heart to heart.

"Ay, twins," he repeated; "one dead, and another living —even you yourself, Henney, who are as like your father as if there never had been a Captain Preston in the world."

And thus was John Cowie precognosced. We need not say that he was that very day examined before the commissioner. He gave an account of all the proceedings of the house in Meggat's Land on the eventful night to which we have referred. The case was no longer a puzzle; and, accordingly, a decision was given in favour of Henrietta, whereby we have one other example of truth and right emerging from darkness into light. Some time afterwards, the heiress, with Mrs Hislop alongside, and John Cowie on the driver's box, proceeded to Eastleys and took possession; where Henrietta acted the part of a generous lady, Mrs Hislop that of a kind of dowager, and John was once more butler in the house of the Napiers. We stop here. Those who feel interest enough in the fortunes of Henney to inquire when and whom she married, and what were the subsequent fortunes of a life so strangely begun, will do well to go to Eastleys.

Mrs Corbet's Amputated Toe.

THE authority I have for venturing so far on the domain of belief, which every one guards with so much care, even while he permits most suspicious-looking squatters thereon, as to claim attention to the all but unbelievable story I am here to relate, was the late Professor John Lizars, who related it, in the outline, to me some years before his death. I do not deny that, even like as I am to the credulous Mylus,—*omnia audiens*,—I might, during the recital, have looked like Pyrrho,—*credens nihil*,—but it is just as likely that I might have allowed my look of incredulity to compose itself among the gravities that hang about the lower part of the face when he assured me he had seen the *object itself* in the room where it was said to be—moreover, that he had got some of his anatomical knowledge from it. However all that may be, it is certain that Lieutenant-Colonel Corbet, an officer who had been in India, lived in Hyndford's Close for a good many years, and along with him Mrs Corbet, a beauty whom he had picked up in Bombay. Like other people who have passed a pretty long time in the East, they did not—as the author of the "Castes of Edinburgh" says of our Indian refugees in general—fit in very well with our people, insomuch as while they remembered the dark slaves they ruled in India, they could never exactly forget that the folks hereaway are generally white; while those whom they could not but admit to be of that hue were apt to view the somewhat dignified couple as being tinged with the colour of gold, in other words, with that of a bad liver. Yet withal they lived in good society—and, what was of more importance, they were—so far as testified to by the wise who know more of the insides of other people's houses than the fools do who live in them—very happy; a state of matters which generally excludes the wry-mouthed genius of scandal.

But, as our story does not hang by the domestic happiness of the Colonel and his wife, we may be excused from dwelling on the beauties of conjugal love ; the more by reason that, as the thing is fashionable, there is more of pretension to it than of reality. Nor blessed and perfect as conjugal happiness may be, is it, alas! exclusive of visits from the angry gods, who, as Plutarch tells us, have woolly, that is, soft feet; and the softer, one would think, the less they are expected. And so in the case of our happy couple. Somehow or other, our Colonel, like most others whose livers are not so sound as that ruling organ of the human body ought to be, was most ingenious in devising remedies for ailments ; and, what is really not more wonderful, he was equally expert at finding out those ailments, whether they existed or not. To give you an instance : he carried about with him, as regularly as a man does a snuff-box, out of which he generously supplies his friends, a nostrum that the most of the ailments of mankind arise from crudities in the blood, which again are the consequence of an over-accumulation of muscular force ; so that if people had just the sense, which is possessed by engine-men when they let off their superabundant steam, to work off that energy, they would seldom or ever be out of sorts. Being of the tribe of theorists, it was of no account to tell him that the hard-working people had ailments as well as the lazy or slothful. He was not bound to believe what he had no wish to believe ; and, therefore, he stuck to his therapeutic remedy of exercising himself every forenoon with a pair of dumb-bells, each weighing some five or six pounds avoirdupois. If he had not been a theorist, the difficulty he had in working these heavy weights might have told him that he had not much overflowing energy to work off. It was enough that he thought he had, and so he toiled for a whole hour at a time, more like a pentathlete of old than a modern gentleman who enjoyed the privilege of living at his ease. Nor was it of any avail that his wife. who saw in his spare body, indexed by a saffron-coloured face, that he had no strength to throw away, remonstrated with him on the absurdity of weakening, with the view of strengthening himself. What has reason to do with theory? and don't theorists know that reason is a mole-eyed baggage, who cannot see an inch beyond the narrow line of a poor limited experience?

So the affair went on ; and we go on so far with it as to say that no man could have told how far it would have gone, had it not been for an accident—so called by mortals, for there are no accidents in nature, even where the woolly-footed powers seem to break in and play the deuce. And how innocently it occurred! Simply by Mrs Corbet trying, in a good-humoured way, and after a little badinage, to take one of the weights out of her husband's hand. A most unfortunate effort. the weight of lead fell with a crash on the lady's toes, and a scream from the sufferer resounded through the whole house. The servants rushed in, and Mrs Corbet was laid upon the arm-chair, in a condition approaching to a faint. On taking off the stocking, it was found that the injury was inflicted on the small toe of the left foot, which was crushed so seriously as to render it doubtful whether the bone was not broken. Probably if a doctor had been there at the moment, and before the small member began to swell, he might have decided the point; but it was not till three hours afterwards that Dr James Russel called, and by that time the injured part had become so swollen and irritable, that skilly as the doctor was, he could not make himself sure on the point; so that, with a little top-dressing, the toe was left to develop itself according to its own temper, or rather that of the old leech, the *vis medicatrix*. Meanwhile the swelling diminished the pain; a result to which a little brandy contributed so much—that being always something more than its real virtue would seem to warrant.

Apparently there was nothing to fear from an accident of so common a character; that is to say if the interesting patient—who by the way carried the blood of a Georgian mother in veins which, in their pale blue lines, could not be concealed by the fair silken skin of that famous people—had been in her constitution perfectly normal; but there are diathetic conditions which no doctor is bound to know, for the simple reason that he has seldom any means of knowing them till they are evolved, and then it is generally too late. Days passed, but without bringing those pathological changes which are looked fo: or expected in consequence of nature's comparative uniformity. On the contrary, the entire foot became swollen to nearly the double of its natural size, and as further time passed Dr Russel waxed more certain in his early suspicion that the bone had been broken at the joint; an opinion which, when communicated to the Colonel, produced an effect as divergent from the normal as the consequences of the injury themselves threatened to be. Nor was the reason here so recondite as the peccant secret of the obdurate toe, for he had from the beginning blamed himself as being the cause of the accident; and this would not have been very formidable to him if his feelings had allowed him—as they never do in such cases—to make the rational distinction between acts that are voluntary and those that are not. So he murmured and tormented himself, with the usual result of an increase of his pain; unless we are to take into account the anxious duty of a continual attendance on the patient, whose every look and sign he watched, as if his fate in the place of punishment depended upon the vibration of a nerve in her pale but beautiful face. Then, even

C

if he had had the power of making the proper distinction, and thus saving him from the self-imputation of any designed harm to one so inexpressibly dear to him, he was met by the subtlety of his own creation, that the angry power who had imposed the misfortune had purposely selected him as the medium of the infliction, for the reason that he was in some secret way obnoxious to Heaven.

So far perhaps in anticipation, yet necessary in order to enable us to understand the effects produced upon one so formed by the condition of the invalid, who shewed no signs of improvement. On the contrary, she became daily worse, till at length the doctor was alarmed by a dark spot, which gave indications of gangrene. There was now no time to be lost in speculation about the condition of the bone, whether fractured or not. The toe was amputated ; but the remedy came too late. That dreaded power, deadness or mortification, which we are so apt to view as a negative, was to shew its stern activities in its antagonism of darkness to light, of silence to sound, of stillness to motion, of ugliness to beauty, of coldness to heat, of death to life. The insidious enemy had got beyond the line of amputation, and had gathered its energies for the reduction of that fair form to base matter. As yet, no communication of the danger was made to her ; and, as we all know that mortification generally involves a relief from pain, we are not to wonder that the patient viewed the change as a token of convalescence. We are sometimes led to think that Nature, usually so beneficent to man, often wears the Myrtean crown of the tyrant, insomuch as she is often cruelest, even by way of refinement, when she appears most kindly. And here the husband was the victim. In the forenoon, he had got the intelligence of the fatal change ; and the self-imputed conviction that he was the cause of the calamity wrought on his heart at the very moment when, sitting by the bed and holding her hand, he was obliged to encounter the light of the false hope which shone in her eye. The day passed amidst the quietude of a solemnity in which all participated, except her on whom all attention was fixed; for the silence which destroys many friendships is not that silence which is enforced by the hovering presence of "the shadow feared of man." The night wore on till nearly twelve. The wax-taper had been renewed, so as to last till the first beam should come with the pæan of the opening morn, wherein Nature would again give evidence of her refined mode of torturing poor mortals. The small light, meanwhile, glimmered on the pale but beautiful face of the victim, as that was presented to the anxious eye of the husband. That look of peace, if not pleasure, would have been to him as a *lumen fausti minis*, replete with all joy, had he been ignorant of the fatal secret. As it was, it scathed him even more than he could have experienced from an expression of the greatest pain. Nor was even this all: he was fated to hear the words of playfulness breaking the silence of the chamber of death. As he held her hand in his, she said—

"George, do you know what I was thinking last night?"

"No," replied he sorrowfully, as he met the happy look.

"Of course not," she proceeded. "I was afraid to tell you at the time; for I may now admit to you, that I was under a fear I was to die: but, when I am free from all pain, and hope to be soon well again, I may state it to you now for our amusement, especially as in this gloom and silence we require something to cheer us."

"Well?" groaned the Colonel

"You know," continued the invalid, "that Edinburgh has always been famous for stories of dead bodies being taken out of the graves."

"I do not believe one half of them, Isabella," replied he.

"But I believe them all," said she. "When I was under the fear of death, (how glad I am that that fear is gone!) a thought haunted me that my body might be stolen ; and, do you know, I was so frightened that I intended to request of you as a great favour, that you would provide means for watching my grave ? I can smile now at my intention, but wasn't it a strange whim ?"

And a faint laugh twittered on the vocal chords, irrespective of the approach of the dark foe, which was gradually proceeding from the point of its first triumph in the left foot, and would soon silence those chords for ever.

" And I am not done yet," she continued in the same strain ; " for, as I thought that as it was from one of those horrid dumb-bells with which you were killing yourself that I received my misfortune, I was to tell you, that if you allowed my body to be stolen, I would, in my disembodied spirit, appear to you during the nights of your watchfulness,—ay, and even during the day,—and scowl upon you just in the way that owls and goblins used to do in the old houses."

The Colonel could yet find no words to reply, and he shrunk from the cheerful expression of her face.

" Nor am I done yet," she continued ; "for I was to tell you also that my spirit, when it appeared to you, would point down to my left foot, just as if it said, ' You will know my body amidst a hundred by the want of the toe.'"

And the laugh was even a little stronger.

" But do not look so sorrowful, my dear," she continued ; " for you know all my danger is over now : ay, and I may yet live to dance one of your Scotch reels with that same foot, to the music of some of your beautiful tunes."

These strange words were the last the Colonel heard ; and this strange play of light in the face he had worshipped, as well for its Eastern beauty as for its indicial manifestations of the love which really existed in her heart towards him,—so like, that light, to the phosphorescence which gleams at night from decaying organisms, with still beauty on the surface,—

was the last symptom he witnessed of her naturally buoyant spirit. He was exhausted ; and the nurse came to take his place, with that impassable calmness which befits her kind for scenes sufficient to drive husbands and wives mad, yea, and would have that effect if mortals were not mad already ; and sure it is, that some may even modulate a groan and a laugh into the paradox, that if man were not mad, he could not live. He rose, and retired to his bedroom ; there probably to wring his hands, or go through some of the other contortions whereby wretched man tries to repress the agonies of the spirit.

Meanwhile, the patient, after that strange manifestation of a deluded hope, was fast undergoing " the unleavening process ;" and with all that regularity, too, which is shewn in the circulation of the blood—every drop of which, as it left the infected part, carried to the heart the means of stilling it for ever. True as it is that the *nunc fluens* with all of us is ever in continual progress towards the *nunc permanens* of eternity : her moments were charged as it were with the periods of years ; and we thus see the difference between the process of taking down from that of building up—how slowly the threads are added one after another to the mysterious texture of life, yet how rapidly unwinded. Before the next midnight, Mrs Corbet was dead ; and, in a few days more, this child of the sunny regions of the East lay under the cold turf in the churchyard of the Canongate. Of such things in their external aspect we have an amount of knowledge, but of the effects which are produced by them on the inner lives of those who are left behind we know comparatively nothing. Man may weave poetry, and think he is expressing his feelings, so that others may know the workings of his spirit ; but he produces only a specimen of art, where the words form a picture, and where the words too are taken for the things they cannot represent ; so that to those who never experienced such a condition of the mind as that to which the bereaved husband was reduced, a description would effect no more than an endeavour to convey to one who never saw a tree the form of the blasted oak by shewing a few of its withered leaves.

Nor for the space of a month could Colonel Corbet have any precise knowledge of the state of his own mind, where every energy was resolved into images of the past, leaving the external senses dead or inoperative. Among the ancients, as Cicero tells us, it was held to be ominous to speak of the dead ; a maxim which modern experience would induce us to reverse, insomuch as we have no better sign of a coming recovery from grief than is afforded by a disposition to speak of the departed. It would seem that we ease the heart by transferring its energy to the tongue. It is the unspoken brooding thought that makes ravage of the heart ; yet, in the case of our bereaved husband, it might be said, all this dark brooding was for the time foregone only the normal condition of ordinary mortal grief. But there was to be a change. We will say nothing as yet of a certain peculiarity of his mind existing theretofore, whereby that change could be explained according to well-authenticated principles of psychology, or rather we should say, physiology, if the matter does not lie between the two ; but we may state, what will doubtless produce surprise, that, amidst all his thoughts, he had never recurred to the extraordinary statement made by his wife on the evening of the day preceding her death. We may account for this on the supposition that, whatever impression these words of hers had made upon him at the moment, the effect was due to the false hope in which she had indulged when evidently dying, rather than to the weak words she so lightly uttered. We have said that his grief was normal ; nor do we need to qualify our expression more than by stating that the aggravation produced by the conviction that he was the means through which she had met her death, was more a temporary triumph when the reason was taken captive by the feelings than a haunting produced by the conscience.

There was to be a change ; and that was ushered in by a strange phenomenon. One morning, when lying in bed, his eye sought the window, where the breaking light of the early dawn was bringing out faintly the green of the curtain, which had been drawn on the previous evening. The look was only a listless one, as if he wished to augur the time of the morning ; nor, indeed, could he see much even of what the room contained, for the partial light seemed to be drunk up by the curtains, leaving the apartment itself nearly as dark as it was before. While his eye was so occupied, it seemed as if some nebulous object had come between him and the drapery ; and of this he could be the more apprised by the apparent darkening of the illuminated damask to an extent co-ordinate with the interrupting medium, whatever it might be. Even yet, his look was listless ; for, with all his fanciful conviction of having been the cause of his wife's death, he was not a superstitious man, if he was not more independent of a belief in supernaturals than most people even with sound livers. But that listlessness began to give way to a sharpening of the eye, as he saw the face of Mrs Corbet slowly evolving from the vapoury medium. At first he could observe only the general contour ; but gradually, and as it were line by line, the features became more and more distinct; and, indeed, so apparently palpable, that the seer (for we think the word appropriate) actually made an exclamation, and held out his hand to touch it. This distinct condition of the object lasted only for a moment or two, and seemed to depend somewhat upon a sympathy with the action of the eye ; for as he began to strain that organ, in order to make himself more sure of the reality of his vision, the face seemed to respond in a diminution of its distinctness — recovering again its former marked line and angles as he relaxed the intensity of his gaze. A moment

or two more, and the green curtain, embued with the dawn
light, recovered its apparency where that had been excluded.
The figure was gone, and had left the Colonel opening and
shutting his eyes, as if he would test by an experiment what
he considered to be an illusion.

On throwing himself again back on the pillow from which
he had partially raised himself, he began to think whether he
had not been *inter res commentitias et frivolas quænus quam
sunt—*

> " Things unreal, and phantoms vain,
> Which morbid minds spew forth as fumes
> That circling rise, and take on lying forms ;"

and he would have been well contented if he could have
rested on this conclusion ; but even while he was making the
effort, the words of his wife flashed across his mind with a
rapidity and vivacity as if derived from a reaction of the force
by which they had been so long excluded : *"If you allow my
body to be stolen, I will, in my disembodied spirit, appear to you
during the nights of your watchfulness."* He repeated them
with trembling lips, over and over again, as if he now felt it a
duty to remember them. And did she not further say, that
her spirit would scowl upon him as the cause of her death?
This, too, he remembered, but he did not forget that the
words were said in playfulness ; and then there was the fact
that the said spirit, if spirit it was, did *not* look angry at him;
so that, after all, it might be that a troubled mind and a
coincidence casual, however strange, had more to do with the
affair than any supernatural agency.

This conclusion, upon which he latterly came to lean, was
at least philosophical, and perhaps he might have remained
satisfied if he could have assured himself that there would be
no recurrence of the vision. This, of course, he could not
do, and having fallen asleep he awoke to a nervousness, if
not unqualified misery, which hung about him throughout the

whole day. He could not assure himself that he was not the object of an unfavourable attention on the part of some superior power. He did not know that even the sturdiest sceptic, when he comes to deliberate on the great question of special interpositions from above, is lost; for reason is only a temporary friend, who leaves you when the mind becomes clouded by adversity, while the instinct, which is always pointing to occult powers, clings to you for ever, even as a quality of the spirit. Yea, proud and supercilious philosophy is forced to admit, that where there are so many blanks in the links of the chain of secondary causes, there is room and verge enough for more than .the subtle finger of a Deity. Of these considerations the Colonel knew nothing—he had simply an experience to deal with ; and so it is with a great part of mankind—they have an inner life, the workings of which are exclusive of postulates, and premises, and formulas, and make them recusants to philosophy. Yet, withal, if there had been no repetition of his vision, our seer would have in time again lapsed into the rational mourner over the beloved dead. Nor was the test very long delayed. In the evening, after he had lain down on the sofa, and just before the bringing in of the candles, when the twilight hung between the light of day and the darkness of night, the vision repeated itself in the distinct form and features of his wife. There could be no mistake : even the changed conditions of the apparition (a word as philosophical as it is superstitious) imparted certainty, if assurance had been wanted. On the former occasion it had appeared as if against the light which faintly tinted the green hangings of the bedroom window ; now it seemed invested with a light of its own, only a little stronger than the crepuscle which lingered in the dining-room—representing, as near as possible, the appearance of her face at that midnight hour when, in the light of the wax taper, she made the remarkable, however frivolous, communication to him. There was another difference which he had time and power to mark as he lay as it were enchanted, with his eye fixed and his mouth open : the face was not of that placid character which it had exhibited before—it was stern and severe, relaxing gradually into soft-ness, only to assume again the more enduring expression ; but, withal, there was again the apparent tendency to appear the less distinct the more he strained his eyes.

Entranced as he was, this latter peculiarity was not passed unnoticed by the Colonel, though he had neither power nor inclination to try to account for it ; nor could he tell, as he suddenly rose from the couch, whether he did so with a view to test further the endurance of the vision under a changed condition of his own nerves, or to try to escape from what truly terrified him. Having got to his feet, he stepped into the middle of the room, and bracing himself, as a military man, of course not without even yet a remnant of courage forcing itself through his superstition, he began to walk from the side board to the window. He even affected not to look for it, but to cast his eye in various directions ; yet his efforts were unavailing : somehow or other the organ would steady itself, and then it was further steadied, even to being riveted, by the vision, which thus seemed to accompany him. That by moving his arms and waving them to and fro, he satisfied him-self that it was impalpable and intangible, afforded him but small relief, for it only assured him that he could not by any physical energy drive it away, besides proving the spiritual character of his visitant. At this moment the servant brought in the candles ; and whether it was that ghosts do not like the light and make off at its approach, or that they have not points of reflection whereby they can appear by borrowed rays, sure it is that the vision was no more seen that evening.

Notwithstanding of this interruption, the Colonel continued his walk along the room. He was disturbed, anxious, and tremulous. The prior arguments he had used for the purpose of satisfying himself that there was no mysterious final cause in the phenomenon were discharged. The conviction settled deeper and firmer that he was obnoxious to powers who had taken his wife under their protection, and his failure of duty in not taking means to watch her grave added its remorse to the self-imputation that he had caused her death. He was, in short, under the influence of that feeling of awe—sufficient to make the boldest of us quake—that he was a particular object selected by divine power for a particular retribution. Like him who slept below the tripod of Apollo, he knew that he had the gods for his masters, and was able by their inspiration to divine his own ruin. Yet, could he not ward off his impending fate by a late repentance and an obedience to the angry spirit who had visited him. While still engaged in these thoughts the door opened, and there entered a young man, who, as a student-assistant to Dr Russel, was present at the amputation of the toe. His name was Davidson, and the object of his visit now was to bring some medicines which the doctor had prescribed for his widower patient. The presence of the student presented an opportunity, suggested by the thoughts which had been passing through his mind.

" Stop," he said, as the young man was about to depart, after laying down the parcel ; " you may do me more good than these drugs, which, alas! cannot minister to the mind."

" Whatever I can," replied Davidson, in something like wonder at being thus selected as a doctor on moral ailments, of which he had but small experience during the time he had been in the world.

" Is it true," said the Colonel, as he fixed his somewhat nervous eye on the student's face, " that dead bodies are stolen from the churchyards in this country ?"

" I am not just the person you should ask," replied Davidson. " You know I study anatomy myself, and we must get our knowledge somehow ; besides, I am afraid to alarm you."

"Alarm me !" cried the Colonel. "What do you mean ? Have you any reason to suspect anything in regard to Mrs Corbet ?"

"Not particularly," was the answer, in a tone which indi- cated that the interrogated had no particular desire to set the Colonel's suspicions to rest.

"Not particularly !" rejoined the questioner, as he laid his hand on the student's arm. "The words are not satisfactory. Have you any reason," he continued, in a voice which betrayed emotion, "for your halting answer ? Have you ever seen the body in any of the rooms ?"

"One cannot say," replied the youth, with the same calm pertinacity ; "they are so changed you know."

"Yes," said the Colonel, as he tried to keep down his voice ; "but there is an unmistakeable mark in the case we are speaking of. You were present at the amputation ?"

"The small toe of the left foot—I mean the want of it," rejoined the student, "would be a good mark if one went for the purpose of identification ; but, you know, we don't go to identify subjects, and then the small toe is so *very* small an affair, that one is apt to overlook it."

"At least," cried the Colonel, somewhat impatiently, "you have met no such body ?"

"I think not," was the reply, but with a smile, which the Colonel no doubt thought very inopportune. "If there had been six toes in place of four, one might have been more certain ; and I need not say that if there had been seven, one would have been more certain still, and——"

But the Colonel, suspecting the student was proceeding to the *eight,* which probably he had no intention of, stopped him, with a request to the effect that if he should meet with any body which appeared to be that of Mrs Corbet, he would lose no time in communicating to him the fact.

"That would be as nearly as possible a matter of course,"

replied Davidson, with still more of a smile on his sinister face;
" but, in the meantime, you should keep an eye upon the green
tumulus in the Canongate, and if you find that the turf, especially about the head of the grave, has been disturbed, we
might be led to expect something in the rooms."

" I intend to visit the spot to-morrow," said the Colonel ;
and, with a deep heaving of the breast, " I have delayed that
duty too long "

" You had better pay a visit to that quarter to-night," added
the youth.

" There is no moon," rejoined the Colonel. " I could
see nothing in the dark.".

" There is such a thing as a lantern," was the quick reply ;
" and, after all, it is perhaps as well if you can avoid the
sexton. These gentry are our best friends."

" I will perform the duty," said the Colonel, speaking perhaps as much to himself as to the student. " It is impera-
tive."

" At what hour ?" asked the youth—a question a little more
particular than the answers he had given to the Colonel's in-
terrogation ; but the Colonel, concerned with deeper thoughts,
did not mark the difference.

" About ten," he replied ; " but how am I to get entry ?"

" Over the low north wall," was the reply.

And the youth, having thus so far satisfied the Colonel, and
perhaps to some extent himself, went away, leaving the solitary
occupant of the room under the fear that that solitude would
be interfered with by the same bodiless companion who had
taken the trouble of visiting him twice that day ; but whether
it was that, as he lay on the sofa, he gazed with more earnest-
ness into the empty space about him than was consistent with
the modesty of these susceptible creatures, or that now he
had resolved on conciliating the angry spirit by obedience,
certain it is that he did not see the image again that night.

The intermediate hours were solemn and heavy, nor had he any wish even to try to lighten them, for he was in that selfishness of misery which throws its gloom over all thoughts that are happy, so as to assimilate them to its own condition. So at half-past nine he made ready his lantern,—an article then much in use,—and wrapping himself up in a large cloak, proceeded to the burying-ground, which he had not visited since that day—known to many of earth's mourners as the true *dies irae* which engulphs the happiness of a life—on which he committed his wife's body to the earth. Nor was he long in getting to the side of the "little hillock," which has in its bosom a story more wonderful than that which might be told by the mountains "earthquake-born." Having made sure of the object, which he knew from the relation it held to a white marble headstone of another grave by the side, he sat down on a tablet covered with green mould, and began to direct the light of the lantern to the tumulus. The beam was made to traverse the joining of the sods, in order that he might discover whether any crevice gave indication of external disturbance. And thus amid the darkness and silence, with bent head and peering eyes he was engaged in this piety of grief for the best part of a quarter of an hour. Regaining his upright position, he got into meditation. He was in the midst of the dead—many of them in their new shrouds, those marriage dresses of death's brides not yet soiled. Even his wife would yet have undergone little change, and thus he conjured up to the eye of his fancy all those children of mortality, who, a little time before, were, as he himself was now, instinct with life, lying extended in their small habitations silent and motionless; yet the consciousness of the presence of these was as nothing to the awe which overshaded him as he thought that the place and the hour were propitious to another visit from his spiritual monitor. He felt unnerved, and even took the precaution of turning the light of the lantern upon his own

face, as if thereby he might shut out the lesser light of the
apparition ; but the moment his face shone amid the darkness,
he was startled by the sound of a voice, which behoved to be
sepulchral among so many graves. The sound was distinctly
articulate, and the words, " Colonel Corbet."

When a man hears his name pronounced as a salutation,
he will naturally doubtless turn his eye to the source of the
sound ; and so would the Colonel on the instant, if it had not
been that he was doing his best by holding the lantern to his
face to keep away the object of his dread, and somehow or
other he confusedly mixed up the party, whoever it might be,
that had pronounced the,words and the apparition of his wife.
A very little power of thinking would have satisfied him that if
Mrs Corbet's spirit chose to address her husband, she would
have used the same kind of voice which was her natural and
peculiar gift when alive, and that the voice he had heard was
not at all in that key, if indeed it did not very clearly come
from a man ; but then it just happened that he had not the
power of comparison, and then, we all know, the effect of fear
in the transmutation of appearances is not more than in that of
sounds. So he felt himself in that most unsoldier-like attitude
of being irresolute—inclined to turn the lantern, yet terrified
that by so doing he would reveal the apparition he so much
dreaded. Even as he thus stood in a position sufficiently
ridiculous, he was soon resolved.

" Colonel Corbet," repeated the voice, " your wife's no
aneath thae sods."

Mrs Corbet did not speak Scotch, and so the lantern was
turned on the object—no other than a man standing on the
other side of the grave. The light brought him out in all his
perfections—a raw-boned cadaverous-looking fellow, who could
hardly have had a more grim and death-like look if he had
at that time come out of the grave on which he stood. He
had a peculiar squint, too, which gave him a leering look,

even when, as at present, he intended to be very serious ; but if he had been as villainous-looking as a solitary ghoul, who invites no one to his feasts of dead bodies, he was at least a being with real flesh and bones; and therefore the Colonel was no longer afraid, however stunned he might have been by the ominous announcement.

"Who are you, and what do you mean?" was accordingly the somewhat firm question.

"As to wha I am," replied the man ; "ye may ken that when we're better acquaint ; and as to what I mean, what, in the name o' a' that 's gude and holy, can be plainer than the words I hae spoken—ay, just thae words—Mrs Corbet's no aneath thae sods ?"

"Where is she then ?" was the natural question.

"I'm no just inclined to answer that question," was the reply, accompanied by a kind of laugh, which could have sounded better nowhere than among these graves. "But, hooly, sir, I dinna mean to say that the secret is so dead close as never by ony means to be revealed ; but I am modest, and if you havena' forgotten your Latin, you might understand me when I say, *Edinæ venalia sunt omnia.*"

"You mean," said the Colonel, "that I may know where the body of my wife is if I will pay for the information ?"

"Weel, you have helped my bashfulness," said the man ; "and if you will meet me at the Tron the morn's night at nine o'clock, you will hear what you will hear, and see what you will see."

And with these words the man disappeared, no doubt to find his way out as quickly as possible.

Some little time elapsed before the Colonel could recover himself from his confusion, and he seemed to be rejected of heaven not to be accepted on earth, with only the problematical relief that if the body was actually stolen, he might, by redeeming it, appease the angry manes of his wife ; and with some thoughts of this kind passing through his mind, he turned his steps homewards—lighting his path over the graves by his lantern, the glimmering of which would no doubt be noticed by some sly ghosts shading themselves behind the head-stones; nor when he got home could he banish from his mind the augury that, according to the old Greek saying, he was doomed either to act a tragedy or go mad. The discovery he seemed to have made satisfied him that the visions he had seen were not only veritable but justified, inso-much as he had not only caused the death of his wife, but, by his supineness and disregard of her injunctions, allowed her body to be taken out of the grave—the circumstance of all others which had filled her with the greatest apprehension. Nor had he been able to shake himself free from these thoughts up to the time when he went to bed; and as foi accomplishing such a feat there, he had no great chance, even though he tossed himself in his own blankets, as if he wanted to inflict upon himself a punishment more usually conferred by others without the special consent of the culprit. It is not unlikely that he thus did himself some service, for he left himself little leisure, and certainly he had no inclination, for witnessing a vision in the dead hours of the night.

The next day was passed in similar nervousness and appre-hension—feelings which were by no means allayed by the non-appearance of his expected monitor. At nine he was at his post at the Tron. The night was again dark, and the glimmer-ing lamps at the heads of the timber posts looked as if a little of the wood at the tops had been charred and ignited into dull embers. The people were passing and repassing like shadows in Hades—that is to say, they presented that appear-ance to the gloomy mind of the Colonel, who now saw every-thing through the clouded medium of his own mind. Pre-sently, as he stood in the middle of the street, some one whis-pered in his ear, "Follow me, but see that nane follow ye."

D

And the Colonel forthwith put himself in motion, following in the rear of the whisperer, who, as he could easily see, was his amiable friend of the churchyard. Their course was first up the High Street, next down Libberton's Wynd, then across the Cowgate, thence far up another close leading to Brown Square, and, lastly, up a kind of entry towards a house standing by itself. As yet there was no conversation, nor even when the man mounted two or three steps which led to the door of that house did he utter a word. It seemed to be understood that the Colonel was to follow whithersoever he was led. The door was opened by the man by means of a key which he took from his pocket, and, proceeding inwards, he was followed by the Colonel. The man, without yet opening his mouth, put his hand on the shoulder of his companion as a sign for him to stand, and then proceeded to lock the door inside ; after which act of apparent precaution, he opened an inner door and entered, the Colonel following—not by sight, for it was pitch dark, but simply by the ear as it conveyed to him the motions of his leader. They were now in a room, at least so the Colonel thought, and taking a step forward he came against some object which seemed to be suspended from the roof, for it moved, and seemed to oscillate backward and forward, giving forth at same time a crepitation of dry bones rattling in chains.

"Never mind that," said his leader ; "stand steddy till I strike a licht."

And by and by the sound was heard of the flint upon the steel : rasp—rasp—a spark--phroo, phroo—whew-w—"The deil's in the tinder"—phroo—"There noo."

And a blue light from the sulphur at the end of the spunk flashed through the room, shewing to the Colonel a small apartment with two prepared skeletons suspended from the roof, one of which—that impinged upon by the Colonel in the dark—being still in motion, and crepitating during its oscillation. Not a word passed yet from the man who was busy getting the light from the match transferred to a candle, which, having with some difficulty got it ignited, he placed in a candlestick, which again he placed in the sole of the window. All this time the Colonel was no doubt in great amazement. He was, moreover, shocked by the sight of the suspended objects, each of which seemed from its empty sockets to look down upon him in grim dissatisfaction; yet he was under the conviction that this was a mere ante-room, from which he would be led to another, where the body he was doubtless brought to see would be presented him—to stun and terrify him, yea, to horrify him'!

So far he was mistaken. The man, after deliberately putting away the tinder-box in a press in the wall, proceeded to take up the candle, and coming round to where the Colonel stood, he took hold of one of the suspended forms, and twirling it round so that its face might confront them, he pointed to the *patella* or knee-pan.

" Read ye thae words there," said he, " and see if ye ken wha *that is.*"

And he essayed pretty successfully a laugh.

The Colonel's eye was meanwhile fixed on the spot, where he read, in pretty legible letters, "MRS COL. CORBET, died 9th Sept. 18—."

It was sometime before he seemed to gather up thought enough to enable him to understand the meaning of the words, and, as he bent his body and gazed with staring eyes, the man seemed inclined to question his perception.

" An auld friend wi' a new face?" said he drawlingly.

But the addition was not needed. The perceptive power had vindicated itself—the Colonel staggered as if he would have fallen; and it is more than likely he would, if there had not been a long seat behind upon which he sank under the influence of a spasm. He clutched the empty space about him, breathed laboriously, and turned more than once a hare-brained look at the object, averting again his eyes and trembling violently. All which indications of misery had no more effect upon "the broken student," as he afterwards turned out to be, than the crackle of the suspended bones.

"And you see the sma' tae o' the left foot is awanting."

Words the truth of which he pointed out by taking hold of the left foot of the figure, and which again threw the Colonel into another fit of laborious breathing—a condition, however engrossing, not now incompatible with an effort to fix his eye on that part pointed out by the man.

"Good God!" he at length exclaimed. "Is all that true? Is it possible that that is *my* Isabella?"

"Your Isabella!" replied the man. "No; she belongs now to Mr M——, the proprietor of the dissecting-rooms; and valuable property she is, for there's no a finer specimen of the genus *homo* in Edinburgh."

"But you are a Christian," cried the Colonel, as he awakened more completely to the reality of his extraordinary position. "And since you have brought me here to witness this terrible spectacle, you can surely put me on some way and means to get possession of these bones, and get them buried." And as these words did not seem to remove the apathy of the man, (probably more affected than real,) he clutched him by the neck of the coat. "I demand of you," he cried, more loudly than the man relished, "to know whether you have authority to give me up the bones of my wife."

"Canny, sir," was the reply; "ye'll mak naething by anger, and I will befriend you if I can ; but," in a low voice, "there maun be money—money :" and whether it was that the broken student thought that some words of Latin would help a scene which was more like an incantation than a mercantile bargain, or that the reduced man was proud of the learning that had done him no good, he added what, certainly, the Colonel did not understand, *Tu mulierem amabas, missa est.   Ego pecuniam dedisti.*"

"Money!" rejoined the Colonel; "I will give *any* money."

"Then, it's a' richt," said the man.   "She's worth fifty guineas, and, if you agree, she shall be at your house within, say, twenty-four hours."

"Ten o'clock to-morrow night," said the Colonel.

"Exactly—settled—completed—dune," drawled the man; "and I can assure you, sir, she's a gude bargain at the money."

With these words this extraordinary meeting terminated. The Colonel, as if anxious to get out of sight of the object of his purchase, hurried out as fast as a nervous groping would permit, and in a short time was in his own house extended upon the sofa, and in a state of mind which, with so few examples of an analogous kind to help our sympathies, it is almost impossible to conceive.   To assure himself that he had so far gained his point was, in reality, next to nothing, for he was conscious that the horror entertained by his wife of being exhumed was no doubt founded on the desecration of the body, and that had been accomplished in a way which had probably never occurred to her; yet, even in the worst cases of crime or culpable negligence, there is a grain of comfort in duty done, even at the eleventh hour; and with this small amelioration of his racked feelings he retired to bed.

Next night, precisely at ten o'clock, a knock, probably expected by at least one individual of the family, was heard at the door of the house in Hyndford C'ose; nor was it long in being responded to.   The door was opened by the Colonel himself, and there stood the broken student with a large box on his shoulders, which, having carried into a dark room, he deposited upon the floor.   There were very few words spoken.

Probably they were not needed, where the occasion neither required the solemnity of set sentences, nor suited the expres-

sion of light thoughts. The money was promptly paid, and
the recipient having wished the Colonel joy of his bargain,
departed with as much rapidity as probably the Colonel
wanted. So far all was as favourable as the Colonel could
wish ; and seeing that there is, at least, one skeleton in every
house, and that one is generally considered to be enough,
it behoved him to get the supernumerary disposed of in the
only one way suited to our customs and our individual feelings.
Next day, accordingly, he bent his steps to the house of the
sexton of the churchyard from which the body had been taken.
Having found the redoubted Andrew Gemmel in, he recounted
to him, with appropriate solemnity, his story, beginning with
that part where he first encountered the broken student. During the recital, he watched the face of the sexton, where he
found solemnity the ruling expression up to the end of the
narrative ; but why, at that point, Andrew should have permitted that most grave of all faces to gather itself into a smile,
was one mystery more added to a story which was mystery all
over.

"And now, sir," said Andrew, " I will finish your story for
you, for I see it wants an end.

And calling his man, he asked the Colonel to accompany
him to the burying-ground. Nor did he say another word
until they came to the desecrated grave, where, having given
the necessary commands to his assistant, the two began to
take off the turf, and thereafter to remove the earth. The
grave was not a deep one, and a very short time only was
required to get down to the coffin. This was laid bare, and
Andrew having applied his screw-driver with all the tact of a
joiner, the lid was taken off. The covering of the face was
next removed, and there, with the Colonel looking down with
staring eyes, lay Mrs Corbet in all the calmness and placidity
of death.

" Now, sir," said Andrew, "there is the end of your story."

The Colonel might now see somewhat more into the mystery, but he was entranced by the object which, in its still
unsullied whiteness, lay in the dark hole before and beneath
him. Old Chaos was busy tugging at those Caucasian lines
of beauty, so like what the fading moonbeams shew on the
sculptured face of Parian stone which genius has made instinct
with life. It is vain to talk of thought in such situations.
The charm wrought by the great wizard Nature is complete
without more of incantation than a look. Yet this fixedness of
anguish must obey the eternal law of motion : " Man must
think ;" and so recovering himself, as from a fearful dream,
he started, and put the question to Andrew, so replete again
with the grotesque *bizarrerie* of life—

"And what am I to do with the box of bones ?"

" Just return them to Sandy Mackay," was the answer ;
" but as for your getting back your £50, you may as well try
to make calf'sfoot jelly out of your purchase."

And so, too, the Colonel probably thought, but the less of
£50 was nothing in an account of debit and credit against the
other world, or at least one spirit therein, and that account
was fated to undergo a further diminution of balance against
him ; for in the evening he was visited by Dr Russel, who, on
hearing the detail of all these strange circumstances, assured
his patient that the vision he had seen was merely the consequence of a deranged stomach. Nay, the Colonel himself
recollected that when he was in India he was troubled with
muscæ volitantes,—a symptom very often indicative of a tendency to that projection into space of images on the retina,
which generally goes under the name of *mon mania,* and is
supposed, by Hibbert, to be the ground-work of most of our
stories of apparitions.

The events of this day were not yet finished. About nine
o'clock, two young men met in the tavern kept by Mrs Gowans
in the High Street. One of them was no other than the

student Davidson, the other Sandy Mackay ; who, to account for his learning and no less his squalidness, we may as well say had been a student at the Edinburgh University, from which he had been expelled, or, as they call it, broken, for some grievous misdemeanour,—a consummation which necessitated his becoming a kind of scullion-assistant at the dissecting-rooms in the place called "Society," with a pittance which he tried to eke out by occasionally procuring a *subject.* The two were clearly bent on a jollification, for they had before them each a large jug of ale, into which they had just dipt when Davidson began a certain count and reckoning :—

"I 'll thank you, Sandy, for the £25," said Davidson, as he stretched forth his hand.

" Na," replied Sandy ; " you forget the £5 I paid to Begbie for the auld frame of Luckie Corner, the woman who murdered Bell Gellatly. Besides, ye 're importunate. It 's *partitio non præfocatio.* I will divide fairly ; £22, 10s. is just your share."

" Well, I'm content," said the other.

And Sandy began to count the money, laughing the while, and punning on the old maxim of the Stoics—*Quod utile honestum.*

"Can you tell me," said he, " why this is honestly won ?"

" Because it is *utile,*" was the reply.

Whereat Sandy laughed again, adding thereafter, with a sigh and a smile, " But it will do me nae gude,—*mendici pera nunquam impletur.* There 's nae keeping fou o' a beggar's wallet. There 's your half."

"And you 've made the skeleton all right at the rooms?" said Davidson, as he pocketed the cash.

" Ou ay," was the answer ; "I 've joined the tae, and rubbed out the letters on the knee-pan. Here 's to ye."

The Brownie of the West Bow.

I CANNOT say so much for the authenticity of the legend I am now to relate, as I have been able to do for some of the others in this collection ; but that is no reason, I hope, for its failing to interest the reader, who makes it a necessary condition of his acceptance that a legend shall keep within the bounds of human nature : not that any of us can say what these bounds are, for every day of our experience is extending them in both the inner and outer worlds ; and we never can be very sure whether the things which rise upon the distant horizon of our nocturnal visions are less unstable and uncertain than those that exist under our noses. True it is, at any rate, that the legend was narrated to me in a meagre form by a lady, sufficiently ancient to be supposed to be a lover of strange stories, and not imaginative or wicked enough to concoct them.

That part of Edinburgh called the West Bow was, at the date of our legend, the tinsmiths' quarter ; a fact which no one who chanced to walk down that way could have doubted, unless indeed he was deaf. Among the fraternity, there was one destined to live in annals even with more posthumous notoriety than he of the same place and craft who long got the credit of being the author of the "Land o' the Leal." His name was Thomas, or, according to the Scottish way of pronouncing it, Tammas Dodds ; who, with a wife going under the domestic euphuism of Jenny, occupied as a dwelling-house a small flat of three rooms. in the near neighbourhood of his workshop.   This couple had lived together five years, without having had any children procreated of their bodies, or any quarrel born of their spirits , and thus they might have lived to the end of their lives, if a malign influence, born of the devil, had not got possession of the husband's heart.

This influence, which we may be permitted by good Calvinists to call diabolical, was, as a consequence, not only in its origin, but also in its medium, altogether extraneous to our couple.   For so far as regards Mrs Jenny Dodds, she was, as much as a good wife could be, free from any great defects of conduct; and, as for the tinsmith himself, he had hitherto lived so sober and douce a life, that we cannot avoid the notion, that if he had not been subject to "aiblins a great temptation," he would not have become the victim of the arch-enemy. Thus much we say of the dispositions of the two parties ; and were it not that certain peculiarities belonged to Jenny, which, as reappearing in an after-part of our story, it is necessary to know, we would not have gone further into mere character—an element which has little to do generally with legends, except in so far as it either produces the incidents, or may be developed through them.   The first of these peculiarities was a settled conviction that she had as good a right to rule Tammas Dodds, as being her property, as if she had drunk of the waters of St Kevin.   Nor was this conviction merely natural to her ; for she could lay her finger on that particular part of Sacred Writ which is the foundation of the generally-received maxim, "One may do what one likes with one's own."   No doubt, she knew another passage in the same volume with a very different meaning ; but then Mrs Dodds did not *wish* to remember that, or to obey it when she did remember it ; and we are to consider, without going back to that crazy school of which a certain Aristippus was the Jominie, that wishing or not wishing has a considerable influence upon the aspects of moral truth, if it does not exercise over them a kind of legerdemain of which we are unconscious, whereby it changes one of these aspects into another, even when these are respectively to each other as white is to black. This "claim of right" does not generally look peaceful. No more it should; for it is clearly enough against nature; and one seldom kicks at her without getting sore toes. True enough, there do appear cases where it seems to work pretty well; but when they are inquired into, it is generally found either that the husband is a simpleton, submitting by mere inanity, or a man who has resisted to the uttermost, and is at last crumpled up by pure "Caudlish" iteration and perseverance. How Tammas took it may yet appear. In the meantime, we proceed with the peculiarities: another of which was, that Mrs Dodds, like her of Auchtermuchty, or Mrs Grumlie, carried domesticity to devotion, scarcely anything in the world having any interest to her soul, save what was contained in the house, from Tammas, the chief article of furniture, down, through the mahogany table, to the porridge-pot; clouting, mending, darning, cleaning, scouring, washing, scraping, wringing, drying, roasting, boiling, stewing, being all of them done with such duty, love, and intensity of purpose, that they were veritable sacrifices to the *lares*. This was doubtless a virtue; and as doubtless it was a vice, insomuch as, if we believe another old Greek pedagogue of the name of Aristotle, "All virtues are medial vices, and all vices extreme virtues." How Thomas viewed this question may also appear. But we may proceed to state, that Mrs Janet Dodds was not content with doing all those things with such severity of love or duty. She was always telling herself what she intended to do, either at the moment or afterwards. "This pan needs to be scoured." "Thae stockings maun be darned." "This sark is as black as the lum', and maun be plotted." "The floor needs scrubbing." "Tammas's coat is crying, 'A steek in time saves nine,' and by my faith it says true;" and so on. Nor did it signify much whether Thomas or any other person was in the house at the time—the words were not intended for anybody but herself; and to herself she persisted in telling them with a steadfastness which only the ears of a whitesmith could tolerate ; even with the consideration that he was not, as so many are, deaved with scandal—a delectation which Janet despised, if she did not care as little for what was going on domestically within the house on the top of the same stair, as she did for the in-door affairs of Japan or Tobolsk. We may mention, also, that she persevered in reading the same chapter of the Bible, and in singing the same psalm, every Sunday morning. In addition to these characteristics, Janet made it a point never to change the form or colour of her dress ; so that if all the women in Edinburgh had been of her taste and mode of thinking, all the colours by which they are diversfied and made interesting would have been reduced to the dead level of hodden-gray ; the occupation of the imp Fashion would have been gone ; nay, the angels, for fear of offending mortals, would have eschewed the nymph Iris, from whom the poets say they steal tints, and dipt their wings in a gray cloud, before appearing in the presence of the douce daughters of men.

With all these imperfections, — and how many husbands would term some of them perfections !—the married life of Thomas and Janet Dodds might have gone on for another five years, and five to that, if it had not been that Thomas, in a weary hour, cast a glance with a scarlet ray in it on a certain Mary Blyth, who lived in the Grassmarket,—a woman of whom our legend says no more than that she was a widow, besides being fair to the eye, and pleasant to the ear. We could wish that we had it not to say, but as truth is more valuable than gold, yea, refined gold, we are under the necessity of admitting that that red ray betokened love, if an affection of that kind could be called by a name so hallowed by the benedictions of poets and the songs of angels. You must take it in your own way, and with your own construction; but however that may be, we must all mourn for the fearful capabilities within us, and the not less awful potentialities in the powers without —the one hidden from us up to the moment when the others appear, and all wrestling with the enemy prevented by what is often nothing less than a fatal charm. From that moment, Thomas Dodds was changed after the manner of action of moral poisons, for we are to remember that while the physical kill, the other only transmute, and the transmutation *may be* from any good below grace to any evil above the devil.

This change in the mind of the husband included his manner of viewing those peculiarities in the mental constitution of Janet to which we have alluded. Her desire to rule him was now rebellion, her devotion to "hussyskep" was nothing better than mercenary grubbing, her adhesion to her hodden-gray was vulgar affectation, and as to her monologues, they were evidence of insanity. Such changes in reference to other objects happen to every one of us every day in the year, only we don't look at and examine them, nor if we did, could we reconcile them to any theory of the mind—all that we can say being, that if we love a certain object, we hate any other which comes between us and our gratification, and thus just as Mr Thomas Dodds loved Mrs Mary Blyth, so in an equal ratio he hated his good helpmate, Jenny. And then began that other wonderful process called reconciliation, whereby the wish gradually overcomes scruples through the cunning mean of falsifying their aspects. Whereunto, again, the new mistress contributed in the adroit way of all such wretches—instilling into his ear the moral poison which deadened the apperception of these scruples at the same time that it brought out the advantages of disregarding them. The result of all which was, that Jenny's husband, of whom she had made a slave, for his own good and benefit, as she thought, and not without reason, arrived, by small degrees, and by relays of new motives, one after another, at the conclusion of actually removing her from this big world, and of course also from that little one to her so dear, even that of her household empire.

A resolution this, which, terrible and revolting as it may appear to those who are happily beyond the influence of "the wish," was far more easily formed than executed, for nature—although improvident herself of her children—swallowing them up in thousands by earthquakes, tearing them by machinery, and drowning them in the sea by shiploads—is very careful to defend one of them against another. Every scheme the husband could think of was surrounded with difficulties, and one by one was laid aside, till he came to that of precipitating his faithful Jenny, as if by accident, into a deep pool in the North Loch, that sheet of water which contained as many secrets in its bosom as that more romantic one in Italy, not far removed from a certain pious nunnery. Even here there was the difficulty of getting Jenny out at night, and down Cranstoun's Close, and to west of the foot thereof, where the said deep pool was, for no other ostensible purpose in the world than to see the moon shedding her beams on the surface of the water—an object not half so beautiful to her as the clear tin pan made by the hands of her own Tammas, and in which she made her porridge every morning. But the adage about the will and the way is of such wondrous universality, that one successful effort seems as nothing in the diversity of man's inventions, and so it turned out to be comparatively easy to get Janet out one evening for the reason, that her husband did not feel very well, and would like his supper the better for a walk along the edge of the loch, in which, if it was her pleasure, she would not refuse to accompany him. So pleasant a way of putting the thing harmonised with Janet's love of rule, and she agreed upon the condition she made with herself by means of the eternal soliloquy that she would put on the stew to be progressing towards unctuousness and tenderness before they went. Was that to be Janet's last act of her darling hussyskep? It would not be consistent with our art were we to tell you; but this much is certain, that Janet Dodds went down Cranstoun's Close along with her beloved Tammas, that shortly after she was plunged by him into the said deep hole of the loch, and cruelly left there to sink or swim, while he hastened back to tell his new love, Mrs Blyth, how desperately he had done her bidding. But sometimes running away has a bad look; and it happened that as Thomas was hurrying up the dark close, he met a neighbour brother of the craft, who cried to him, "What, ho! Tammas Dodds; whaur frae and whaur tae, man?" To which, seeing how the act of running away would look in the Justiciary Court, he replied with wonderful invention for the moment, that Janet had fallen into the deep pool of the loch, and that though he had endeavoured to get her out, he had failed by reason of his not being able to swim, and that he was running to get some one to help to save her, whereupon he entreated his brother craftsman to go with him to the spot, and help him to rescue his beloved wife, if she weren't yet dead. So away they went, in a great hurry, but to no purpose, for when they came to the said pool, no vestige of a creature being therein could they see, except some air-bubbles reflecting the moonbeams, and containing, no doubt, the living breath of the drowned woman.

Nor when the terrible news was spread through the city, and a boat and drags were made to do their uttermost, under the most willing hands could the body be found. It was known that the bank there was pretty steep in declivity, and the presumption was that the body had rolled down into the middle of the loch, where, in consequence of the muddiness of the waters, it would be difficult to find it. The efforts were continued next morning, and day by day, for a week, with no better success, till at last it was resolved to wait for "the bursting of the gall-bladder," when no doubt Mrs Janet Dodds's

body would rise and swim on the top of the waters. An event
this which did not occur till about three weeks had passed, at
the end of which time a crowd of people appeared at Mr
Dodds's door, bearing a corpse in a white sheet. It was
received by the disconsolate Thomas with becoming resignation, and laid on the bed, even the marriage-bed, realising
that strange meeting of two ends which equalises pain and
pleasure, and reduces the product to *nil.* Nor were many
hours allowed to pass when, decayed and defaced as it was,
it was consigned to a coffin without Mr Dodds being able to
bring his resolution to the sticking point of trying to recognise
in the confused mass of muscle and bone, forming what was
once a face, the lineaments of her who had been once his
pride, and now, by his own act, had become his shame and
condemnation in the sight of Heaven. Next day, she was
consigned to the tomb, in so solemn a manner, that, if man
were not man, one would have had a difficulty in recognising
in that gentle hand that held the head-cord, and dropped
it so softly on the coffin, the same member which drove the
innocent victim into the deep waters.

There is a continuous progress in all things—a fact which we
know only after we get hold of the clue. And so, when Mrs
Mary Blyth appeared as Mrs Mary Dodds. in room of the
domesticated Jenny, it was in perfect accordance with the law
of cause and effect. No doubt, they did their best to be
happy, as all creatures do, even the devil's children, only in a
wrong shaft; but they had made that fearful miscalculation,
which is the wages of sin, when they counted upon conscience
as a pimp to their pleasures, in place of a king's evidence
against them, that king being the Lord of heaven and earth.
And so it turned out in the course of several years, that, as
their love lost its fervour, their respective monitors acquired
greater power in pleading the cause of her who was dead, and
convincing them against their will, (for the all-powerful wish

has no virtue here,) that they had done a cruel thing, for which they were amenable to an avenging guardian of the everlasting element of good in nature's dualism. Yet, strange enough, each of the two kept his and her own secret. Their hearts burned, even as the fire which consumes the wicked, under the smother of a forced silence—itself a torment and an agony —yea, neither of the two would mention the name of Jenny Dodds for the entire world. And there was more than a mutual fear that one should know what the other thought. Each was under a process of exculpation and inculpation—a mutual blaming of each other in their hearts, without ever yet a word said to indicate their thoughts. It was the quarrel of devils, who make the lesser crime a foil to shew the greater, and call it a virtue for the reason that they would rather be the counterfeits of good than the base metal of evil; yet, with no advantage, for hypocrisy, is only the glow which conceals the worm in its retreat within it. The plea of the wife was, that she was courted by the man, and that, although she might have wished Jenny out of the way, and hinted as much, she never meant actual murder; while his, again, was the old Barnwell charge, that his better nature had been corrupted by the woman, and that he did it at her suggestion, and under the influence of her siren power. They thus got gradually into that state of feeling by which the runaway convicts from a penal settlement were actuated, when, toiling away through endless brakes and swamps where neither meat nor drink could be procured, they were so maddened by hunger, that each, with a concealed knife under his sleeve, watched his neighbour for an opportunity to strike, nor could one dare to fall behind without the suspicion being raised in the minds of his companions that he was to execute his purpose when they were off their guard. So like, in other respects too, for these men, afraid to speak their thoughts of each other, jour-neyed on in deep silence, and each was ready to immolate

E

his friend at the altar of selfishness, changed into a blood-thirsty Dagon by the fiends Hunger and Thirst.

The years were now to be counted as seven since Janet Dodds was plunged into the deep pool of the North Loch, and the state of mind of the married criminals, which we have tried to describe, had been growing and growing, for two of these years, as if it threatened to get stronger the older they grew, and the nearer the period of judgment. One morning when they were in bed, for even yet while they concealed their thoughts from each other and the name of Jenny Dodds was a condemned word in their vocabulary, even as the sacred name among the Romans, they had evinced no spoken enmity to each other, they heard a tirl at the door. The hour was early, and the douce genius of the gray dawn was deliberating with herself whether it was time to give place to her advancing sister, the morning. Mrs Mary Dodds rose to answer the knock, and Thomas listened with natural curiosity to know who the early visitor was, and what was wanted. He heard a suppressed scream of fear from his wife, and the next moment she came rushing into the room; yet the never a word she uttered, and her lips were so white and dry that you might have supposed that her silence was the result of organic inability. Nor even when she got into bed again, and tried to hide her head with the bed-clothes, did her terror diminish, or her lips become more obedient to the feeling within, so that Thomas knew not what to think, except it was that she had seen a ghost—not an unnatural supposition at a time when occult causes and spiritual appearances were as undoubted as the phenomena of the electric telegraph are in our day. But he was not destined to be left many minutes more in ignorance of the cause of Mrs Mary Dodds's terror, for, upon listening, he heard some one come into the kitchen, and bolt the door on the inside—so much for his ears; then he turned his eyes to the kitchen, into which he could, as well

as the light of the gray dawn would permit, see from where he lay, and what did he see?

> " How comes it? whence this mimic shape?
> In look and lineament so like our kind.
> You might accost the spectral thing, and say,
> ' Good e'en t'ye.'"

No other than the figure of Mrs Janet Dodds herself. Yes, there she was in her old gray dress, busy taking off that plaid which Thomas knew so well, and hanging the same upon the peg, where she had hung it so often for five long years. Thomas was now as completely deprived of the power of speech as she who lay, equally criminal as himself, alongside of him ; but able at least to look, or rather, unable to shut their eyes, they watched the doings of the strange morning visitor. They saw that she was moving about as if she were intent upon domestic work ; and, by and by, there she was busy with coals and sticks brought from their respective places, putting on the fire, which she lighted with the indispensable spunk applied to the spark in the tinder-box. Next, she undertook the sweeping of the floor, saying to herself—and they heard the words—" It looks as if it hadna been swept for seven years." Next she washed the dishes, which had been left on the table, indulging in the appropriate monologue implying the necessity of the work. Thereafter it appeared as if she was dissatisfied with the progress of the fire, for she was presently engaged in using the bellows, every blast of which was heard by the quaking couple in bed, and between the blasts the words came, " Ower late for Tammas's breakfast." So the blowing continued, till it was apparent enough, from the reflection of the flame on the wall, that she was succeeding in her efforts. Then, having made herself sure of the fire, she went to the proper place for the porridge goblet, took the same and put a sufficient quantity of water therein, placed it on the fire, and began to blow again with the same assiduity as before, with still interjected sentences expressive of her confidence that she would overcome the obstinacy of the coals. And overcome it she did, as appeared from the entire lighting up of the kitchen. Was ever Border brownie so industrious! Some time now elapsed as if she were sitting with due patience till the water should boil. Thereafter she rose, and they saw her cross the kitchen to the lobby, where the meal was kept, then return with a bowl containing what she no doubt considered a sufficient quantity. The stirring utensil called a "theedle" had also been got in its proper place, and, by and by, they heard the sound of the same as it beat upon the bottom and sides, guided by an experienced hand, and, every now and then, the sweltering and tottling of the pot. This process was now interrupted by the getting of the gray basin into which the porridge behoved to be poured; and poured it was, the process being followed by the sound of "the clauting o' the laggan," so familiar to Scotch ears. "Now it's ready for him," said the figure, as it moved across the kitchen again, to get the spoon and the bowl of milk, both of which they saw her place beside the basin.

All things being thus completed according to the intention of the industrious worker, a period of silence intervened, as if she had been taking a rest in the chair which stood by the fire. A most ominous interlude, for every moment the couple in bed expected that she would enter the bedroom, were it for nothing else than to "intimate breakfast"—an intimation which, if one could have judged by their erect hair and the sweat that stood in big drops on their brows, they were by no means prepared for. They were not to be subjected to this fearful trial, for the figure (so we must persist in calling it) was seen again to cross the kitchen, take down the plaid, and adjust it over the head according to the manner of the times. They then heard her draw the bolt, open the door, and shut the same again after her as she departed. She was gone.

Mr Thomas Dodds and his wife now began to be able to breathe more freely. The hair resumed its flexibility, and the sweat disappeared; but, strange as it may seem, they never exchanged a word with each other as to who the visitor was, nor as to the morning's work she had so industriously and silently (with the exception of her monologues) executed. Too certain in their convictions as to the identity, whether in spirit or body, of the figure with that of her they had so cruelly put out of the way, they seemed to think it needless to question each other; and, independently of this, the old terror of the conscience was sufficient to seal their lips now, as it had done for a period before. Each of them supposed that the visitor was sent for the special purpose of some particular avengement of the crime upon the other; the appearance in so peaceful a way, in the meantime, being merely a premonition to shew them that their consciences were not working in vain : and if Thomas was the greater sinner, which he no doubt suspected in spite of himself, he might place against that conviction the fact that the inscrutable visitor had shewn him the kindness at least of preparing his breakfast, and entirely overlooking the morning requirements of his spouse. Under these thoughts they rose and repaired with faltering step and fearful eyes to the kitchen. There everything was in the order they had anticipated from what they had seen and heard. Each looked with a shudder at the basin of porridge as if it had been invested with some terrible charm—nay, might it not have been poisoned !—a thought which rushed instantaneously into the head of Thomas, and entirely put to flight the prior hypothesis that he had been favoured by this special gift of cookery. The basin was accordingly laid aside by hands that trembled to touch it, and fear was a sufficient breakfast for both of them on that most eventful morning.

This occurrence, as may readily be supposed, was kept a profound secret. They both saw that it might be the forerunner of Divine means to bring their evil deeds to light; and, under this apprehension, their taciturnity and mutual discontent, if not growing hatred, continued broken only by occasional growls and curses, and the ejaculations forced out by the inevitable circumstances of their connexion. The effect of the morning visit was meanwhile most apparent upon the man who committed the terrible act. He could not remain in the house, which, even in their happiest condition, was slovenly kept, shewing everywhere the want of the skilled hands of that queen of housewives, Mrs Janet Dodds—so ill requited for her devotion to her husband. Nay, he felt all this as a reproof to him, and sorely and bitterly lamented the fatal act whereby he had deprived of life the best of wives, and the most honest and peaceful of womankind. Then the awe of Divine vengeance deepened these shadows of the soul till he became moody and melancholy, walking hither and thither without an object, and in secluded places, looking fearfully around him as if he expected every moment the spectre visitor of the morning to appear before him. Nor was he less miserable at home, where the growing hatred made matters worse and worse every hour, and where, when the gray dawn came, he expected another visit and another scene of the same description as the last.

Nearly a week had thus passed, and it was Sabbath morning. The tinsmiths' hammers were silent, the noisy games of the urchins were hushed, the street of the Bow resounded only occasionally to the sound of a foot;—all Edinburgh was, in short, under the solemnity enjoined by the Calvinism so much beloved by the people, and surely the day might have been supposed to be held in such veneration by ministering spirits, sent down to earth to execute the purposes of Heaven, that no visit of the feared shadow would disturb even the broken rest of the wicked. So perhaps thought our couple; but their thoughts belied them, for just again as the dawn broke over the tops of the high houses, the well-known tirl was heard at the door. Who was to open it? For days the mind of the wife had been made up. She would not face that figure again; no, if all the powers of the world were there to compel her; and as for Thomas, conscience had reduced the firmness of a man who once upon a time could kill to a condition of fear and trembling. Yet terrified as he was, he considered that he was here under the obligation to obey powers even higher than his conscience, and disobedience might bring upon him some evil greater than that under which he groaned. So up he got trembling in every limb, and proceeding to the door, opened the same. What he saw may be surmised, but what he felt no one ever knew, for the one reason that he had never the courage to tell it, and for the other that no man or woman was ever placed in circumstances from which they could draw any conclusion which could impart even a distant analogy. This much, however, was known: Thomas retreated instantly to bed, and the visitor, in the same suit of hoddengray, again entered, passed the bolt, took off her plaid, hung it up, and began the duties which she thought were suited to the day and the hour. So much being thus alike, the couple in the bed-room no doubt augured a repetition of the old process. They were right, and they were wrong. Their eyes were fixed upon her, and watched her movements; but the watch was that of the charmed eye which is said to be without motive. They saw her once more go deliberately and tently through the old process of putting on the fire, and they heard again the application of the bellows, every blast succeeding another with the regularity of a clock, until the kitchen was illuminated by the rising flame. This was all that could be called a repetition; for in place of going for the porridge goblet, she went direct for the tea-kettle, into which she poured a sufficient quantity of water, saying the while to herself, "Tammas maun hae his tea breakfast on Sabbath morning"—words which Thomas, as he now lay quaking in bed, knew very well he had heard before many a time and oft. Nor were the subsequent acts less in accordance with the old custom of the dwelling. There was no sweeping of the floor or scouring of pans on the sacred morning—in place of all which she had something else to do, for surely we must suppose that this gentle visitor was a good Calvinist, and would perform only the acts of necessity and mercy. These she had done in so far as regarded necessity, and now they saw her go to the shelf on which the Bible was deposited—a book which, alas! for seven years had not been opened by either of the guilty pair. Having got what she wanted, she sat down by the table, opened the volume at a place well thumbed, and began to read aloud a chapter in the Corinthians, which Thomas Dodds, the more by reason that he had heard it read two hundred and fifty times, knew by heart. This being finished she turned up a psalm, yea, that very psalm which Janet Dodds had sung every Sunday morning; and, presently, the kitchen was resonant with the rising notes of the Bangor, as they came from a throat trembling with devotion—

> " I waited on the Lord my God,
>   And patiently did bear ;
> At length to me he did incline
>   My voice and cry to hear.

> " He took me from a fearful pit,
>   And from the miry clay,
> And on a rock he set my feet,
>   Establishing my way."

The service finished, they saw her replace the book where she had found it, and by this time the kettle was spewing from the mouth thereof a volume of steam, as if it were calling to its old mistress to relieve it from the heat of the fire ; nor was she long in paying due obedience. The tea-pot was got where she seemed to know it would be found, so also the tea-canister.

The quantity to be put in was a foregone conclusion and steadily measured with the spoon. The water was poured in and the utensil placed on the cheek of the chimney in order to the indispensable infusion. Next, the cup and saucer were placed on the table, then followed the bread and butter an.l the sugar and the milk, all being finished by the words to herself, " There's nae egg in the house." Having thus finished her work she took down her plaid, adjusted it carefully, opened the door, and departed.

The effect produced by this second spectral appearance could scarcely be exaggerated, yet we suspect you will not find it of that kind which is most in harmony with human nature, except in the case of Mrs Dodds the second, who lay, as on the former occasion, sweating and trembling. It was now different with the husband, on whom apparently had fallen some of the seeds of the Word, as they were scattered by the lips of the strange visitor, and conscience had prepared the soil. The constitutional strength of character which had enabled him to perpetrate a terrible deed of evil, was ready as a power to achieve his emancipation and work in the direction of good. So, without saying a word of all that had been acted that morning, he rose and dressed himself, and going into the kitchen he sat down without the fear of poison and partook of the breakfast which had been so strangely prepared for him, nor was he satisfied till he read the chapter and psalm with which he had been so long familiar. He then returned to the bedroom, and addressing his wife—

"You now see," said he, "that Heaven has found us out. That visitor is nae ither than Mrs Janet Dodds returned frae the grave, and sure it is that nane are permitted to leave that place o' rest except for a purpose. No, it's no for naething that Janet Dodds comes back to her auld hame. What the purpose may be, the Lord only knows, but this seems to me to be clear enough—that you and I maun pairt. You see that nae breakfast has been laid for you. I have taen mine and nae harm has come o't, a clear sign that though we are baith great criminals, you are considered to be the warst o' the twa. It was you wha put poison into my ear and cast glamour ower my een ; it was you wha egged me on, for ' The lips of a strange woman drop as a honeycomb, and her words are smoother than oil ; but her feet take hold of hell.' That I am guilty I know, and ' though hand join in hand, the wicked shall not go unpunished.' I will dree my doom whatever it may be, and so maun you yours ; but there may be a differ- ence, and so far as mortal can yet see, yours will be waur to bear than mine. But, however a' that may be, the time is come when you maun leave this house. ' Cast out the strange woman, and contention shall go out ; yea, strife and reproach shall cease ;' but ' Go not forth hastily to strive, lest thou know not what to do in the end, when thy neighbour hath put thee to shame.' Keep your secret frae a' save the Lord, and may He hae mercy on your soul."

With which words, savouring as they did of the objurgations of the black-pot to the kettle, Mr Thomas Dodds left his house, no doubt in the expectation that Mrs Dodds *secunda* would move her camp and betake herself once more to her old place of residence in the Grassmarket. Where he went that day no man ever knew, further han that he was seen in the afternoon in St Giles's Church, where, no doubt, he did his best to make a cheap purchase of immunity to his soul and body in consideration of a repentance brought on by pure fear, produced by a spectre ; and who knows but that that was a final cause of the spectre's appearance. We have seen that it was a kindly spirit, preparing porridge and tea for him at the same time that it made his hair stand on end and big drops of sweat settle upon his brow or roll down therefrom— a conjunction this of the tawse and the jelly-pot, whereby kind and loving parents try to redeem naughty boys. Nor let it be said that this kindly dealing with a murderer is contrary to the ways of Heaven; for, amidst a thousand other examples, did not Joshua, after the wall of Jericho lay flat at the blast of a trumpet, save that vile woman Rahab at the same time that he slew the young and the old, nay, the very infants, with the edge of the sword? All which, though we are not by token of our sins able to see the reason thereof, is doubtless consonant to a higher justice—altogether unlike our goddess, who is represented as blind, merely because she is supposed not to see a bribe when offered to her by a litigant. So, the penitence of Mr Thomas Dodds might be a very dear affair after all, in so much as terror is a condition of the soul which, of all we are doomed to experience, is the most difficult to bear, especially if it is a terror of Divine wrath. On his return to his house in the evening he found that Mrs Mary had taken him at his word and decamped, but not without providing herself with as good a share of the "goods in communion" as she could, perhaps, at two or three returns, carry off. So was she like Zebulun in all save her righteousness, for she "rejoiced in her going out," nay, she had some reason, for she had discovered that in a secret drawer of an old cabinet there was a pose of gold collected by the industrious hands of Mrs Janet, and unknown to her husband, every piece of which she carried off in spite of all fear of the spectre, which, if a sensible one, might have been supposed to be more irritated at this heedless spoliation than at all the Jezebel had yet done, with the exception of the counselling her death in the deep hole of the North Loch. On seeing all this robbery Mr Dodds became more and more aware of the bad exchange he had made by killing his good spouse to enable him to take another, who had merely found more favour in his eyes by reason of her good looks, and we may augur how much deeper his feeling of regret would have been had he known the secret pose, so frugally and prudently laid up, perhaps for his sake, at least for the sake of both, when disease or old age might overtake them, in a world where good and evil, pleasure and pain, appear to be fixed quantities, only shoved from one to another by wisdom and prudence, yet sometimes refusing to be moved even by these means.

After satisfying himself of the full extent of the robbery, which, after all, he had brought upon himself, and very richly deserved, he sat down upon a chair and began to moralise after the manner of those late penitents who have found them-selves out to be either rogues or fools—the number of whom comprehends, perhaps, all mankind. He had certainly good reason to be contrite. The angel in the house had become a spectre, and she who was no angel either in the house or out of it, had carried off almost everything of any value he pos-sessed ; nor did he stop at mere unspoken contrition — he bewailed in solemn tones his destiny, and then began to cast up all the perfections of good Janet, the more perfect and beautiful these seeming in proportion as he felt the fear of her reappearance, perhaps, next time in place of making his breakfast to run away with him to the dire place of four letters. All her peculiarities were now virtues— nay, the very things which had appeared to him the most indefensible took on the aspect of angelic endowments. While her careful house-wifery was all intended for his bodily health and comfort, her perseverance in adhering to the one chapter and the one psalm was due to that love of iteration which inspires those who are never weary of well-doing. And what was more ex-traordinary, one verse of the psalm — that which we have quoted—had special reference to the manner of her death, and her deliverance from condemnation in the world to come. No doubt the man who meditates upon his own crime or folly at the very moment when he is suffering from its sharp recal-citrations, is just about as miserable a wretch as the reforma-tory of the world can present ; but when to the effects upon himself he is compelled to think of the cruelty he has exercised towards others—and those perhaps found out to be his best friends—we doubt if there are any words beyond the vocabulary of the condemned that are sufficient to express his anguish. Even this did not comprehend all the suffering of Mr Dodds, for was he not under doom without knowing what form it was to assume, whether the spectre (whose cookery might be a sham) would choke him, burn him, or run away with him.

Deeply steeped in this remorseful contemplation, during which the figure of his ill-used wife flitted before the eye of his fancy with scarcely less of substantial reality than she had shewn in her spectral form, he found that he had lost all regard to time. The night was fast setting in, the shadows of the tall houses were falling deeper and deeper on the room, and the Sabbath stillness was a solemn contrast to the perturbations inside the chamber of his soul, where "the serpents and the cockatrices would not be charmed." Still, everything within and without was dreary, and the spoliation of his means did not tend to enliven the outer scene or impart a charm to the owner. While in this state of depression, Tammas heard a knock at the door. It was not, as on the former occasions, what is called a tirl. It might be a neighbour, or it might be an old crony, and he stood in need of some one to raise his spirits, so he went to the door and opened it ; but what was his horror when he saw enter a female figure, in all respects so like his feared visitor that he concluded in the instant that she was the same ; nor could all his penitence afford him resolution enough to make a proper examination ; besides, it was gray dark, and even a pair of better eyes than he could boast of might, under the circumstances soon to appear, have been deceived. Retreating into the kitchen, he was followed by this dubious, and yet not dubious visitor, who, as he threw himself upon a chair, took a seat right opposite to him.

" Ye 'll no ken me, Tammas Dodds ?" said she.

Whereupon Tammas looked and looked again, and still the likeness he dreaded was so impressive that, in place of moving his tongue, he moved, that is, he shuddered all over.

"What—eh ?" at length he stuttered ; "ken ye ; wha in God's name are ye ? No surely Mrs Janet Dodds in the likeness of the flesh !"

"No, but her sister, Mrs Paterson," replied the other. " And is it possible ye can hae forgotten the only woman who was present at your first marriage ?"

' Ay, ay," replied Tammas, as he began to come to a proper condition of perceiving and thinking ; "and it was you, then, wha was here this morning ?"

"No, no," replied she , " I have not been here for seven long years, even since that terrible night when you pushed Janet into the North Loch."

"And may Heaven and its angels hae mercy upon me !" ejaculated he.

"Aiblins they may," said she, " for your purpose was defeated ; yea, even by that Heaven and thae angels."

"What mean you, woman ?" cried the astonished man. "What, in the name o' a' that 's gude on earth and holy in heaven, do ye mean ?"

" Just that Janet Dodds is at this hour a leevin' woman," was the reply.

" The Lord be thanked !" cried Tammas, again, "for ' He preserveth all them that love Him.' "

" But all the wicked He will destroy," returned she ; "and surely it was wicked to try to drown sae faithful a wife and sae gude a Christian."

" Wicked !" rejoined he, in rising agony. " Let the righteous smite me, it shall be a kindness ; and let them reprove me, it shall, as Solomon says, be an excellent oil."

" I am glad," continued the woman, "to find you with a

turned heart; but whaur is the Jezebel ye took in her place?"

"Awa this day," replied he. "I have found her out, and never mair is she wife o' mine."

"Sae far weel and better," said she.

"Ay, but speak to me o' Janet," cried he, earnestly. "Come, tell me how she escaped, whaur she is, and how she is—for now I think there is light breaking through the fearfu' cloud."

"Light indeed," continued Mrs Paterson; "and now listen to a strange tale, mair wonderfu' than man's brain ever conceived. When ye thought ye had drowned her, and cared naething doubtless, for ye see I maun speak pl in, whether her spirit went to the ae place or the ither, ay, and ran awa to add to murder a lee, she struggled out o' the deep, yea—

> ' He took her from the fearfu' pit,
> And from the miry clay.'

And when she got to the bank, she ran as for the little life that was in her, until she came to the foot o' Halkerstone's Wynd, where she crossed to the other side of the loch. When she thought hersel' safe, she took the road to Glasgow, where I was then living wi' my husband, wha is since dead. The night was dark; but self-preservation maks nae gobs at dangers, so on she went, till in the gray morning she made up to the Glasgow carrier, wha agreed to gie her a cast even to the end o' his journey. It was the next night when she arrived at my door, cold and hungry, and, what was waur, sair and sick at heart. She told me the hail story as weel as she could for sobs and greeting; for the thought ay rugged at her heart that the man she had liked sae weel, and had toiled for night and day, should hae turned out to be the murderer o' his ain wife."

"And weel it might hae rugged and rugged," ejaculated Tammas.

"I got aff her wet clothes," continued she, "and gave some strong drink to warm her, and then we considered wha was to be dune. My husband was for aff to Edinburgh to inform on ye, even if there should hae been a drawing o' the neck on 't; but Janet cried, and entreated baith him and me to keep the thing quiet. She said she couldna gae back to you, and as for getting you punished, she couldna bear the thought o 't. And then we a' thought what a disgrace it would be to our family if it were thought that my sister had been attempted to be murdered by her husband. We knew weel enough ye would say she had fallen in by accident; and when afterwards we heard that ye had buried a body that had been found in the loch, we made up our minds as to what we would do. We just agreed to keep Janet under her maiden name. Nane in Glasgow had ever seen her before, and her ain sorrows kept her within doors, so that the secret wasna ill to keep. Years afterwards, my husband was ta'en from me, and Janet and I came about twa months syne to live at Juniper Green, wi' John Paterson, my husband's brother. wha had offered us a hame."

"And is Janet there now?" cried Tammas, impatiently.

"Ay," continued Mrs Paterson; "but, alas! she's no what she was. She gets at times out o' her reason, and will be that way for days thegether. The doctor has a name for it ower lang for my tongue; but it tells naething but what we ken ower weel. When in thae fits she thinks she is here in the Bow, and living with you, and working and moiling in the house just as she used to do langsyne. Mairower, and that troubles us maist ava, she will be out when the reason's no in, so that we are obliged to watch her. Five days syne, she was aff in the morning before daylight, and even so late as this morning she played us the same trick; whaur she gaed we couldna tell, but I had some suspicion she was here."

" Ay," replied Mr Dodds, as he opened his eyes very wide ; " she was here wi' a vengeance."

Thus Mrs Paterson's story was finished ; and our legend of the Brownie, more veritable, we opine, than that of Bodsbeck, is also drawing to a conclusion. Tammas, after a period of meditation, more like one of Janet's hallucinations than a fit of rational thinking, asked his sister-in-law whether she thought that Janet, in the event of her getting quit of her day-dreams, would consent to live with him again. To which question she answered that she was not certain ; for that Janet, when in her usual state of mind, was still wroth against him for the attempt to take away her life ; but she added that she had no objection, seeing he was penitent, to give him an opportunity to plead for himself. She even went further, and agreed to use her influence to bring about a reconciliation. It was therefore agreed between them that the sister should call again when Janet had got quit of her temporary derangement, and Thomas might follow up this intimation with a visit. About four days thereafter, accordingly, Mrs Paterson kept her word, and next day Mr Dodds repaired to Juniper Green. At first Janet refused to see him; but upon Mrs Paterson's representations of his penitence and suffering, she became reconciled to an interview. We may venture to say, without attempting a description of a meeting unparalleled in history, that if Janet Dodds had not been a veritable Calvinist, no good could have come of all Mr Dodds's professions ; but she knew that the Master cast out the dumb spirit which tore the possessed, and that that spirit attempted murder not less than Tammas. Wherefore might not *his* dumb spirit be cast out as well by that grace which aboundeth in the bosom of the Saviour ? We do not say that a return of her old love helped this deduction, because we do not wish to mix up profane with sacred things. Enough, if we can certify that a very happy conclusion was the result. The doctor did

E

his duty, and Janet having been declared *compos mentis*, returned to her old home. Her first duty was to look for " the pose." It was gone in the manner we have set forth; but Janet could collect another, and no doubt in due time did, nor did she fail of any of her old peculiarities, all of which became endeared to Thomas by reason of their being veritable sacrifices to his domestic comfort.

The Ancient Bureau.

THE sources of legends are not often found in old sermons; and yet it will be admitted that there are few remarkable events in man's history, which, if inquired into, will not be found to embrace the elements of very impressive pulpit discourses. Even in cases which seem to disprove a special, if not a general Providence, there will always be found in the account between earth and heaven some "desperate debt," mayhap an "accommodation bill," which justifies the ways of God to man. It may even be said that the fact of our being generally able to find that item is a proof of the wonderful adaptability of Christianity to the fortunes and hopes of our race. That ministers avoid the special topics of peculiar destinies may easily be accounted for otherwise than by supposing that they cannot explain them so as to vindicate God's justice; but if ever there was a case where that difficulty would seem to the eye of mere reason to culminate in impossibility, it is that which I have gleaned from a veritable pulpit lecture. I have the sermon in my possession, but from the want of the title-page, I am unable to ascertain the author. The date at the end is 1793, and the text is, " Inscrutable are *His* judgments."

Inscrutable indeed in the case to which the words were applied—no other than an instance of death by starvation, which occurred in Edinburgh in the year we have just mentioned. In that retreat of poverty called Middleton's Entry, which joins the dark street called the Potterrow and Bristo

Street, the inhabitants were roused into surprise, if not a feeling approaching to horror, by the discovery that a woman, who had lived for a period of fifteen years in a solitary room at the top of one of the tenements, had been found in bed dead. A doctor was called, but before he came it was concluded by those who had assembled in the small room that she had died from want of food, and such was the fact. The body—that of one not yet much past the middle of life, and with fair complexion and comely features—was so emaciated, that you might have counted the ribs merely by the eye ; and all those parts where the bones are naturally near the surface exhibited a sharpness which suggested the fancy, that as you may see a phosphorescent skeleton through the glow, you beheld the form of the grim figure of death under the thin covering of the bones. She realised, in short, the description which doctors give of the appearance of those unfortunate beings who die of what is technically called *atrophia famili-corum*—that Nemesis of civilisation which points scornfully to the victim of want, and then looks round on God's bountiful table, set for the meanest of His creatures. So we may indite ; but rhetoric, which is useless where the images cannot rise to the dignity or descend to the humiliation of the visible fact, must always come short of the effect of the plain words that a human creature—perhaps good and amiable and delicate to that shyness which cannot complain—has died in the very midst of a proclaimed philanthropy, and within the limits of a space comprehending smoking tables covered with luxuries, and surrounded by Christian men and women filled with meat and drink to repletion and satiety.

Some such thoughts might have been passing through the minds of the assembled neighbours ; and they could not be said to be the less true that a shrunk and partially-withered right arm shewed that the doom of the woman had been so far precipitated by the still remaining effects of an old stroke of palsy. And the gossip confirmed this, going also into particulars of observation—how she had kept herself so to herself as if she wished to avoid the neighbours—a fact which to an extent justified their imputed want of attention ; how almost the only individual who had visited her was a peculiar being, in the shape of a very little man, with a slight limp and thin pleasant features, illuminated by a pair of dark, penetrating eyes. For years and years had he been seen, always about the same hour of the day, ascending her stair, and carrying a flagon, supposed to contain articles of food. Then the gossiping embraced the furniture and other articles in the room, which, however they might have been unnoticed before, had now assumed the usual interest when seen in the blue light of the acted tragedy : the small mahogany table and the two chairs—how strange that they should be of mahogany !—and some of the few marrowless plates in the rack over the fireplace, why, they were absolute china ! but above all, the exquisite little bureau of French manufacture, with its drawers, its desk, and pigeon holes, and cunning slides—what on earth was it doing in that room, when its value even to a broker would have kept the woman alive for months? Questions these put by a roused curiosity, and perhaps not worth answer. Was not she a woman, and was not that enough ?

Not enough ; for legendary details cluster round startling events, and often carry a moral which may prevent a repetition of these ; and so had it not been for this apparently inexplicable death by starvation, our wonderful story might never have gathered listeners round the evening fire. We must go back some twenty years before the date of the said sermon to find a certain merchant-burgess of the city of Edinburgh, David Grierson, occupying a portion of a front land situated in the Canongate, a little to the east of Leith Wynd. It would be sheer affectation in us to pretend that this merchant-burgess had any mental or physical characteristic about him to justify

his appearance in a romance, if we except the power he had
shewn of amassing wealth, of which he had so much that he
could boast the possession of more than twenty goodly tenements, some of wood and some of stone, besides shares of
ships and bank stock.　And no doubt this exception might
stand for the thing excepted from, for money, though com-
monly said to be extraneous, is often so far in its influences
intraneous, that it changes the feelings and motives, and
enables them to work.　And then don't we know that it
is by extraneous things we are mostly led?　But, however all
that may be, certain it is that our merchant-burgess was a great
man in his own house in the Canongate, where his family
consisted of Rachel Grierson, his natural daughter, by a
woman who had been long dead, and Walter Grierson, his
legitimate nephew, who had been left an orphan in his early
years, and who was his nearest lawful heir.　Two servants
completed the household ; and surely in this rather curious
combination there might be, if only circumstances were favourable to their development, elements which might impart
interest to a story.

So long as the shadow of the dark angel was, as Time
counted, far away from him, Burgess David was comparatively
happy ; but as he got old and older, he began to realise the
condition of the poet—

> "Now pleasure will no longer please,
> 　And all the joys of life are gone ;
> I ask no more on earth but case,
> 　To be at peace, and be alone :
> I ask in vain the winged powers
> 　That weave man's destiny on high ;
> In vain I ask the golden hours
> 　That o'er my head for ever fly."

Then he waxed more and more anxious as to what he was
to do with his money.　He tried to put away the thought ; but

the terrible *magistra necessitas* went round and round him with ever-diminishing circles, clearly indicating a conflict in which he must succumb. He must make a will, an act which it is said no man is ever in a hearty condition to perform, unless mayhap he is angry, and wishes to cut off an ungrateful dog with a shilling; and besides the general disinclination to sign the disposal of so much wealth, of which he was more than ordinarily fond, and to give away, as it were, *omnia præter animam*, in the very view of giving away the soul too, he was in a great perplexity as to how to divide his means. Nor could he reconcile himself to a division at all, preferring, as the greatly lesser evil, the alternative of destinating his fortune all of a lump, with some hope of its being kept together. As for Walter, though he had some affection for him, he had not much confidence in him, for he had seen that he was hare-brained as regarded things which suited his fancy, and pig-brained as respected those which solicited and required sound judgment; while Rachel, again, was everything which, among the lower angels, could be comprehended under the delightful title of " dear soul," an amiable and devoted creature, as stead-fast in her affections as she was wise in the selection of their objects. So by revolving in his mind all the beauties of the character of her who, however disqualified by law, was still of his flesh and blood, yea, of his very nature, as he complacently thought in compliment to himself, he became more and more reconciled to his intention, if the very thought of making a will, which had been horrible to him, did not become even a pleasing kind of meditation. So is it—when nature imposes an inevitable duty, she gives man the power of inventing a pleasing reason for his obedience; nay, so much of a self-dissembler is he that he even cheats himself into the belief that his obedience is an act of his own will. In all which he at least proved the value of one of the arguments in favour of marriage, for trite it is to say a bachelor bears to no one a love which reconciles him to will-making, while a father, in leaving his means to his children, feels as if he were giving to himself. But this plan of our merchant-burgess had in addition a spice of ingenuity in it which still more pleased him—he would so contrive matters that the daughter and the nephew would become, after his death, man and wife. He had only some doubts how far their tastes agreed, probably an absurd condition, in so much as we all know that love is often struck out by opposition, and that there is a pleasant suitability in a husband preferring the head of a herring and the wife the tail.

Having thus arrived at a sense of his duty by the pleasant path of his affection, Mr David Grierson seized the first oppor-tunity which presented itself of sounding the heart of R chel, in order to know in what direction her affectiôns ran. Sitting in his big chair, all so comfortably cushioned by the hands of the said Rachel herself, and with a good fire alongside, due also to her unremitting care, he called her to him, and placing his arm round her waist, as he was often in the habit of doing, said to her—

"Rachel, dear, I feel day by day my strength leaving me, and it may be, nay, will be, that I will not be very much longer with you."

Rachel looked at him for a little, but said nothing, for, as the saying goes, her heart came to her mouth, and she could not have spoken even if she would; but the father understood all this, and preferred the mute expression of a real grief to a hysterical burst—of which, indeed, her calm genial nature was incapable.

"Forgive me, dear," continued he, "for I would not will-ingly cause you sorrow, but I have a reason for speaking in this grave way. Who is to fill the old arm-chair when I cannot occupy it?"

And he smiled somewhat grimly as he sought her eye, in

which he could observe the most real of all nature's evidences of emotion.

" What mean you, father ?" she replied, with something like an effort to respond to his humour.

" Why, then, Rachel," he said, " to be out with it, I want to know whether you have fixed your heart on any one."

" Only upon you, dear father," she replied, with a smile which struggled against her seriousness.

" Nay, Rachel," continued he. " It is no light matter, and I must have an answer. I intend to leave you my whole fortune, but upon one condition, which is, that if Walter Grierson shall sue for your hand you will consent to marry him."

To this there was a reply given with an alacrity which shewed how her heart pointed—" Yes : " then, adding that wonderful little word, " but," which makes such havoc among our resolutions, she paused, while her eyes sought the ground.

" What 'but' can be here?" interjected the old man. " Surely you do not mean to doubt whether *he* would consent ?"

" And yet that is just my doubt," she replied, as if she felt humiliated by the admission.

" Doubt !" cried the father, in rising wrath , " doubt—doubt if a beggar would consent to be made rich by marrying *you !* Why, Rachel, dear, if the fellow were to breathe a sigh of hesitation, he would deserve to be a beggar with more holes than wholes in his gabardine, and too poor even to possess a wallet to carry his bones and crumbs. Have you any reason for your strange statement ?"

" No," replied the girl, with a sigh. " It is only my heart that speaks."

" And the heart never lies," said he, sharply ; " but I shall see," he muttered to himself, " whether a certain tongue in a certain head shall speak in the same way."

"But would it not bring me down," said she, "were he to think that he was forced by a promise?"

"A promise," rejoined he; "why, so it would, my dear. I see you are right." But then he thought he could sound him without putting any obligation upon him. "And a pretty obligation it would be," he continued, "for a young fellow cut off with a shilling to bind himself to consent to be the acceptor of two such gifts as a fine girl and a fortune."

And Burgess David tried to laugh, but the effort was still that of a heavy heart, and, reclining his head upon the back of the chair, he relapsed into those thoughts which, as age advances to the term where Hope throws down her lamp, press in and in upon the spirit. Rachel glided away quietly, perhaps to think, and certainly she had something to think about.

So, too, doubtless had Mr David Grierson, who, after indulging in his reverie, wherein the subject of will-making suggested a match between himself and a certain bridegroom who never says nay, awoke to the interest of his scheme of match-making in this world. So far he had accomplished his object, for he could rely upon his faithful Rachel's performance of her promise, and if the two should be married, he knew how to take care to give her the power of the money, and keep a youth in whose prudence he had no great faith in proper check. Next he had to sound the nephew. Nor was it long before he had an opportunity—even that same afternoon.

"Walter," he began with an abruptness, for which probably the young man was scarcely prepared, "I am getting old, and must now think of arranging my affairs so as to endeavour to make my fortune serve the purpose of rendering those happy in whom I have a natural interest. So I have some interest also as well as, I suspect, some right to put the question to you, whether you ever thought of Rachel Grierson for your wife?"

" Upon my word," replied the nephew, with just as little *mauvais honte* as suited his nature, "I never thought of aspiring to the *hon ur.*"

A word this last which grated on the ear of the rich merchant-burgess, inasmuch as it suggested a suspicion of the figure of speech called irony, seeing that Rachel Grierson was a bastard, and the youth carried the legitimate blood of the Griersons in his veins.

" Honour or no honour," replied he, sharply, and perhaps contrary to his original intention, " Rachel Grierson is to inherit my fortune, ay, every penny thereof."

" Every penny thereof," echoed the youth, as if his mind had flown away with the words, and dropt them in despair as it flew.

" Yes," rejoined the angry uncle, " lands, tenements, hereditaments, shares, dividends, stock, furniture, bed and table linen."

" And table linen," echoed the entranced nephew.

" Yes ; everything," continued the uncle, and, calming down as he saw the white lips and blank despair of the youth, he added—"And to you I will leave and bequeath my natural-born daughter, Rachel Grierson."

And as he uttered these significant words, he watched carefully the face of the youth, where, however, all indications defied his perspicacity, inasmuch as blank astonishment was still the prevailing expression. But after some minutes, the young man stuttered out—

" A legacy worthy of a nobleman."

Words that sounded beautifully, because they were true as regarded Rachel, whatever they might be as respected his secret intention ; yet, as the children vaticinate from the examination of each others' tongues, if the uncle had examined that organ, he might have discovered some of those blue lines which produce an exclamation from the young augurs

" *Words* worthy, too, of a nobleman," cried the old man, in a trembling voice ; and holding out his hand, which shook under his emotion of delight at hearing his beloved Rachel so praised, he seized that of his nephew—

"Yes, Walter," he added, "you have by these words redeemed yourself, and I will take them as an offering of your willingness to accept my legacy ; but, remember, I extort no promise, which might reduce the value of a young woman's affection,—a gift to be accepted for its own sake.

"I am content," said Walter.

"And I am satisfied," added the uncle. "But here is wine on the table," he continued, as he turned his eye in the direction of a decanter of good claret, just as if Rachel had, by her art of love, anticipated what he wished at this moment. "Ah, Walter, if she shall watch your wants as she has done mine, you will live to feel that you cannot want *her*, and live ; so, fill up a glass for me, and one for yourself, that we may drink to the happiness of the dear girl when, after I am dead, she shall become your wedded wife."

"With all and sundry lands, tenements, hereditaments, and so forth," cried Walter, with a laugh which might pass as genuine, and which was responded to by a chuckle from the dry throat of the uncle, which certainly was so.

So the pledge was taken, and Walter Grierson went away, leaving the old merchant-burgess as happy as any poor mortal creature can be when so near the term of his departure. Such is our way of speaking. and yet we are forced to admit, that at no period of life, however near the ultimate, abating the advent of the great illumination which breaks, like a new dawn, upon the internal sense of a favoured few, can you say that the hold of this world upon the spirit is ever renounced. Whether the young man was as happy, we may not venture to say , but this we might surmise, even at this stage of our story, and in reference to the classical proverb, that the bastard might be the beautiful Nisa, and the lawful heir the ill-favoured Mopsus.

These things we may leave to development; and with a caution to the reader not to be over-suspicious, we will follow our Nisa, Rachel Grierson, as she proceeds from the house of the merchant-burgess up the High Street, at a period of the evening of the same day when the shadows of the tall lands wrapped the crowds of loiterers and passengers almost in utter darkness; not that she chose this time for any purpose of secrecy,—for she had no secret, except that solitary one which every young woman has, and holds, up to the minute of conviction, that she is engaged, after which it becomes a fame blown by her own breath, but simply because it suited the routine of her duties. Her night-cloak kept her from the cold, and the panoply of her virtue secured her from insult; so, threading her way amidst the throng, she arrived at the head of the old winding street called the West Bow, where, at a projection a little to the north of Major Weir's entry, she mounted a narrow stair. On arriving at a door on the third landing-place, she tapped gently, and, in obedience to a shrill voice, which cried "Come in," she lifted the latch, and entered a small room, where, at a bench, sat a very peculiar personage. This was no other than the famous Paul Bennett, an artist in jewellery, who, at that time, excelled all his compeers for beauty of design and exquisite refinement of minute elaboration. And this, perhaps, a good judge of mankind might have augured of him; for while his body was far below the middle size, his long, thin fingers, tapering to a point, seemed to be suitable instruments intended to serve a pair of dark eyes, so lustrous and sharp that nothing within the point of the beginning of infinitesimals might seem to escape them. Nor was his pale face less suggestive of his peculiar faculties; for it was made up of fine, delicate features, harmonised into regularity, and so expressive, that it seemed to change with every feeling of the moment, even as the flitting moonbeams play on the face of a statue. In addition to these peculiarities, his appearance was rendered the more striking, that, working as he did under a strong reflected light, cast down immediately before his face by a dark shade, the upper part of his person, and a circle on the bench, were in bright relief, while the other parts of the room were comparatively dark.

"Still at work, Paul," said Rachel, as she entered; "how long do you intend to work to night?"

"Till the idea becomes dim, and the sense waxes thick," replied he, as he turned his eyes upon her.

"I have something to tell you," she continued, as she sat down on a chair between him and the fire, if that could be called such which consisted of some red cinders.

"Some other wonder," replied he; "another cropping out of the workings of fate."

Words these, as coming from our little artist, which require some explanation, to the effect that Paul was a philosopher, too, in his own way. Early misfortunes, which mocked the resolutions of a will never very strong, had played into a habit of thinking, and brought him to the conviction that every movement or change in the moral world, not less than in the physical, is the result of a cause which runs back through endless generations to the first man, and even beyond him. Paul was, in short, a fatalist; not of that kind which romance writers feign in order to make the character work through a gloomy presentiment of his own destiny, but merely a believer in a universal original decree, the workings of which we never know until the effects are seen. A fatalist of this kind almost every man is, less or more, in some mood or another; only to save himself from being a puppet, moved by springs or drawn by strings, he generally contrives to except his *will* from the scheme of the iron-bound necessity. But Paul would permit of no such exception. The will, with him, was merely the *motive in action;* and as he compelled you to admit that no thought is, in man's experience, ever called into being, only developed from prior conditions, and that, even as to an idea, the doctrine, *Nihil nisi ex ovo,* is true, and therefore that no man can manufacture a motive, so he took a short way with the maintainers of a moral liberty. This doctrine, so gloomy, so grand, yet so terrible, was, to Paul, a conviction, which he almost made practical; nay, he seemed to realise a kind of poetic pleasure from reveries, which represented to him the universe, with the sun and the stars, and all living creatures —walking, flying, swimming, or crawling—going through their parts in the great melodrama of destiny, no one knowing how, or why, or wherefore, yet every human being believing that he is master of his actions, at the very moment that he might be conscious that his belief is only a part of the great law of necessity. Then it seemed as if this delusion in which men indulge, and are forced to indulge, was an element of the farce introduced into the play, so as to relieve the mind from the heavy burden of contemplating so terrible a theory.

"Something to tell me, Rachel," continued he, "and what may that be ?"

"My father has told me to-day," replied she, "that he is to leave me all his fortune, and, however grieved I may be at the thought of losing him, I am glad to think that it may be in my power to be of service to you, Paul, as my only relative on my mother's side."

"Service," muttered Paul to himself, while he looked into her face as wistfully as a lover, which indeed he was, though in secret; "and what is to become of Walter Grierson ?" he asked.

"When he finds that the entire fortune is mine," replied she, "he will propose to marry me ; and this is what my father wishes to bring about by putting the fortune in my power."

"So the events crop out from the long chain of causes," thought Paul; "but who shall tell the final issue? Look here, Rachel," he continued, as he laid his hand on a golden locket which lay before him of the shape of a heart; "I have made this to order," and as he spoke he touched a spring, whereupon a lid opened, and up flew a pair of tiny doves, which, with fluttering wings of gold and azure, immediately saluted each other with their long bills, and piped a few notes in imitation of the cushat. The touch of another spring immediately consigned them again to the cavity of the heart,—a conceit altogether of such refined manufacture and ingenuity of design, as to remind us of the saying of Cicero, that there is an exquisiteness in art which never can be known till it is seen fresh from the hand of genius.

"And who ordered that beautiful thing?" inquired Rachel.

"Walter Grierson," replied Paul, fixing his eyes upon her sorrowfully, as if he felt oppressed by that gloomy theory of his.

Nor did he fail to perceive the effect his few words had produced upon the heart of his cousin, where there was a fluttering very different from that of cooing turtles; for the fate of her happiness seemed to her to be suspended on the answer to a question, and that question she was afraid to put.

"Be patient, and learn to hear," continued the little philosopher. "Ere yet Cheops built the Pyramids, or Joshua commanded the sun to stand still; yea, before the first sensation tingled in the first nerve made out of the dust, the beginnings were laid of these events of this day and hour, and, in particular, of that one which may well astonish you and grieve you,—viz., that the locket is intended for and inscribed to Agnes Ainslie."

"Agnes Ainslie!" repeated Rachel, with parched lips and trembling voice, "the daughter of Mr John Ainslie, my father's agent, to whom I am even now going, by Mr Grierson's command, to request him to call to-morrow for the purpose of preparing the settlement."

"A strange perplexity of events," said Paul; "but what is this mingling of threads to the great web of the universe, which is eternally being woven and unwoven, unaffected by the will of man? and then these small issues, the loss of a fortune by a man, and that of a lover by a woman, how mighty they are to the individual hearts and affections!"

"Mighty indeed," sobbed Rachel, who had loved Walter so long, and rejoiced to have it in her power to bestow a fortune upon him, and now found all her hopes dissolved into the ashes of grief and disappointment. "Mighty indeed; and these thoughts of yours are so dreary, how can one believe in them and live!"

"We are compelled to live," replied he, "even by that same decree which binds us to the infinite chain. Were it not so, man would imitate the day flies, and die at sun-down, that he might escape the dark night which reveals to him the mystery of his being, whereat he trembles and sobs; and all this is also in the decree."

"But if all these things are so," said Rachel, "what do you say of happiness? Is there no joy in the world?—are not the birds happy, when, in the morning, the woods resound with their song, and so, too, every animal after its kind? Are not children joyful when the house rings with their mirth? and have not men and women their pleasures of a thousand kinds? nay, might not I myself have been one of the happiest of beings if, with the fortune which is to be left to me, that locket had been engraved with the name of Rachel Grierson in place of Agnes Ainslie?"

"Yes," replied he, "happiness is in the decree as well; "and," he added, with a smile, "it is always cropping out around us; but no one can manufacture the article. If you wait for it, you may feel it—if you run after it, you will most

G

probably not find it, because it is not ready by those eternal
laws which, at their beginning, involved its coming up at a
certain moment of long after years. Then, at the best, pleasure and pain are mere oscillations; but the first movement
is downwards—for we cry when we come into the world; and
the last is also downwards—for we groan when we go out of
it. It is the old rhyme—

> ' We scream when we 're born,
> We groan when we 're dying;
> And all that 's between
> Is but laughing and crying.' "

A parade of philosophy all this which at another time might
have had but a small effect upon a youthful mind; but Rachel
was in the meantime occupied by looking at the inscription
on the fatal toy, and we all know that the feeling of the
dominant idea of the moment assimilates to its own hue the
light or shade of all other ideas of a cognate kind; and there
is in this process also a se'ection and rejection whereby all
melancholy ideas cluster in the gloomy atmosphere, if we may
so term it, of the prevailing depression, and all joyful ones
come together by the attraction of a joyful thought; and so
Rachel was impressed by views which, if they had been modi-
fied by the comforting doctrines of Christianity, might have
enabled her at once to bear and to hope. Even when Paul
had finished, she was still gazing on the locket. A moment or
two more, and she laid it down with a deep sigh, saying,
almost involuntarily, "If my name had been there, I would not
have repined at the loss of all my expected fortune." Then
shaking hands with this peculiar being, whom she could not
but respect for his ingenuity, as well as for a kindliness and
sympathy which lay at the bottom of all his abstract theories,
she left him to his work, at which he would continue till
drowsiness made, as he said, the idea dim and the nerve
thick.

Retracing her steps down the long dark stair, not a very efficient medium for the removal of impressions so unlike the results of our natural consciousness, Rachel Grierson found herself again among the bustling crowds of the High Street. Nor could she view these busy people in the light by which she saw them before entering the little dark room of the philosopher. Though she did not know the classical word, she looked upon them as so many *automata;* and the long chain of causes came into her mind so vividly, that she found herself repeating the very words of Paul. Then there was the reference to her own individual fate—and was it not through the self-medium she saw all these people in so strange a light? —with Hope's lamp dashed down at her feet, and extinguished at the very moment when, by the communication of her father, she thought she had the means of recruiting it with a store of oil never to be exhausted till possession was accomplished. Still under these impressions, she came to the door of Mr Ainslie's house. There were sounds of mirth and music coming from within, and so plastic is the mind when under a deep and engrossing feeling, that she found no difficulty in concentrating and modifying these sounds into joyful articulations from the very mouths of Walter Grierson and Agnes Ainslie themselves. Such are the moral echoes which respond to, because they are formed by the suspicions of, disappointed love. No longer for the moment were Paul's thoughts true. These happy beings inside were happy because they had the hearts and the wills to enjoy ; but she could draw no conclusion that she herself could dispose her mind for the acceptance of the world's pleasures also when her gloom should be away among the shadows, and nature's innumerable enjoyments placed within her power. Yet, withal, she could execute her commission, and upon the door being opened, she could enter in the very face of that mirth of which she fancied herself the victim.

On being shewn into a parlour, she was presently waited

upon by Mr Ainslie, who seemed to her to have come from the scene of enjoyment in the drawing-room. She could even fancy that he eyed her as in some way standing in the path of his daughter's expectations through Walter—a fancy which of course would gain strength from the somewhat excited manner in which he received the words of her commission, to the effect that he would repair the next forenoon to the house of the merchant-burgess, for the purpose of preparing his last will and testament. The notary agreed to attend, and thus, still construing appearances according to the assimilating bent of her mind, she departed for home. After going through the routine of her domestic duties, and caring for her invalid father, she retired to bed—that place of so-called rest, where mortals chew the cud of the thoughts of the day, or of years ; and how unlike the two processes, the physical and the mental ; in the one is brought up for a second enjoyment the green grass of nature, still fresh and palatable and nutritious ; in the other, the seared leaves of memory, feeding unavailing regrets, and filling the microcosm with phantoms and dire shapes of evil, the types whereof never had an existence in the outer world. Walter Grierson was lost to her for ever, and the dire energies of fate, as described by the artist-philosopher, seemed to hang over her, claiming, in harsh tones, her will as a mere instrument in the working out of her own destiny.

Next day Mr Ainslie called, and was for a long time closeted with Mr Grierson ; but so careless was she now of the fortune about being left to her, and which she was satisfied would not now be a means of shewing her affection for Walter, that she felt little interest in an affair which otherwise might have appeared of so much importance to her. Her attention was notwithstanding claimed by an incident. After the interview, the notary visited Walter Grierson in his room, where the young man seemed to have been waiting for him. In ordinary circumstances it might have appeared strange that a man of business, bound to secrecy, would divulge the terms of a will to any one, but far more that he should take means for apprising a nephew that he was deprived of any share of his uncle's means. Nor could she account for this interview on any other supposition than that Mr Ainslie knew of the intentions of Walter towards his daughter, and that he took this early opportunity of intimating that a disinherited young man, of the grade of a merchant's clerk, would not, as a son-in-law, suit the expectation of an ambitious writer. Yet out of this interview there came to, if not drawn by, her fancy a glimmer of hope, insomuch as, if the young man were rejected by the notary in consequence of the ban of disinheritance, he would be left to the attractions of her wealth; but this supposition involved the assumption that her triumph would be over a mind that was mercenary, and not over a heart predisposed to love ; nay, her generosity revolted at the thought of gratifying her long-concealed passion at the expense of the sacrificed love of another. That other, too, had a better right to the object than she herself, in so far that Agnes Ainslie's love had been returned, while hers had not. But these speculations were to be brought to the test by words and actions.

No sooner had Mr Ainslie left than Rachel was visited in her private parlour by Walter Grierson himself. He had seldom taken that liberty before, for her secret passion had been ruled by a stern virtue. A natural shyness, remote from coyness, demanded the conciliation of respect, though ready at a moment to pass into the generosity of confidence where she was certain of a return ; but his presence before her might have been accounted for by his appearance, which was that of one whose excitement was only attempted to be overborne by an effort—a result more mechanical than spiritual. His manner, not less than his countenance, composed to gravity, was belied by the tremulous light of his eye ; and, as he seized her hand and pressed it fervently, she could feel that his trembled more than her own. Her manner was also embarrassed, as it well might be, where so many conflicting feelings, some revived from old memories, and some produced by the singular events of the day and hour, agitated her frame.

"I am going to surprise you, cousin," he said, while he fixed his eye upon her, as if to watch the effect of his words.

Rachel forgot for a moment the philosophy of Paul—why should one be surprised when the thing that is to be is a result of a change in something else as old as Aldebaran, let alone "the sun and the seven stars." She was indeed prepared for a surprise.

"It is just the old story of the heart," he resumed. "Our intercourse began so early, and partook so much of that of mere relations, that I never could tell when the mere social feeling gave place to another which I need not mention. You know, Rachel, what I mean."

She was silent, because she was distrustful, yet her heart beat bravely in spite of her efforts; for was not this man the object of her love, and is not love moved with an eloquence which makes reason ashamed of her poor figures and modes?

"Yes," he went on, "I take it for granted that you know I am only labouring towards a confession. Yes, dear heart, for years I have considered you as the one sole object in all this world of fair visions formed to make me happy. You see I cannot get out of the ordinary mode of speech. The lover is fated to adjure, to praise, and to petition always in the same set form of words—yet is not the confession enough?"

"So far," said she; "but I have never seen any evidence of all this," as if she wanted more in the same strain—sweet to the ear, though distrusted by the reason.

"No more you have," he continued, "yet you know that love is often suspicious of itself. I have watched with my eye your movements and attitudes when you thought I was not observing you. My ear has followed your voice through adjoining rooms when you thought I was listening to other sounds. I have admired your words without venturing the response of admiration. Often I have wished to fold you in my arms when you dreamt nothing of my inward thoughts. In short, Rachel, I have loved you for years! yes, I have enjoyed, or suffered, this gloating, yea, delightful misery of the heart when it feeds upon its own secret treasures, and trembles at the test which might dissolve the dream."

"And why this suppression and secrecy, Walter?" she asked. "How could you know," she continued, as she held down her head, "that I would be adverse to your wishes; nay, that I was not even in the same condition as yourself?"

"Surely you do not mean to say that!" he cried, with something like the rapture of one relieved by pleasure from pain. "I am not worthy even of the suspicion that you speak according to the bidding of your heart. Have I not watched your looks, and penetrated into your eyes, to ascertain whether I might venture to know my fate, and yet never could discover even the symptom of a return; and then was I not under a conviction that your affections were engaged elsewhere?"

"Where?" asked Rachel, with a look of surprise.

"We are apparently drifting into confessions," responded he. "I may say that I never could construe your visits to Paul, the ingenious artist, merely as dictated by admiration of his wonderful genius."

"You do not know that Paul is the son of my mother's sister," replied she. "Your uncle knows; but there may be reasons why you don't."

"Then I am relieved," was the lover's ejaculation, in a tone as if he had got quit of a great burden.

"Yes, that is the truth," continued she; "but I also confess that I have been attracted to his small dark workshop by the exquisite curiosities of art on which he is so often engaged, and which, by occupying so much of his time, keep him poor.

It was only yesterday I saw on his bench a locket which seems to transcend all his prior efforts."

The young man smiled and nodded. What could he mean? Why was he not dumbfoundered?

" It is in the shape of a heart," she continued ; " and upon touching a spring there fly up two tiny figures, which, with fluttering wings, seem to devour each other with kisses."

Words which forced themselves out of her in spite of her shyness; but which she could not follow up by more than a side-look at her admirer.

" And upon which," said he, still smiling, " there is engraven the inscription, ' From Walter Grierson to Agnes Ainslie.' "

" Yes," sighed Rachel, " the very words. I read them again and again, and could scarcely believe my eyes."

" And well you might not," said he ; " but your simple heart has never yet informed you that love finds out strange inventions. I have been guilty of a *ruse d'amour*, for which I beg your pardon. Knowing that you were in the habit of visiting Paul's workroom, and seeing all the work of his cunning fingers, I got him to make the locket out of a piece of gold I got from my uncle, and the inscription was "—and here he paused as if to watch her expression; " yes, designed to quicken your affection for me by awakening jealousy. I confess it. Agnes Ainslie was and is nothing to me; and I used her name merely because I thought that you would view her as a likely rival."

" Can all this be true?" muttered Rachel to herself, as the wish to believe was pursued by the doubt which revolted against a departure from all natural and rational actions.

Perhaps she was not versed in the ways of the world ; but whether so or not, the difference in effect would have been small ; for what man, beloved by a woman, ever yet pled his cause before his mistress without other than a wise man for his client?

" And if it is your wish, my dear Rachel," he continued, "the inscription shall be erased, and replaced by the name of Rachel Grierson—what say you?"

His hand was held out for that acceptance which betokened consent. It was accepted, yes, and more. His arms were next moment round her waist; the heart of the yielding girl beat rarely; the wistful face was turned up as even courting his eyes; the kiss was impressed—why, more, Rachel Grierson was surely Walter Grierson's, and he was hers—and surely to be for ever in this world.

Rachel was now in that state of mind when the pleasantness of a contemplated object excludes any inquiry whether it is true or false, good or evil; and, in spite of Paul's fatalism, she was satisfied that it was with Walter's own free will that he had done what he had done, and said what he had said. The changed inscription on the locket, and the delivery of that pledge to her, would complete the vowing of the troth whereby she was to become his wife. Entirely ignorant of what had taken place between the nephew and the uncle, by means of which she might have been able to analyse his conduct, she had only the closeting of Mr Ainslie and Walter to suggest to her that the young man's sudden declaration was the result of his knowledge that she was to be sole heiress. The heart that is under the influence of love, as we have hinted, is too credulous to the tongue of the lover to doubt the sincerity of his professions. So all appeared well. The motives in action were adequate to the will of the parties who used them; and, as she felt that her love was in the power of herself, so she could not doubt that Walter's affection was the result of his approval of her good qualities. Paul was now no longer an oracle. She would be pleased to have an opportunity of shewing him that his genius lay more in his fingers than in his head. She had now, however, something else to do; she went to her father's room. He was in one of those reveries to

which, as we have said, all the thinking of the extremely aged
is reduced — when the world and its figures of men and women,
its strange oscillations, and changes, its passions, pleasures,
and pain;, seem as made remote by the intervention of a long
space—dim, shadowy, and ghost-like.   It is one of the stages
through which the long-living must pass, and, like all the other
experiences of life, it is true only to one's-self—it cannot be
communi ated by words.   " O'd memories are spectres that
do seem to chase the soul out of the world,"—an old quotation,
which may be admitted without embracing the metaphysical
paradox, that "subjective thought is the poison of life," or
conceding the sharp sneer of the cynic—

> " Know, ye who for your pleasures gape,
> Man's life at best is but a scrape."

But the entry of his daughter brought the old man back to the
margin of real living existences.   He held out his hand to her,
and smiled in the face that was dear to him, as if for a moment
he rejoiced in the experience of a feeling which connected him
with breathing flesh and blood.   The object of her visit was
soon explained.   Whispering in his ear, as if she were afraid
of the sound of her own words, she told him that Walter had
promised her a love-token, and that she wished to give him
one in return, for which purpose she desired that she might be
permitted to use one or two old "Spanish ounces" that lay in
the old bureau.

"Yes, yes, dear child," said he.   "Get a golden heart made
of them.   It will be an emblem of the true heart you have to
give him, and a pledge to boot."   Then, falling into one of
his reveries, in which his mind seemed occupied by some
strong feeling, "I am thus reminded," he continued, " of the
old song you used to sing.   There is a verse which I hope will
never be applicable to you as it was to me.   I wish to hear it
for the last time," he added, with a languid smile, "in consideration of the ounces."

Rachel knew the verse, because she had formerly noticed that it moved some chord in his memory connected with an old love affair in which his heart had been scathed; but she hesitated, for the meaning it conveyed was dowie and ominous.

"Come, come," said he, "the fate will never be yours."

She complied, yet it was with a trembling voice. The tune is at best but a sweet wail, and there was a misgiving of the heart which imparted the thrilling effect of a gipsy's farewell—

> "If I had wist ere I had kisst,
> That true love was so ill to win,
> I'd have lock'd my heart in some secret part,
> And bound it wi h a silver pin."

"Now you may take the ounces," said he, with a sigh. "The verse has more meaning to me than you wot of, and surely I hope less to you."

And having thus gratified his whim—if that could be called a whim which was a desire to have repeated to him a sentiment once to him, as he hinted, a reality connected with the young heart when it was lusty, and his pulse strong and thick with the blood of young life—she went to the bureau, and, taking three of the ounces, she left the room. In the gloaming, she was again on her way to Paul's workshop, where she found the artist, as usual, with his head bent over the bright desk on the bench, engaged in some of his fanciful creations. Having seated herself in the chair where she had so often sat, she commenced her story of the circumstances of the day—how Walter Grierson had acted and spoken to her; how he had accounted for the locket and inscription; how he inte ded to change the latter, and substitute her name for that of Agnes Ainslie; how he had sought her love, and succeeded in his seeking; how she was satisfied that he was sincere in his professions; and how she had got the ounces from her father to make a love-token, to be given in exchange for Walter's. All which Paul listened to with deep attention, now and then a faint smile passing over his delicate face, and followed by the old pensive expression which was peculiar to one so deeply imbued with the conviction that he was an organism in nature's plan, acted upon to fulfil a fate of which he could know nothing.

"And so the powers work," said he, as he looked in the hopeful face of his friend. "You are now happy, Rachel, because you believe what Walter has said to you, and you have no power over your belief. But," he continued, after a moment or two's silence, "I *may* have power over you, but not over myself. Walter Grierson has told you a falsehood, and his motive for it is adequate to his nature. Since he gave me the order for the locket, he has learnt that you are to inherit the whole fortune of your father, on the condition that you are to marry him; and his love for Agnes has been overborne by another feeling—the desire to possess your wealth. Neither the one nor the other of these feelings could he manufacture or even modify, any more than he could charm the winds into silence, or send Jove's bolt back to its thunder-cloud; and now, look you, his game is this—if you succeed to the money, he will marry without loving you. If not, he will marry the woman he loves, Agnes Ainslie."

"You alarm me, Paul," said she, involuntarily holding forth her arms, as if she would have stopped his speech.

"And you cannot help your alarm," said he, calmly; "neither can I help *not* being alarmed by your alarm."

"Oh, you trifle with my feelings," she cried, with a kind of wail. "What have all these strange thoughts to do with this situation in which I am placed? Even though all things are preordained, neither you nor I is absolved from doing our duty to God and ourselves."

"Absolved!" echoed Paul. "Why, Rachel, look you, we are forced to do it, or not to do it, precisely as the motive culminates into action, but we are not sensible of the compulsion; and so am I under the necessity to tell you that

Walter Grierson is playing false with you, according to the inexorable law of his nature. It is not an hour yet since Agnes Ainslie called here with some old trinkets, and requested me to make a ring out of them ; nor was I left without the means of understanding that it was to be given in exchange for the locket."

" Is it possible !" cried she. " And can it be that I am deceived, and that secret powers are working my ruin ?"

" Not necessarily your ruin," said he; " no mortal knows the birth of the next moment. The womb of fate is never empty ; but no man shall dare to say what is in it till the issue of every moment proves itself. Nor does all this take away hope, for hope is in the ancient decree, like all the other evolutions of time, including that hope's being deferred till the heart grows sick ; and," he added, as he looked sorrowfully into her face, " that is the fate of mine, for, know you, Rachel Grierson, I have long loved you, and have now seen that the riches you are to inherit put you beyond the sphere of my ambition. I have often wished—pardon me, Rachel—yes, I have often wished you might be left a beggar, that I might have the privilege of using the invention with which I am gifted to astonish the world by my handiwork, and bring wealth to her I loved."

" I am surrounded on all sides by difficulties," sighed the young woman, as she seemed to find herself in the mazes of an unseen destiny. As she looked at her cousin, she thought that one of her evils was that the capture of her affections so early by Walter had prevented her from viewing Paul in any other light than that of an ingenious artist, and a man of kindly sympathies, however much he was separated from mankind by a theory of the world too esoteric for ordinary thought, and which yet at some time of man's life forces its way amidst palpitations of fear to every heart.

On reaching home she met there the notary, Mr Ainslie, who

informed her, probably at the request of her father (for information of that kind is seldom given gratuitously) that the will had been signed, and left in the possession of the old man. Even this com. munication, so calculated to shake from the heart so many of the sorrows of life, had no greater effect upon her generous nature than to increase the responsibility of fulfilling the condition upon which the inheritance was to be received and held. If she had not been under the effect of an early prepossession in favour of Walter, she might have doubted the sincerity of his statement, as it came from his own mouth. Suspicion attached to every word of it; but after the communication made by Paul, it was scarcely possible for her to resist the conclusion, that he had told her a falsehood, and that he was aiming at the fortune, without the power or the inclination to give her in return his love; nay, that he was heartlessly sacrificing to his passion for gold two parties—the object of his real love, and that of his feigned. Yet she did not resist that conclusion, and so good an analyst was she of her own mind, that even when in the very act of throwing away these suspicions of his honesty, she knew in her soul that her love was in successful conflict with an array of evidence establishing the fact which she disregarded. Then the consciousness of this inability to cease loving the man whom she could hardly doubt to be a liar, as well as heartless and mercenary, brought up to her the strange theory of Paul. The motive which no man or woman could make or even modify, was the prime spring as well as ruler of the will, cropping out, to use his own words, from moral, if not also physical, causes laid when God said, "Let there be light, and there was light." A deeper thinker than most of her sex, she felt "the sublimity in terror" of this view of God's ways with man. If she could not resist the resolution to love Walter, how could he resist the love he bore to another? The thought shook her to the heart; nor was she less pained when she reflected on the hapless Paul, with his long-concealed affection, so pure from the

sordidness of a desire for money, that he would have toiled for
her under the flame of the midnight lamp, continued into the
light of the rising sun.

During the night the persistency of her resolution to remain
by her past affection was maintained ; yet, as it was still merely
a persistency implying the continuance of a foe ready to assert
the old rights, she was so far unhappy that she wanted that
composure of mind which consists in the absence of conflict
among one's own thoughts.

In the morning she found the locket lying on her parlour table,
with the inscription changed from Agnes Ainslie to Rachel
Grierson. She took it up and fixed her eyes upon it. At one
time she would have given the world for it, now it attracted
her and repelled her. It came from the only man she loved ;
but another name had been on it, which ought, for aught she
could be sure of, to have been on it still. It might be the
pledge of affection, but it might also be the evidence of falsehood to her and unfaithfulness to another. And then, as she
traced the lines of her name, she thought she could discover
the signs of a tremulousness in the hand that traced them.
Amidst all these thoughts and conflicting feelings, she could
not help recurring to the circumstance that he had not presented the locket with his own hands. She was unwilling to
indulge in an unfavourable construction ; and perhaps the more
so that it so far pleased her as relieving her from the dilemma
of accepting it with more coldness than her love warranted, or
more warmth than her reason allowed. Nay, though she
gloated over his image when she was alone, she felt an unde-
fined fear of meeting him. Might he not be precipitated into
some further defence or confession, which might fortify suspi
cions still battling against her prepossessions, and diminish her
love ? Nor was this disinclination towards personal interviews
confined to this day—it continued ; and it seemed as if he also
wished his connexion with her to stand in the meantime upon

the pledges and confessions already made. This she could also notice, but as for rendering a true reason for it, she couldn't, even with the great ability she possessed in construing conduct and character.

But meanwhile time was accumulating antagonistic forces which would explode in a consummation. Her thoughts were to be occupied by another, who claimed her affections and care by an appeal as powerful as it was without guile. Her father was seized with paralysis. He was laid speechless on the bed where she sat, a watchful and affectionate nurse, ready to sacrifice sleep, and peace, and rest, to the wants of him who, all through her life, had been her friend and benefactor, and who had provided for her future days at the expense of hopes entertained by his legitimate heirs. For three days he had lain without speaking a word, and Rachel could only guess his wants by mute signs. During all this time her thoughts had scarcely glanced at Walter. He seemed anxious about the condition of his uncle, calling repeatedly at the bedroom door, and going away without entering. But his manner indicated no affection, if it did not rather seem that he considered the old man had done his worst against him, and that sorrow was not due from one he had disinherited. Her affections were too much engrossed by her patient to permit her thinking of what was being transacted in the outside world. Yet, when she looked upon the face of the invalid, so pale and motionless, where so long the shades of grief and the lights of joy had chased each other, by the old decree of human destiny, the words of Paul would occur to her. Was the death that was there impending the result of a more necessary law than that which had ruled every other condition of body or mind which had ever been experienced by the patient sufferer? Then there came the question, Could Walter Grierson so regulate his heart as to force it to love her in preference to Agnes Ainslie? Could she, Rachel herself, so rule her feelings as to cease loving the man she still suspected

of falsehood and treachery? It was even while she was thus ruminating over thoughts that made her tremble, that she observed, on the third night, a change in her patient. He seemed to start by the advent of some recollection. His body became restless, and he waved his hand wildly, as if he wanted her to bend over him, to hear what he might struggle to say. She immediately obeyed the sign. He fixed his eyes upon her, made efforts to articulate, which resulted only in a thick, broken gibberish. She could only catch one or two indistinct words, from which it seemed that he wished to tell her *where she would find the will;* but the precise phrase whereby he wished to indicate the deposit was pronounced in such an imperfect manner that she could not make it out. Strangely enough, yet still consistently with the generosity of her character, she did not like to pain him by indicating that she did not understand him. Nay, she nodded pleasantly, as if she wanted him to be easy, under the satisfaction that he had succeeded in his efforts to articulate. Yet so far was she from thinking of the importance of the communication to herself, that she flattered him into the belief that, as he could now speak so as to be understood, he was in the way of improving. Alas for the goodness which is evil to the heart that produces it !

> "There are of plants
> That die of too much generosity—
> Exhaling their sweet life in essences."

Paul would have said that this, too, was a cropping out of the old causal strata. In two hours more, David Grierson was dead, and Rachel was left to mourn for her parent and benefactor.

Now the issues were accumulating. A very short time only was allowed to elapse before Mr Ainslie, accompanied by Walter, came to seal up the repositories, an operation which was gone through in a manner which indicated that both of them thought they were locking up and making secure that which would destroy their hopes.   They seemed under the conviction that the will was in the bureau ; and if they had been men otherwise than merely what, as the world goes, are called honest, they might have abstracted the docu. ment; for the generous Rachel never even looked at their proceedings, grieved as she was at the death of her father. They were, at least, above that.

In a few days David Grierson was consigned to the earth, and, after the funeral, Mr Ainslie, accompanied by Walter, again attended to open the repositories and read the testa- ment.   Rachel agreed to be present.   When the seals were removed, she was asked by the notary if she knew where the document was deposited.   She now felt the consequence of the easy manner in which she had let slip the opportunity so dearly offered by her father, of knowing the *locale* of a writ in all respects so important ; for it cannot be doubted that, if she had persevered, she might have succeeded in drawing out of him the word, articulated so as that she might have comprehended it.   She accordingly, yet without any anticipation of danger, answered in the negative, whereupon the notary and nephew, who seemed to be on the most friendly terms, set about a search.   Rachel remained.   A whole hour was passed in the search, the will was not yet found.   Every drawer of the bureau was examined,—the presses, the cabinets, the table- drawers, the trunks.   And so another hour passed—no will. Rachel began to get alarmed, and, perhaps, the more, that she saw upon the faces of the searchers an expression which she could not comprehend.   Their spirits seemed to have become elated as hers became depressed ; yet why should that have been, if Walter Grierson was to be " true to his troth ?"

" We need search no more," said Mr Ainslie.   " The will is not in the house.   I should say it is not in existence, and that Mr Grierson, having changed his mind, had destroyed it."

" Not so," replied Rachel, " for a few minutes before his

death he tried to tell me where it was, but the name of the place died away upon his tongue, and I could not catch it."

"Neither can we catch the deed," said Walter, with a laugh which had a spice of irony in it.

And so the search was given up. The two searchers left the house, apparently in close conversation. Rachel sought her room and threw herself on a sofa, oppressed by doubts and fears which she could not very well explain. The manner of Walter appeared to her not to be that of one who was pledged to marry her. Her mind ran rapidly back over doubtful reminiscences which yielded no comfort to the heart; nay, she felt that he had never been as a lover to her; and far less, that day when, as it appeared, he was to be master of his uncle's wealth. Yet again comes the thought, Was he pledged to her? Ay, that was certain enough; and then she was so little versed in the subtle ways of the world, that she could not doubt of his being "true to his troth."

As soon as she recovered from her meditation she sought again the work-room of the artist, to whom she told the issue of the search for the will; Paul looked at first greatly struck, but under his strange philosophy he recovered that calmness which belongs to those of his way of thinking.

"Have I not often preached to you, Rachel," said he, as he lay back on his chair, "that all these things were fixed ere Sirius was born? Yea," he added, as a smile played amid the seriousness of his face, "ere yet there was space for the dog-star to wag his tail. The croppings out will now come thick, and you will know whether you are to be a lady or a beggar."

Rachel might have known that the consolation offered by fatalists is only the recommendation of a resignation which, as fated itself, is gloomy, if not awful, for it amounts to an annihilation of self, with all hopes, energies, and resolutions. She heard his words, and forgave him, if she did not believe him, for she knew that he was true in his friendship, and benevolent in his feelings—parts these, too, as he would have said, of the decree. She left him in a condition of sadness for which she could not yet account, and the hues of her mind seemed to be projected on all objects around her. She retired to rest ; but she could not banish from her mind that the realities of her condition required to be read by the blue light of Paul's philosophy. It was far in the morning before she fell asleep, and when nine came she felt unrested. The servant came in to her and told her the hour. The breakfast was ready, but Walter, who had not returned on the prior night, was not as usual waiting for her. The announcement was ominously in harmony with the thoughts she had tried to banish. She scarcely touched the breakfast, and the day passed in expectation of Walter. Night came, but it did not bring him. The next day passed in the same way. People called to condole without knowing how much she stood in need of condolence; but still no Walter to redeem the pledge of his love. Yet still she hoped ; nor till an entire month had gone over her head did she renounce her confidence that he would be " true to his troth."

At the end of this period Paul advised her to take counsel. He told her that the law had remedies for losses of deeds ; and she accordingly consulted a legal gentleman of the name of Cleghorn. The result was not favourable. It appeared that Mr Ainslie denied that there was any copy, or scroll, of the will, through the means of which it might have been " set up," by what is called a proving of the tenor. There was no hope here, and by and by she saw advertised in the *Caledonian Mercury* that the furniture of the house was to be sold within a week. She was there on mere tolerance ; and now she had got a clear intimation to flit. As for money or effects, she had none, except her wardrobe, for she never thought of providing for an exigency which she was satisfied never would occur. Again she applied to Paul, who, with her consent, went and

took for her a solitary room in the close we have already mentioned. It was her intention to acquire a livelihood by means
of her needle, at that time almost the only resource for genteel
poverty. Some articles of furniture were got, principally by
Paul; and there, two days before the sale, she took up her residence. Nor did the kindness of Paul stop here. He attended
the sale, and considerately judging that some articles belonging to her father would be acceptable to her, he purchased, for
a small sum, the old bureau of which we have already spoken.
The article was removed to Rachel's room.

For a period of fifteen years did Rachel Grierson live in that
room plying her needle to obtain for her a subsistence. Her
story, which came to be known, procured her plenty of work ;
and the ten fingers, which were sufficiently employed, sufficed
for the wants of the stomach—small these wants, probably, in
her who had heard of the marriage of Walter with Agnes
Ainslie ; yea, she who could bear to hear that intelligence
might claim a right to be a pupil of Paul's school of philosophy.
Paul she indeed loved as a friend, but she never could bring
herself to the resolution of marrying the little artist. There
was a train of evils ; the "croppings out" of her fate, as Paul
called it, were thick enough and to spare ; for she fell into bad
health, which was the precursor of a fit of palsy, depriving her
for ever of the power of working for herself. Then it was that
Paul's affection was shewn more clearly than ever. Day by day
he brought her all the food she required ; but at length he
himself was taken ill, and his absence was fatal. Pride prevented her from making her necessity known to the neighbours,
with whom she had but little intercourse. We have told how
she was found dead ; and when we say that Paul recovered to
be present at her funeral, we have only one fact more to state.
It is this—Paul took the old bureau home to his own little
room to keep as a memorial of the only woman he ever loved.
One day, when repairing the internal drawers, he found in a

hollow perpendicular slip, which looked like a broad beading, a document which was thus entituled on the back :—

LAST WILL AND TESTAMENT

BY

DAVID GRIERSON,

IN FAVOUR OF

RACHEL GRIERSON.

1778.

A Legend of Halkerston's Wynd.

IT has often occurred to me that if we were, by the loan of some divine gift for a short time, to get to know how many truths are disbelieved and how many fictions are accepted as veritabilities, we would come to be as sceptical as those peculiar people called Pyrrhoneans, who believe in nothing, and of whom it is said by Cicero that there is always a stock kept up, as if the truth of no truth were a truth that Nature was unwilling to let die out. Among her stage properties she always retains a number of masks, to enable her to keep up the play of life. It even happens often that many veritabilities pass through the mind without leaving any trace whereby we can know whether they have been there or no, just as many kinds of food do not fatten us a whit, and may just as well have remained outside, so like in this respect are our minds and bodies. These delicate and fastidious little agents called the absorbents often won't nibble at very fair chyme, and the still smaller nerve filaments, which are the absorbents of the mind, shew often a most whimsical distaste to very beautiful moral and physical truths. Hence I suspect the different fates of legends not depending on the degrees of their truthfulness, but on some affection of the mind itself, as difficult to account for as any other of the secrets which Nature keeps to herself. So it may be with respect to a story which I had utterly forgotten for years, but which must have been pretty favourably received by those said fastidious door-keeping sprites ; for upon the occasion of my

sitting down, not long ago, to read a certain famous trial, with a woodcut of the hero, (a faithful copy of which illustrates our legend), the whole wonderful affair came into my memory just as if it had been coiled up as a panorama in some recondite part of my brain, and unfolded by quick machinery.

And so pictorially too! I actually seemed to myself to be in Widow Buchan's house, in the second flat, entering by the second door on the right hand as you go down Halkerston's Wynd. And, no doubt, if one fond of the *chiaro-oscuro* wished to select a very suitable place for the locale of a domestic romance, where would he succeed better than in that dark, narrow close,—I mean as it stood at the time of the said trial, for it is very much altered now? Still there is the lofty land, of five or six storeys, dark and dingy; and if you examine the entrance to the spiral stair, and try to make your way up, you would fancy that the architect had some philanthropic notion in his head, that the goers up and down might, from some unsteadiness of the brain connected as effect with the price of claret—at that time sixpence a bottle—require to have a hand on each side. Certain it is, at least, that he never troubled himself about the difficulty of getting down a heavy coffin. But then it is just as undoubted that about a year before—a certain night very memorable to the widow—a sonsy corpse, in the shape of John Buchan, had been carried down from the second landing-place or flat of that long spiral stair, on its way to the Canongate churchyard.

Yes; so wonderful are the ways of God that the quietest and most reposeful hour is often the prelude to an occurrence which is to be as a mystery among the common, every-day things of life. The winged spirits that muffle the occult causes, and work effects as miracles to us poor purblind wretches, take spiteful occasion of heart-quiet, serene moments. It was eleven o'clock by the clang of St Giles'. The five-flight stair resounded to no unsteady step; and though it had, the good

widow would not have heard it, for she had something else to
think of. Grief—that selfish passion, which man forgives in
his neighbour if he does not hold it very sacred, for the reason,
perhaps, that he is pretty·sure to have a tasting of it himself,
and also because sympathy takes no money from him—ensconces
itself within closed doors. The little flat of three rooms had
become a temple, where the deity was a souvenir and the offering tears. Yes, the shrine was empty—no other than the arm-
chair, where no one dared to sit, except, perhaps, bawdrons,
purring her threnody, so well heard where all was silence.
Yet not empty in that deeper, more mysterious sense which
recognises all our knowledge as resolvable into signs of things.
Surely though we see everything we see nothing. Our visions
are merely more palpable conditions of the mind-matter ; the
images projected as they are, are really beings in the world of
spirits ; nay, sometimes they take on forms, and stand or flit
before us, making us rub our eyes, as if we could thereby rub
out the world of *real* realities which lie beyond the merely
visible.

Of all which notwithstanding, I am, I hope, as hardened a
sinner in my unbelief of a spirit-world existing around us, in
the sense of ancient or modern visionaries, as ever laughed at
the Swedenborgian notion that a warming-pan has a spiritual
counterpart, only we can't see it for the warming-pan itself; or
the spirit-rapping miracles of mediumism, where, like lightning-
conductors, Mr Home and other thin and meagre people
(easily seen through) convey spiritual intelligences between
the two worlds ; or the Catholic miracle of Father Geronimo,
who, though very fat, could raise himself by the inspired afflatus
of the Holy Spirit some feet from the ground, and remain
there until the faith waned—the greater miracle being why he
did not mount at once up to heaven. But what then ? It
would be a pretty world to live in if a man's unbelief were any
reason for the non-existence of the thing not believed. And,

therefore, when Mrs Margaret Buchan did not at that hour so near the witching one see under the dim light of her cruse the figure of honest John, was that any reason why she should not have been deceived on the previous night when she saw him standing by the side of her bed in that very square hat, and broad-tailed coat with crown buttons, he used to wear of a Sunday when he went to hear his minister at the Tron? Verily, those scant-brains who deny ghosts may be excused their fun when they ask why don't these fitful creatures come and pull our noses, and thus pinch us into belief, for the very reason of our advantage over them when we reduce them to the scrape of asserting their real meaning that spirits are nowhere. Yea, it is not a question of an *alibi*, but of a *nilibi*.

And so it was not to keep honest John out that Margaret went and carefully examined the door to see that the lock was bolted. She took especial care, too, to take the key out, as John used to do, and hang the same on the nail at the back of the door—a proceeding perfectly consistent with her notions of bodiless beings, for she had sense enough to know that a spirit such as that of John Buchan never could descend to such meanness as to take advantage of a key-hole to get into his widow's house. But she had another reason independent of security in thus withdrawing the key: her only son George— we beg pardon, " Geordie "—who, as she thought, had gone for the night to his uncle's at Dalkeith, carried a duplicate, whereby he could always enter, when he chose to come home, after his mother had gone to bed. Next she looked through the three small rooms, and even glanced in under Geordie's bed and her own,—not that she expected to find anybody there, far less a spirit, but just that it was a custom derived from her father's house, where once upon a time, when she was a pretty bloom- ing maid, a thief of no less valuable a commodity than her own heart was detected by her father, and very heartily thrashed out of the house as one who had intended to rob it of material things, which thief—no other than John Buchan—afterwards repaid that drubbing so well by marrying the fair Peggy. At the instant, the incident which had been the origin of the custom glanced across her mind, and brought a deep sigh as she thought that that once sportive lover now lay under another bed—even one of turf; and shall we say that there are many customs better justified by their beginnings?

So all was right; and that awe which is the offspring of silence and solitude at the very hour of twelve was busy with her soul as she undressed, so that she was involuntarily rehearsing the prayer that was to come in set words. It is at these moments when the bereaved spirit is sad, and yet hopeful, that religion is felt as a necessity and a solace. How true is it—to speak with the wisdom of folly—when we say it is an instinct, and thus get quit of all the subtleties of philosophy! Then came the sobbing adjuration, as she knelt at the side of the bed where she had lain on the night of the day on which she was a bride, and where, thirty years after, she had seen her husband extended as a corpse,—"Lord, remember me in my sorrow as Thou didst in my joy! and even now, when the greatest of human grief is heavy on me, teach me to know that behind thy providence, which sometimes frowns, there is a face which for ever smiles in love to Thy creatures! Give me this night rest to my body, and sanctify my hope for eternal rest to the spirit, even for Christ's sake! Amen." And with this best of sleeping draughts, Margaret Buchan was in less than a quarter of an hour dead asleep.

But somehow or other, the temporal portion of the widow's prayer was not answered, though everything boded at first well for rest. She had slept soundly for two hours; nor even in a dream did honest John Buchan, with the said square hat, and broad coat with crown buttons, appear to her. At the end of that time she was awakened, yet without knowing what had disturbed her—little it might be, no doubt, for the sleep of the aged is a kind of somnolent vigil. The clock in the kitchen strikes one, and again another one—it was two o'clock; but strange as the sound of that old wooden time-piece always was —more resembling a scream of some weird creature in agony —each toll accomplished, too, with a straining as if the difficulty of striking increased by every effort, than any merely artificial note—there was something about it now which terrified her. The first knell seemed subdued and distant; the other, loud, sharp, screechy, and dolorous. At any other time this might have been easy of explanation. The door between the kitchen where the clock stood and the room where Margaret lay must have been opened between the first stroke and the second. But then there was no other human creature in the house—bawdrons required only small apertures, and ghosts none; yet it appeared certain to her that that door had been opened.

Under this impression she lay for a minute or two. The whole energies of her spirit seemed collected and concentrated in her ear, wherein the sense became so painfully acute that she could detect even the low breathing of some one in the room. She strained her eyes in the direction of the sound, and even in the darkness of the apartment she thought she discovered a moving body, but so indistinctly that she could assign to it no form. But there was little time given to her for speculation, even if she had been able to exercise any thinking faculty of her mind. There were two distinct footfalls in the direction of the bed. Again a breathing, so well heard that she could even be certain that the body was within a few feet of where she lay. Yet not a word was spoken; and so overcome was honest Peggy with mysterious fear, that she could not even turn her thoughts in the direction of Heaven, whereto it had been her constant habit to look in all emergencies. It was with no aid of her will, properly called, that her eyes were fixed on the supposed spot of the intruding body or spirit.

The act was a charmed effect, over which she could exercise no more control than she could over the motionless limbs that lay as if palsied ; and palsied for the time they were. While the orbs were thus strained looking into darkness, a gleam of light was suddenly thrown into her face. The eyes shrunk ; the lids quivered, so that for an instant she was unconscious of aught save that the light glared upon her ; nor even when she again so far recovered herself could she observe any object behind the gleam, which seemed to be reflected from the burnished back of a lantern, the slide of which had been drawn up. There was still no speech or sound of any kind, as if the pause was the consequence of irresolution, though it might have been to give time for examination.

The power of the charm had now reached its utmost, when, either from some unsteadiness of the hand or an effort to change the direction of the gleam, the lantern was moved so that the top of it was turned back, and she could now see the face and the upper portion of the figure of a man. Who was he ? It was not the figure of John Buchan ; and though a modern reader may think that it would have been a strange thing if it had, he is to remember that his widow, with the notions of the time, thought it a very strange thing that it was not. The gleam had not only shewn her that the figure was very unlike that of her husband, but, having glanced on John's picture on the wall, brought out by the light, the contrast was vividly apparent. These deep-seated eyes were shaded by bushy eyebrows ; the cold, stern look of the bronzed face was not that of her husband. But if she had required time for comparison, that was not afforded, for the words rang out rough and surly—

" Do you know me ? "

The widow paused.

" Come, I insist upon an answer," he continued. " My fate,

death, and something after, depend upon it. Speak! speak! I demand, do you know me?"

"Ay, weel do I ken ye," replied the widow fearfully; "yea, though ye tak' on mony a strange shape."

"And will you hold my secret then?" continued he, not understanding the allusion she had made to a certain personage who has dominion among us, and who, if our actions were properly construed, would seem to have the upper hand in the affairs of our world.

"Ay, if you dinna harm me," replied she.

"I won't harm you," continued the man. "But," and he now spoke threateningly, "you must swear before Heaven."

"Heaven!" ejaculated she; "and do *you* hae faith in Heaven?"

"I have," responded he, as he put his hand on "the Book," which lay on the top of the old chest of drawers. "Swear that you will never reveal that you saw me here."

"I swear," echoed the widow.

"And I now reward you," said he, as he laid his hand again on the Bible, and deposited something thereon. "If you fail of your oath," he continued, with a stern look, "you may repent it through time and eternity."

The light was then turned, as the figure wheeled slowly round. It made again for the door, which she heard creak, and was shut after him. She watched the other retreating sounds—the step, the opening of the outer door, the locking of it; all was again silent.

Somewhat relieved of her terror, the widow rose from her bed, and, with limbs scarcely yet obedient to her will, sought the kitchen, struck a light, and went to examine the outer door. She found it locked, and her own key still suspended from the nail whereon she had hung it. She had heard the bolt move, and she knew of such things as picking locks, and returning the bolt by the same art. So far appearances were against the miraculous, even to her who had the belief of the time; but in the view of there being nothing supernatural, the difficulty was to know the object of the strange intruder, who, in place of robbing the house, had even spoken of a reward. Nor was this difficulty lessened when, upon returning to her room, and looking about with her cruse, she observed upon the top of the Bible a little bit of paper. On examining it through her spectacles, she discovered that it was a British Linen Company's one-pound note. Curiosity made her turn it over to see whether there were not some devil-singed mark upon it; and there, on the back, was something which she could no more decipher than she could understand the language (said to be Hebrew) in which the devil spoke when he first rebelled. Then she got into vapours a little, and shook, as she thought the writing was a charm intended to work evil upon her. What was she to do with it? "There," said she, as she inserted it between the leaves of that sacred volume, so great a disinfecter of earthly things, if not of things under the earth; and having thus made herself safe from an evil charm, she betook herselt to bed, not to sleep, until the exhaustion she had suffered should lapse into forgetfulness, and nature vindicate her remedy.

But there was an outside to all the mystery. It used to be said that it was one thing to dance within the charmed ring of the chorus and another to walk in the light of day. The thickness of a door divides faiths, and, what is even r)re, characters. Leaving Dalkeith at half-past twelve, George Buchan arrived at the foot of the stair in Halkerston's Wynd much about the time when these strange things were being enacted up in the small flat. It was dark, and George groped his way up the spiral entrance. On getting to the landing-place, he observed, by the dull light of the st ir window, the door of the house open; and starting up a couple of steps on the next ascent, he watched for what should occur. There was at least no deception in George's vision. He saw a man issue from the house, very deliberately pull the door after him, and, after having groped in his pocket for a key, or some other instrument, apply it to the key-hole, and, after one or two apparently adroit efforts, turn and fix the lock. People act differently in identical positions. Another young fellow might, and in all likelihood would, have sprung at the man and seized him. But George was usually in the habit of acting after consideration ; and consideration, till completed, is irresolution, and irresolution in emergencies gets into nervousness. So George stood and saw all this going on without a movement ; and if it had not been that the man turned round, and having seen some one ensconced in the corner, got in his turn nervous, and dropt the instrument whereby he had locked the door, he might have been off without leaving outside the house any trace of having been there or having done those things, except the impressions made on the senses of George himself. Then fear is sometimes nature's prudence. The man took no time to search for that which he had lost, but hurrying down the stair, left George to take possession of the instrument. This he accordingly did ; and having deposited it in his pocket, he bethought himself of the propriety of giving chase. There is no great courage required to run after a man if there is no chance of the pursued turning back and running after you ; so George Buchan began his pursuit. But the man having the whole stair between him and his follower, had so managed to be at the head of the wynd when George had turned his head at the stair-foot to get at least a glimpse of him whom he sought, and yet perhaps was afraid to find. On arriving at the head of the wynd, the man was out of sight.

With some kind of a notion, so comfortable to those who make tentative efforts, that he had done his duty as far as he could, and without analysing the "could," he returned to the house, examining as he proceeded the instrument he had so strangely got possession of, and every now and then shuddering at the thought that his mother had been murdered. Why was there no sign within the house ? Why was not her voice heard calling for assistance ?—not even an involuntary shriek of fear? Then came the imprints of images representing her as extended a mangled corpse, imbedded in her own blood. So overcome was he by these terrible thoughts that when he arrived at the door he could scarcely apply the key, (his own duplicate,) and something like a spasm helped the almost impotent effort. The door was opened, and what was his surprise to find his mother's cruse shining from her bedroom into the kitchen! It cheered him, and terrified him. Pausing for a moment, he listened for some sounds of life, and was even more surprised when he heard her groaning and articulating.

"Come again!" she said ; "may the Lord have mercy on me !"

"Come again!" repeated George to himself. "Then she must have seen him, and the light burning too."

But Margaret Buchan was surely beyond the suspicion of being visited by midnight lovers, and would explain all.

"Mother," cried George, as he entered her room, "why do you groan ? Who has been here ?"

"No *body*," replied Margaret, laying some stress on the word, to save her conscience by a piece of jesuitry.

To which George could have said in the instant that he had seen a man issuing from the house, but the words stuck in his throat—fixed there by the wonder of his mother's denial; for of the mental reservation implying the distinction between body and spirit he never thought. Then he sat and looked wistfully in the face of his mother, praying internally that she would make some explanation of this inexplicable mystery ; but she would not utter a word for very fear of that visitor who had extorted from her an oath of silence. To question farther was a liberty he could not take, for Mrs Buchan was a stern, though a good mother ; and, besides, he knew that she had committed

I

herself to an answer, and that was irrevocable. He had even looked in her face too long for her patience; and observing the lowering indications of displeasure—

"I will go to bed," he said; "but first I will read my chapter."

And laying his hand on the Bible, he was about to open it, when Margaret, stretching forth her hand, clutched the volume nervously, snatching it from his hold, and laying it open in her spasmodic effort so far that the bank note fell out upon the floor. George took up the paper, and holding it before his eyes, looked, and looked, as if he could not wonder enough, for he knew there was no money in the house when he left—nay, it was for money he had gone to his uncle's.

"How did this come here, mother?" said the lad, fearfully.

"Perhaps the back of it will tell you," said she, with some difficulty of utterance.

And George turning round the note, observed some lines of writing, probably inscribed, according to a custom which prevailed when bank notes were few, for the purpose of inducing the custodier to turn the root of evil to good account. The idle words were read by George with some difficulty :—

> "I buy pleasure, I buy pain ;
> Take your choice—or loss or gain ;
> Good and evil, none refuse me,
> Fiend or angel, as you use me."

"A good maxim," said the lad.

"Of the devil's inditing," groaned Mrs Margaret Buchan.

And George's eyes, wide and curious, were again fixed on the writhing face of his mother.

"George Buchan," she cried, after a pause, "you must burn that paper. I will not eat o' the bread, or drink o' the drink it buys, nor shall you. Burn it at the cruse that *he* may smell the reek."

A request which, however passionately expressed, the lad

felt no great inclination to comply with, but the wits of very simple people are sometimes quick, and George, rising and turning his back to the bed, set fire to a bit of paper which he had adroitly taken from his pocket. It flared up and was gone.

"So may burn all charms," said Margaret; " yea, surely it is better that the gifts that come from the evil one should be consumed in a moment than that the soul which comes from the Lord should be burnt for ever."

George rejoined Amen; but even in the midst of his increasing wonder what all this could mean, and not even contented with the blessing, he sat down and read his chapter with as much unction—such is the facile duplicity of the human heart—as if, in place of putting into his pocket, as he had done, the said note, he had deposited there a leaf of the Bible.

The young man, with this deceit in his heart, and the note in his pocket, went to bed. He heard his mother muttering words which he could not comprehend, and by and by sounded that scream of the clock which, in spite of all knowledge that it was a mere inanimate thing of man's making, produced the effect usually consequent on an expression of suffering. Nor was there more of unison in his soul. Simple-minded as he was, he could not fail to be deeply moved by what he had witnessed. Who was that man, and whence came the money so opportunely to one who required it, and yet rejected it with fear? He tried all theories, while he tumbled from one side to another as if he would thereby leave some thought that pained or confused him. The man could not be a robber, for he had stolen nothing,—on the contrary, he had, according to the lad's suspicion, left something, and then the silence of the mother was inconsistent with that theory. Neither could he be a friend, for friends do not enter neighbour's houses with skeleton keys; and what motive, again, could his mother have had for concealing a friendly visit, unless, indeed, she were wicked? Peggy Buchan wicked! Does religion breed the vices which it was sent to prevent or scare away? What then? Spirits do not carry picklocks to get into the living, any more than they use pickaxes to return to the dead. How many turns from right to left, and from left to right, with intermediate reclinations on his back, were required to eliminate or get quit of these thoughts and fancies will never be known.

Nor were these the whole of his cogitations. The rasping wail of the clock, still as lamenting the passing of time, gave forth four, and, worn-out with his brain-fancies, he felt heavy at his heart the weight of his first sin. He had deceived his mother, whose kindness to him as her only child was to be measured alone by the care she took of imbuing all the feelings of his heart with the doctrines and hopes of that blessed book which he had misused. The thought forced groans from him, which, striking on the ear of his parent, brought again the mutterings of the half-awakened spirit, and those mutterings were like the responses of vengeance to his self-impeachment. But the heart-throes worked themselves into weakness. Then came symptoms of pleading for himself. He took refuge in the very words which he threw on his own ear, that it was still for that mother's sake that he had preserved the note. And what will a son not venture for her at whose breast he has hung?

> " The day will wag, the world will wane,
>   Friends change like April weather ;
>   Light loves you may hae mony a ane,
>   But minnie ne'er anither."

And so there was the old devil's logic about means and the end whereunto they lead—that end a good reflected back on him who projects it. He got easier as the unction stuck, and even waxed ingenious as he meditated exchanging the note for silver, and pretending to his mother—the while he applied it to her comfort—that he had got it from his hard uncle at Dalkeith. The subtlety pleased him. In the softness of love he forgot the stern virtues; in the luxury of pride he lost the sense of his sin, and in this frame of mind he gradually fell over into sleep.

One might think that the avenging angel would smile as he looks at sleeping mortals and reads the decree which is recorded, even as they sleep and dream of bliss shining through sin. Margaret Buchan was early up, to prepare from her scanty means the breakfast of her son and her own ; but her first act was prayer, even the prayer of the somewhat morose Calvinist. Yea, it is only to the world the Calvinist is morose ; and, however unseemly that may be to the Arminian, it may be doubted whether that moroseness is not as often the sign of a sturdy habit of virtue, as the more pleasing levity is the unwitting exponent of a lax morality. At least Peggy Buchan's adjuration was that morning contrite, soft, and unctuous ; yet surely she had offended Heaven, for as she looked down on the floor when in the act of rising up, she saw the cinder of the burnt paper, with a small circle of white at the end, and unfolding it curiously, she observed a few words of common print. George Buchan, your deceit is exposed, your sin laid open, and you must awake from your dream of a son's affection to the reality of a mother's reproach. Perhaps not. Peggy staggered to a chair and meditated. The prior night's adventure gave way to the poignancy of sorrow and to the exactions of duty. If she put George on trial by questions, he might confess or deny : she knew all the advantages of the one, and dreaded the evils of the other—nay, hopeful as she was of him, she shuddered as she contemplated the possibility of his taking a stand upon a falsehood ; for while she knew the proneness of the impeached spirit to harden under the impeachment, she knew also that that hardness is confirmed by denial.

On going into the kitchen she discovered two things. In the first place, there was scarcely any article in the house to make up a morning's meal to herself and her son ; and, in the second place, George had not only been before hand with her in getting up, but he had gone out; whereupon she began, as she moved about in the operation of putting on the fire, to meditate upon the question, what might be his object; nor was this mere curiosity, for she was oppressed by a suspicion which she was almost afraid to utter to her own ear. Meanwile, the fire having been lighted, she put on the kettle for tea, albeit there was no tea in the house; but then at the tail of her said suspicion their lurked a hope that George might have succeeded in his mission to his uncle, and brought home some money, (not of the devil's coining,) wherewith he might purchase the necessary articles for not only their breakfast that day, but their meals for some time to come, and until George should get work. Otherwise all around her betokened peace and rest. The kettle by and by began to sing, as if it was conscious that it had a part to play in the domestic economy, and the cat purred in philosophic composure, as if perfectly aware that Madame Muet had left for an individual of her race a yearly pension, with a servant to wait upon the favoured Grimalkin. The only unrest was in the spirit of the mistress, which was not to be alleviated even if her son should return with what was necessary for the requirements of the mere body; —and return he did about nine o'clock, wearing a cheerful countenance, whether assumed for the purpose of keeping up the spirits of his mother, whom, in spite of the deceit imputed to him, he loved beyond all human creatures, or worn as the livery of a successful purveyor.

Of that success he very soon brought forth evidence, as he laid upon the table a pound of ham, half-a-dozen of eggs, a pound of sugar, half a pound of tea, and bread to serve, at least, for the day; on all which the widow cast an eye of suspicion, even while she feared to test his honesty by putting it to him in her usual unflinching way, whether these things were got by the mysterious note, or by the means of a sum given by the uncle. That George understood her look might have appeared from a shadow that passed over his face, but he quickly resumed his cheerful manner, and in a little further time there was only to be heard the bubble and squeak from the frying-pan,—a sound sufficient at least to disperse all those vapours that came from an empty stomach, whatever influence it might have over the feelings of a burdened heart. The breakfast was now prepared, and when they had taken their places, the mother lifted her hands, "We offer our humble thanks to Thee, O Lord, for what Thou hast provided for us out of Thy bountiful providence, and may the means whereby it has been brought to this house be such as to deserve Thy blessing, for the sake of Thy Son. Amen." The grace in this form was an extension of that which she usually said, and George felt the reproof so sharply that he forgot any resolution he might have formed to keep silence as to the source of the money.

"It is honestly come by, dear mother," said he, assuringly. "Eat and be happy."

The charm was broken.

"Na, na," she exclaimed. "There is food for the body, and there is food for the soul, but that which is good for the flesh may be the death of the spirit. George Buchan," she continued, "I have wi' sair travail brought ye up in the fear and admonition of the Lord, and I look for the fruit that comes o' the sowing to the spirit, and of the sowing to the flesh. Whaur got ye the money for thae things? Was it from your uncle?"

"No," replied the youth. "I used the pound-note which you told me to burn, and I did not burn. I was tempted. I knew there was no meat in the house; and you know that if 'any one provide not for his own, and especially for those of his own house, he hath denied the faith, and is worse than an infidel;' and who was she of my own house but the mother who bore me?"

"Ay," replied she; "but you are not told to provide even for your mother by unholy means. I have sworn to keep the secret o' him who left that note, and I will keep it. Albeit my oath was forced; but, George, you deceived me. A bit o' the paper you burned was left by the flame as a witness against you. I will not eat or drink o' what that money has bought, for it is twice cursed—first, by the hand that left it; and, second, by the hand that concealed it. Yea, 'shall not the conscience of him only which is weak be emboldened to eat those things that are offered to idols?'"

"It was only a slight deception, and for your good," replied George, sorrowfully, as he looked at the well-supplied table, and thought of the firmness of his Cameronian mother.

"Slight!" rejoined she. "If the man who deceiveth his neighbour is called by holy writ mad, casting fire-brands, arrows, and death, what is he who deceiveth the mother who bore him? And it was for my good, you say? I would rather have dreed starvation than that you had done this thing;" and rising up, till she became as rigid as a statue of one of the old lights, she said, with a deep emphasis of command, "Nor shall you eat; I forbid it, in the name of Him who fasted and was hungry for forty days, and said unto the tempter, 'Man doth not live by bread alone'"

With which words she left him, retreating into her bed-room, where she betook herself to spiritual food, in place of that which her son had provided for her. Meanwhile, George sat silent and sorrowful. He felt hungry, so that he could have devoured two men's meals; but the injunction of the mother he loved lay heavy on him, made heavier by his consciousness of having deceived the best of parents, and, in addition, he was sorely perplexed by the mystery of the previous night, rendered darker by her statement that she had been obliged to swear secrecy by some one, he knew not who, or for what end or purpose. There was thus a conflict within him—one power suggesting the gratification of his stomach, another contrition of the heart. Again and again he stretched forth his hand as the bodily want increased to pain, and again he withdrew it, even as if these good things had been poison.

In this comfortless, if not painful, condition, the widow and her son remained till it was near twelve o'clock, at which time a pretty loud knock was heard at the door. George started from the reverie in which he had been as one in a confused and painful dream, and proceeded to open the door. Whatever there was within to render him unhappy, he had no fear from without; for he was not conscious of having offended the laws of his country. It was therefore with no little surprise, yet still without dismay, that he saw two men enter and shut the door behind them.

"You are George Buchan?" asked one of them.

"I am," replied George, fearlessly.

At the same moment, his mother appeared before them. She knew the professional character of the men, and looked at them with that calmness of resignation peculiar to a class of religionists (not so common now) who viewed all the doings in this world as mere direct effects of a working of certain machinery above.

"We are come upon a business which is as unpleasant to us as to you," said the man. "It is to apprehend you on a charge of housebreaking and robbery."

"When, and where?" inquired George.

"Last night," rejoined the officer; "and in the house of George Carruthers, in Niddry's Wynd."

George tried to laugh in the exultation of innocence.

"And we are authorised to search you," again said the officer. "Please to turn out your pockets."

Nor did George hesitate to obey; for he still relied upon

his innocence. He first laid on the table fifteen shillings and fourpence in silver and coppers. The officer proceeded to count them carefully.

"You paid four-and-eightpence to Mr Menelaws this morning?" said the man.

"Yes," was George's reply. "I gave him a pound, and that is the change."

"Very correct," rejoined the man, as he took up the money. "What more?"

And George's hand, as he groped in his coat-pocket, laid hold of the skeleton key which had been dropt by the midnight visitor, and taken up by him. He pulled it fearlessly out.

"That is a skeleton key," said he, "which I found on the stair last night, when I returned home from Dalkeith."

"A *skeleton* key, indeed," echoed the officer. "I am sorry to see it, and still more sorry to be obliged to take it with me. Any more?"

"No more," said George.

"Except yourself," responded the officer. "You will now go with us."

"I am ready," was the reply.

And so he was at the moment; for, so long as his mind was engrossed by his obedience to the officers, he was as firm, if not cheerful, as a conviction of innocence could make him; but the feeling which is for the time in the ascendant is the dictator of the soul. When he turned to his mother, that ascendency was changed. A new feeling became the master, and, bursting into tears, he flung his arms round her neck; then, as if ashamed of a strength which is called weakness—

"There is not judge or juryman in broad Scotland," said he, "who can touch a hair of my head for any fault, if it be not that I am poor, and loved my mother so well that I appropriated for her good what Heaven seemed to have sent us in our extremity. I am ready."

And without more preparation he went away in the custody of the officers.

It was now that the widow came to see more clearly the history of this strange affair. She sat down in John Buchan's chair—made by its former occupant sacred to strong sense and stern morality—and meditated upon this inscrutable visitation of Divine wrath. The soft mother struggled against the rigid Covenanter; and tears were the evidence of the triumph of nature against a creed, to some extent, it may be feared, conventional. His deception was the instinct of a son's love, and now seemed to carry small proportions when contrasted with the crime with which he was now charged. She was even sorry that she had made so much of it; for she was bound to acknowledge, that if duty has its obligations so has love its privileges, and though a qualm came over her heart when she thought of the skeleton key, it was followed by the assurance, that the young man had spoken the truth, the evidence of which lay, in the first place, in the fact that all the mysterious pound was accounted for, even to a penny; and, secondly, in a dim recollection she had of having heard the clink of an iron instrument on the stair, all which considerations brought her a new light, whereby she could read more clearly the history of the night. The visitor, whom she had viewed as an emissary of the author of evil, sent, according to her view of the economy of Heaven, to tempt her and test her—no matter whether she required the extraordinary touch-stone or not—was now, in her more earthly, and certainly less irrational view, a midnight robber, who, having calculated that no one was in the house, had, upon finding himself mistaken, left the bribe for the sake of screening himself from discovery and punishment. The note which constituted the bribe had been extracted from Carruther's house, and traced to George through Mr Menelaws, the grocer, with all which George's statement in reference to the finding of the key completely tallied. Nor did her quick sense

fail to shew her the danger of her only boy. Nay, it seemed
to her that he was doomed beyond the influence of any earthly
power to save him. But was there no hope in Heaven?

"Yes," she exclaimed, "the Lord knoweth how to deliver
the godly out of temptations, and to reserve the unjust unto
the day of judgment to be punished."

And just as if this devotional exclamation was to be confirmed
through the working of her own mind, she began to bring before
the eye of her memory the exact form and expression of that
face which she had seen so vividly by the upturned light of the
lantern. Formal images become bright and sharp through the
light, if we may use the expression, of feeling and emotion. She
saw the face before her, even as if it had been part of the living
body, but only the face, for of the other parts of the person she
had seen nothing, by reason of their having been in the shade;
and what was still more strange, she was certain *she had seen it
before*, nay, that she actually knew the man, only she could not
identify him either by name, profession, residence, or acquaint-
ance :—an illumination this in perfect harmony with natural,
though in exceptional workings, but the mind divines for itself
according to its desires. It is its own mystagogue, as well as
hierophant. Mrs Buchan saw Heaven's agency in the resusci-
tation of this bright image; and it was a sign to herald her to
the discovery of the man who had been the means of bringing
her son into the strong clutches of the law, from which, if she
did not make an effort in obedience to what she deemed a
message from the God of mercy, he might not be able to escape
with life. However vain might appear to be a search in a city
like Edinburgh for one solitary individual, whom she could
recognise only by an image of his face impressed upon her
memory, she was determined to find him if she should wander
from day to day, and from night to night, cold and hungry, and
peer into every face she met. The hope was wild; but we are to
remember she was a Christian and a mother, and who is igno-

rant of the achievements of either against obstructions which have been deemed unsurmountable.

The untouched breakfast was still upon the table. She looked upon the eatables with horror, even though nature's craving was upon her. Every article was laid aside, but the kindness of a ruling Providence runs zig-zag in every direction through the variegated web of human destiny. You see it where you do not expect it. The blue hair on the head of the king of the Megarenses was the token of his strength, and his daughter Scylla cut it away; but even Atropos of the shears cannot take away that thread of light which is seen on the cloud of virtue under trial. About two o'clock the uncle from Dalkeith entered, and having heard the story, blamed himself for leaving George to the temptation under which he had succumbed. He left her money, and promised to interest himself in the fate of her son ; at the same time, that he secretly felt that any prospect of success was gloomy, if not desperate.

She could get no access to George that day. He was firmly immured in the Old Tolbooth, where so many innocent prisoners had been kept, and from which so many guilty had escaped. In the latter part of the afternoon she put on her plaid to go forth in the execution of that strange and hopeless purpose upon which she had invoked the blessing of Him whose ears are ever open to the prayers of the just. It has been said, that if you wish to know love—what it is and what it worketh—look to your mother. We all know the yearning of the woman of Canaan. And so she commenced her pilgrimage. Was it not for a lost son? and would she be dismayed so long as her heart beat hope? There was once a search for an honest man, but no account has been left as to the success attending the enterprise, and we are left to laugh at what we call an orthodox paradox. How easy her task would have been if the object of her inquiry had been for a merely dishonest one, an *individuum quod*, if she might not have laid hold of the first man she met, whose natural wants were in the inverse ratio to his guineas. She could be satisfied only with one—with a face whose image had been, as it were, burned into her soul with the red light of a lantern. That one she no where saw, though she looked and peered into every face she met. Nor did she give up hope where she had, as it were, only begun : she continued her wanderings next day, and the day after, and the day after that without success, and yet without even a diminution of an ardour which derived its strength from the heart, even from the blood of the coronaries themselves.

Meanwhile, the authorities were busy in *their* search, making all fast, that the grim god at the head of Liberton's Wynd, more bloody than Dagon, or Chemosh, or Moloch, might have his living victim. They had the pound note with the written doggrel on the back thereof, sworn to by Carruthers, who, in accordance with a singular practice of the times, had written the same as a specimen of his poetical morality. They had the skeleton key, whereby they satisfied themselves by the experiment of a smith, the doors of the house in Niddry's Wynd, and that in Halkerston's Wynd, might be opened. They had, further, the testimony of two witnesses to the effect, that George had been seen to go up Niddry's Wynd at a late hour, but not to the effect that he was then only continuing his road from Dalkeith. And if all this was not sufficient to hang a man in those days, when hanging was a species of pastime to both the hangers-up and the hangers-on, then no man that had ever been executed had been condemned upon sufficient evidence. But well might the men in authority be zealous in their prosecution of George Buchan, for at that time all Edinburgh began to ring with the news of a strange, if not romantic event. There are people yet alive who can remember it. Numbers of the inhabitants were daily applying to the authorities with complaints that their houses and shops had been entered during the night in a manner which shewed that these burglaries were all effected by one man. It appeared, too, that the work was performed so adroitly that, unless for the articles that were taken away, you could not have known that any entry had been made ; but what seemed most extraordinary, was the fact that the ingenious burglar was as much a philosopher, who liked to dive into the inside of things for mere curiosity's sake, as a thief who liked to carry those things off for, according to all the accounts of the time, he went, by the help of his universal key, into many houses and warehouses without taking anything away—a fact the more to be wondered at, that there were in these places plenty of valuable articles which he might have abstracted without difficulty ; nay, more strange things were said of him, such as that one night he went in upon a lady who was so much, occupied in writing a letter that she never knew he was at her back till she saw his face in a mirror opposite to her—when she turned round he was gone.

It was no great wonder, then, that the men whose duty it is to guard the lieges should have looked upon George Buchan as a prize. Meanwhile, the widow, engaged in her peregrinations, which she continued from day to day, heard also of this extraordinary person, and though at first she was staggered at the recollection of the skeleton key, she recovered the steadfastness of the conviction of his innocence by her knowledge of his habit of being home at good hours—a circumstance amounting to an *alibi*. Nay, the intelligence yielded her hope, for she could clearly enough see that her midnight visitor was the very man who thus occupied the tongue of the public. All her wanderings and wanderings up and down did not enable her to find that face. What would she not have given for a glimpse of it ! No opening ray of hope to the dying could match the joy of a reflected beam from that countenance which haunted her, and yet eluded her watchful eye. Nor did she of high lineage in Palestine, who, according to the beautiful story, wandered to England, with no more knowledge of English than the name of him she sought, sigh more ardently to meet her lover than this loving mother did to meet her enemy.

More days passed, and still all was vain. She had seen George since the news of the midnight burglar had broken on the city, and she would go to the Tolbooth to cheer him with what seemed to be an explanation of the mystery as connected with him. She got admittance at once, and was introduced into that place which so well merited the short name with which it was honoured. The night had set in, and the dingy lamps inside threw their light on the bloated faces of those prisoners who occupied the largest room, where they were allowed to mix, and drink, and swear, according to the lax discipline of the time. *Her* boy had been among these—he whom she had so zealously guarded from the example of the wicked, but he had been put, the jailer told her, into one of the small rooms up stairs, set apart for special criminals. In going along an obscure passage, with some cells on each side, she came to a grating through which a light shone. She stopt to look in. There was a man there sitting at a table poring over a book, which she supposed to be the Bible. The light of a lamp shone on his face, she gave an involuntary scream, and sunk on the floor. That face was the very one of her midnight visitor. *The famous Deacon Brodie had been apprehended that day.*

This circumstance was made known to the authorities in due time by the uncle, and was at once seen by them to fit in, not only with George's examination, but with the history of the deacon. Another circumstance tended in the same direction. The skeleton key was compared with others taken from Brodie, and was found to be of the same make, only longer in the hook, as if intended to reach deeper guards. Every one knows the fate of the deacon, who was hanged for his curiosity; but few know of the hairbreadth escape of George Buchan, whose adventure we have thus related.

Lang Sandy Wood's Watch.

OF the many stories and anecdotes told of the celebrated Dr Alexander Wood, otherwise known by the familiar name of Lang Sandy Wood, I do not know if the curious legend connected with his watch has ever been put in a proper storied form ; but whether so or not, having succeeded in hunting up some of the more recondite facts connected with the law case in which the virtues of the chronometer figured so prominently, I hope to be able to impart some new interest to the subject. Before entering upon the strange history, I may, at the risk of repeating what may be very well known, set forth that the great doctor had, if we may so term it, a kind of friendship for his gold repeater—a feeling which, if we examine into the nature of our social friendships generally, may appear not so irrational as many may think. We know that objects not much removed from the mere inanimate have shared strangely the affections of both men and women. The classical reader will recollect the sparrow of Lesbia, the cat of Madame de Gournay, Melior's paroquet, Stella's dove, Madame de Houlier's spaniel, Lady Eglintoun's rats, the lamprey of Hortensius, and so forth ; and if he chooses to acknowledge, with Descartes, that these creations are mere machines, he will be at no loss to account for an affection entertained by a man for so beautiful and useful a piece of mechanism as a watch ; nay, if we go to the ultimate of the nature of friendship among our superior race, we doubt if it would not be found that our amities are not very different

K

from our predilections, which are often no better than whims, and only to be accounted for by qualities sought out by us after we are caught. A response of sympathy forms the whole affair ; and what return to an inquiry as to how time is passing with you could be made with more precision and less fuss than by a good timepiece ? The doctor's watch was, in short, punctual to time, and he was punctual to it. We wish we could say the same to the credit of that sense of obligation which remains in our day of civilisation.

It might be about the period when the doctor usually rolled up his mute monitor, not far from midnight, and when he was sitting in his library thinking of some difficult case which had interested him during the day, that a servant brought him the message that he was wanted at the house of Mr James Gillespie, writer, in Advocates' Close. He had called there in the fore-noon, and knew that the case—that of the young wife, Mrs Gillespie—was a hopeless one. "I can do her nae gude," he muttered to himself, in his broad way; "a decided case of marasmus. The deil a lacteal in a' her body will sip ane o' its ain mouthfuls, if you should tempt it wi' nectar." And putting on his wig and square hat, and taking up the indispensable long cane, he sallied forth for the house of the patient. A few of his long strides soon brought him to the sick-room, where he found Mr Gillespie himself, and the sick-nurse, hanging over the patient, and a young woman, her sister, sitting on a chair by the bedside. A single glance told the doctor how matters were progressing with the invalid; and if he took the chair vacated for him by the sister, and began to feel the pulse of the dying woman, it was rather to measure how near she was to that point where the silver cord breaks, than with any desire to ascertain any particular pathological condition. In going through which mechanical process, Dr Wood, of all men, be-hoved to have in his hand that gold repeater; not that that cunning bit of mechanism could, at the moment, be of any ser-

vice, to one who could, by a few throbs, ascertain all that he wanted to know, but that, in the then janty style of the craft, it was held to be an indispensable part of the process to count by the watch—if, indeed, the friends of the patient could be got to think the examination complete without it. We have in our days changed all this ; and by trying to become more simple in the sign, we have become more complex in the thought, without being more certain of the thing. However all that may be, we are to know that Dr Wood, having held the watch in his hand for a minute or two, observed some change come over the face of the patient ; and with a view to examine more nearly the nature of that change, he rose from the chair, laying down, as he did so, the watch on a side-table, whereon were placed the empty phials and boxes—the virtues of whose contents, no doubt, lay more in the Latin names than in the nature of the essences. In addition to this minuteness of detail, we may state that Mr Gillespie, the husband, was, at the moment when the doctor laid down his watch, standing so close by the side-table that, if he had chosen, he might have taken up the article and examined it ; but we cannot say that he did so ; nay, we would rather incline to the opinion that, with his whole soul engrossed with the fate of his young wife, not even the fame of the doctor's repeater would have moved him to an act partaking so much of the mere by-play of the melodrama of life. But then, on the other hand, we are told that the most strange things in the world are done during lapses or intervals of the great play, when the minds of the actors are off their guard, even by the very interest of the plot they are working out, perhaps more as puppets than we can well be aware of.

But, leaving all dubieties, we get again among verities, where we proceed to narrate that the doctor hung over the changing face of the dying woman for the period of five or six minutes, a portion of time measured by the faint and fainter breathings of receding life. All was now over. The spirit had taken flight, even at that moment when the pupil of the eye was turned in the direction of the husband, and the doctor, seizing between his thumb and fore-finger the upper lids, pulled them down over the stark fixed balls. " There," said he, as he raised his head, " it is ended ; and may the hope of the good fructify in that better Eden where sin daurna enter ;" and, amidst a sudden burst of grief from the two women, turned to the side-table and took up his watch. The doctor had acted his part, and now the husband had to perform his—even that pantomimic part of fixing his gaze upon the face of a dead young wife ; feeling within his brain that shock of the mind as it were revolting against itself, with the frightened ideas shooting forth out of the natural channels of thought, and placing his hand upon his brow as if he would restrain the mad-like energies.

The doctor, meanwhile, was preparing to depart, the more willingly, no doubt, that, like the rest of his profession, he was morbidly averse to witnessing scenes among relatives, where the realities of suffering patients are sufficient for the bearing of even those whom practice is supposed to render callous. He had got to the door of the death-chamber, and was in the act of opening it, when Mr Gillespie, starting suddenly out of his trance of grief, proceeded to follow him.

"Just one moment, doctor," said he, as he came up to the rather impatient physician, when the latter was taking up his hat and cane. "Come here !"

And he led the doctor into a parlour where there was a candle burning on the table, with paper, pen, and ink, duly laid, as if for the occasion.

" I want from you, doctor," said the writer, " a certificate of the hour of the death of my beloved wife."

"The first time I was ever asked for such a document," replied the doctor. " Has the death driven you mad, man ; or, rather, has there no been enough o' misery within this hour, that you want it written down upon paper to harrow up your soul in after-time, when you would be better employed in attending to the interests o' your clients ?"

"I have a better reason for it," rejoined the writer; "and which I will explain to you after the funeral."

"Weel, weel," was the characteristic reply, "you lawyers have your ain secrets, just as ministers have theirs, when they frighten the deil wi' prayers; or we doctors, when we pretend to terrify death by Latin names written on bottles and pill boxes."

And taking up a pen, he wrote on a clean sheet of paper— "I hereby certify, on soul and conscience, that Mrs Isabella Gillespie departed this life at"—("Let me see," as he pulled out his watch,)—' half-past twelve o'clock, on this the 29th day of April,"—

"The 30th," interjected the writer; "you know this is morning."

"Quite right," proceeded the doctor; "I am a day nearer the grave than I thought;"—" this 30th day of April, in the year of grace" ("Precious little o't in our day—except before meat,") "17—." "There it is," he continued; "and if any mortal man daur to question it, tell him that Dr Wood's watch will guarantee it in the face o' the sun—a timepiece that may gae wrang, but his never."

And with this speech, which, for a certain reason yet to appear, might have produced a smile on the writer's face, if his wife had not been lying in the next room dead, the doctor departed; nor did his watch progress another half-hour till it was wound up for the night, and he was stretched out in bed, snoring lustily away the effects of the day's multifarious labours.

Next morning he was duly admonished by his familiar under his pillow of the time to get up; but whether it was that he did not consider himself very well rested, or that he had got into the middle of a difficult diagnosis, certain it is, that he took some quarter of an hour of bed more than he was in the habit of doing. No great matter, at worst, to a man so active that he could put himself right by a tug at time's fore-lock at any juncture ; but though he had sacrificed this quarter of an hour to his ease, that was no reason why he should not have got his breakfast at nine o'clock as he used to do. Clear enough that yet there was no breakfast served at that hour, nor indeed for three-quarters of an hour afterwards, a circumstance, no doubt, due to the laziness of the domestics, who had too clearly followed the example of their master, and honoured it by adding two quarters to his one. But, as we all know, Lang Sandy was excessively good-natured and long-suffering, qualified only at times by sudden bursts, which were over in a moment ; and if we are bourd to say that there were some long strides, as if he intended to stalk out at the window, and some growls as if he would have bitten something else than his morning roll, we are forced to admit a justification, when a doctor's visits were to be thrown out of joint for an entire day. At length he was gratified ; and if he ate quickly, and snarled at the time, the servants could only wonder at the unreasonableness of their excellent master, who was fed that morning with all the regularity enjoyed by the inmates of a menagery whose feeding-time has been advertised by special bill.

So out he went, and if his long lank figure was always re-markable to the good burgesses of Edinburgh, it was now more so than usual, for he took longer strides than he was wont, and brandished his gold-headed cane as if he would use the same to force his way through the crowds of people—more than he usually saw at ten o'clock ; nay, he could not under-stand the economy of the streets that morning at all, for the people seemed all to be hurrying to breakfast, in place of re-turning from it ; and the agents and advocates with their blue bags, so ominous of a colour likely to overtake the faces of their clients, were all hurrying to the Parliament House, as if they had been more anxious that morning than usual to bring their *protégés* to the happiness that awaits them in that elysium; all which might very well be for some occult reason or other, into which he had no time to inquire; but reason here or reason there, there could be no sufficient reason (maugre Leibnitz) why he should doubt the dictum of his repeater, which had never deceived him for twenty years, but had always given him the true point of time with as much certainty as could be imparted by the great archangel when he declares to the spirit the truth of eternity.

Nor was the conviction that he was rather too late than an hour too soon upon his rounds affected by certain ejaculations which met him at the opening of certain doors, such as, "You are early, doctor!" "Bless me! is it that time already?" and the like—all of which were verified by the condition of the patients' bed-rooms, where, in some instances, he even found the breakfast apparatus not yet removed. The error, indeed, seemed to run through the whole route; and no doubt it was the more easily observable as our Æsculapius was so regular that you could not have found the scales in the classic representation of the god more uniform. Several small collateral tests are sometimes more convincing than a great experiment; but even something of this latter kind awaited him, as, when he got to the shop of Bridges, the auctioneer, who was that day to shew some medical books of the very kind wanted by the doctor, the shop was not even open; but then it was well known that the auctioneer was not so regular as men of his public character ought to be, and generally are. And this, again, explained why the work-people were not yet on their move to dinner. Yet these were, in comparison of another, only small tests. Did not St Giles's only shew "one," and Bridges's bill shewed "two." There could be no doubt that the saint's hands did so indicate; but, then, how often had the doctor seen these hands pointing to wrong figures—nay, so dogmatically perverse, that they would stick to some beloved arithmetical signs for a whole day ; nor could less be expected of a saint who, according to the old chronicle of him, said he would die at a certain hour of a certain day, and yet lived and ate and drank for a year after—assigning as a reason, that he had got a reprieve for the purpose of taking to heaven with him a great sinner, so loaded with crimes that it took all that time for him to repent.　There was no faith to be placed in a criterion so changeable.　No more is the revolving wheel turned by the fly that sits upon it, than is the sun regulated by such wooden hands of a crazy machine ; and so, the doctor, taking out his watch, was so daring, that he absolutely laughed in the face of the saint, repeating to himself the while the words of Horace—

" Nocturnâ versate manu, versate diurnâ ; "

after which he put the repeater into his fob, and continued his rounds, with the belief that though the sun once went out of his way under the hand of the son of Clymene, and once stood stock-still under the command of the son of Nun, his watch was void of all such erratic whims.　In all this, Dr Alexander Wood just acted upon a kind of instinct, which, less or more, all mankind obey—and that is, the habit of following the intuition of an old conviction ; and, indeed, this is one of the modes whereby nature gets us to go through all the windings of this dreary world ; for if we were under the necessity of doubting, and inquiring into the truth of everything we encounter, we would never get through our work at all.　Even the libertarians, who shudder at the doctrines of necessity, will so far admit that each of us is just the fly upon the wheel, that thinks it has a considerable capacity for turning ; and we ourselves are only by this observation playing the part of a small metaphysician, who makes a hole in the canvas, through which he may see the true secret of the painted figures on the picture.

So the sun condescended to move more and more that day, under the tutelage of Sandy's regulator, till came " the hour of dine ;" and it happened that he was engaged to be one of a large party pledged to attend at the hospitable board of Dr James Hamilton, even that famous man, we suppose, who was called the expurgator, for the reason that he wrote a book to prove that all mankind stood in need of drastics. The hour of meeting was four—that is, by St Giles's ; but the adoption of that unsafe criterion was no reason why Dr Alexander Wood's watch should be considered a false reckoner ; and so, for a certainty, he was at the house precisely at the proper sun time, or rather a kind of " mean time," for he would allow the party to assemble before he made his appearance ; but we need not try to describe his wonderment when he found that not a single soul was in the ante-room, notwithstanding that he had conceded five or ten minutes to their most unpunctual habits. " Why," he muttered to himself, as he sat down and seized, in desperation, a book, " it would seem that a' the watches in Edinburgh are mad the day ;" and apparently he had a good right to make that observation, for even his host, one of the most punctual men of his generation, was not yet come in from his rounds ; then every one knew how janty the bachelor had to make himself, with his breast-ruffles and wrist-ruffles, his knee-buckles, and shoe-buckles, his wig, and the powder thereon, and the tie thereof, let alone various scents to which he was addicted. " And he has been led by the nose by St Giles's, too," said the impatient doctor again, as he lifted his eyes from the book, which had got only as yet a small hold of a head surmounting, yet governed by, an empty stomach. Whereupon, as a refuge from his impatience, he bored his eyes again into the page, until he got his thoughts to follow the author—a feat which made him so far independent that, with the exception of a growl or two, he did not hear his own voice again till some of the company began to assemble. Yet any one might have observed that the hearty doctor was not altogether himself; but, then, that any one would not have been

entitled to wonder if he had known that the worthy physician
had been doomed to wait there more than three-quarters of an
hour for a parcel of slow-goes and loungers who had not had the
courage to take an old crazy saint by the beard and turn his
head round a full revolution.   In short, Dr Wood was im-
plicitly satisfied that the clock in the High Street had cheated
not only his friends, but the whole town ; and this conviction
was so much of the nature of an instinct, that he despised to
allude to the circumstance, just after the fashion of certain
wiseacres, who think it beneath them to try to instruct a pig-
headed generation by imparting to them the subject of their
own hullucinations.

'This *contretemps* notwithstanding, our doctor, after being
seated for some time at the table, became very obediently, if
not cheerfully, amenable to the suavities of a good dinner,
and the best claret which the cellars of Leith could send forth,
under the influence of the money talisman.   At a time when
scandal and metaphysics formed the staples of all genteel conversation, and good wine was helped by the one and needed
by the other, the hour came when they arrived at that point
at which the truth is said to be in a man, for the reason that
drink is not out of him ; and as Sandy conscientiously believed
that Edinburgh had been, in a chronological sense, all wrong
that day, he did not hesitate to say so, even in his own rough
way—viz., that " Auld St Giles's had led them a' by the nose,"
whereupon he was set down as being deeper in Bacchus's wine-
tub than he really was, and accordingly a hearty response of
mirth greeted the announcement.   No one ever thought of
sending out to see how the saint's hands were pointed, for the
good reasons—first, that these hands could not be seen in the
dark ; and, secondly, because they were satisfied that the
doctor was either funning, or under a delusion ; but in the
midst of the uproar Dr Hamilton bethought him of testing
the affair by the doctor's watch itself, the which Sandy handed

over to the expurgator without deigning to look at it. What the host did to the repeater was not seen by the company, and, by the rules of our art, we are not at liberty to say; but the watch having been returned to its owner, and safely deposited in its proper place, the experimenter proceeded to favour his guests by joining them in their humour, which was no other than that of chiming in with Sandy, and declaring that they had all been deceived by the saint, some saying they were too soon for their work by an hour; others that they had quar-relled with their wives about the time of the day; some that they could not get their shirts and ruffles ready for the time of dressing for dinner and so forth. It was now time for their host to betake himself to his legs, not very steady, by reason of their strict allegiance to their master, the head.

" Why, gentlemen," said he, "the thing may be demonstrated. Let us see; Dr Wood declared—and who ever doubted Lang Sandy Wood?—that he this day compared his watch with the clock of St Giles's, and found the saint's hands pointing an hour behind the said watch. That is, as you must know, behind the sun. That being granted, I may ask you the question, Did any of you set your watches by St Giles's this day?"

" No," replied one, who, in speaking truth, did not require to be chief priest of Momus; and "No," said another and another, till the round table was exhausted.

" Then," continued the host, " it behoves that your watches will all point to the same hour as Dr Wood's."

" Most certainly," cried Sandy, as he in his turn betook himself to his legs; "and ye will allow me to say that ye behoved either to have had very bad timepieces or very in-different headpieces if ye could have allowed yourselves to be led by a crazy clock; the which clock I hae seen standing for a haill day pointing to the same hour wi' a' the dogmatism of a philosopher; yea, nae farther than yesterday week, I saw a countryman, wha, after staring at the dial-plate for full two minutes, held up his hands to heaven, gave a wild shriek, and fled to Jamieson's coach-office, whaur he was an hour ower sune. Now for the test, gentlemen," he continued, as he drew out his famous regulator; " I pronounce that it is now exactly five minutes and two seconds past nine."

On hearing which every one took out his watch, and all declared the time properly announced, there being no more difference than the occasional discrepancies so common among horologes.

" There it is, ye see," continued the doctor, when he heard the verdict; " I am right, and St Giles's is wrong."

And Dr Wood was again applauded. Yet it is doubtful whether any one of the company understood how this harmony of chronometers was brought about except the host himself, who retained his secret with much gravity; nor, when the party broke up at the announced hour of twelve, was our possessor of the unfailing timepiece left without greater gratification at his triumph, for in going home he heard St Giles's chime the very hour at which they had parted; and even the watchmen seemed anxious to impress his ear with the welcome sounds; all of which indicated that the High-Street authorities, who had the charge of the time of the city, had come to find they had been an hour wrong during the day, and had taken the trouble to move the saint's hands an hour forward. Accordingly, next morning everything as regards time was brought into harmony. The doctor's breakfast was not too late, nor his visits too soon; the working people went and came at the right time, and the gentlemen with the bags of papers began their professional labours at the proper hour. Nor did this happy condition of things undergo any change up to the time of Mrs Gillespie's funeral, at which the doctor was, as a matter of course, present, and at which the chief mourner, Mr Gillespie himself, roused again his suspicion of being still held in the wrong, by asking him the exact time. Then, to make matters no better, the writer seemed, even in the depth of his grief and the length of his crape, to be pleased to find that the doctor's time tallied so well with the town clock, just as if he had rejoiced at the doctor's having got out of a scrape,—not that he hinted at any discrepancy having ever existed, but that the doctor so construed his looks, as if he had been sure that the writer pitied him for having been in the false position of a man out of time.

An incident so simple could doubtless have had no effect on any mind not predisposed to taking offence by reason of suspicions verging on monomania; but, then, the doctor was at the very least touchy upon this particular point, and unfortunately, too, Mr Gillespie's conduct was only a beginning. No sooner had the doctor left the burying-ground, and proceeded a short distance on his way homeward, than up comes Mr James Arnot, a leather merchant, and one of the trustees under Mrs Gillespie's father's settlement, who, actuated by Heaven knows what motive, put the question to him, how his watch had been going for the last two or three days. The trustee was a serious man certainly, not given to practical joking, otherwise the doctor would have resented on the instant a question which seemed to have some view to make him ridiculous. As it was, he was inclined to be humorous.

"Tell a' your friends, Mr Arnot," said he, "that Dr Wood's watch is just going on as well as can be expected."

And with these words he brushed past his interrogator; but the latter had no wish to be left by so great a man under the suspicion of tomfooling him, and therefore he kept trotting after the Anak, and trying to assure him that he put the question as a matter of business connected with the trusteeship, all which seemed to our doctor to make the matter worse, inasmuch as it was an attempted justification of impudence.

For a man with such legs it was no difficult matter to get quit of this importunate joker, and seeing that as yet only two questioners had appeared on the field, the danger of being made a butt of was not great: so far there was consolation, but the doctor had not got far away from Mr Arnot when he was saluted by another, a Mr David Edgar, a tea-merchant, who was, as he himself admitted, also connected with the trust, and who, with a kind of apology, came slap out with the question, whether, on the morning of the 30th of the last month, the doctor had found his watch an hour too fast. The question produced a stare of perfect amazement, for we may as well let it be known now, that however genial the doctor was, he had an utter horror at being made an object of banter, and as this third attack was a clear proof of a conspiracy to make public game out of that innocent foible of his—a perhaps undue love for his watch—he required to resent it, and so to be sure he did.

"No," replied he, even louder than he was in the habit of speaking ; " my watch hasna deceived me for twenty years ; but I'll tell you what, Mr Edgar, *you* have *un*deceived me even this minute, for I aye took ye for a serious man, at least far abune a fule."

And again the doctor strode on, probably a little appeased by the consciousness of having put an end for ever to a conspiracy ; but as it is in the way of Providence that we are nearest danger when we think ourselves farthest away from it, so the doctor had no sooner got to the door of his house than Mr Scott the writer accosted him blandly, with the intelligence that he had a few questions to ask him, his apology for putting which lay in his professional capacity.

"What anent?" replied the doctor, now thoroughly roused against interrogatories.

"Why, sir," replied the agent, "just your watch, which we all know is famous for being the best within the sound of St Giles's."

" My watch again!" echoed the doctor.

"You have been questioned before, then?" continued the writer ; "so much the better, as it shews I am not on a solitary fool's errand."

" Gude heavens !" cried the doctor, "are ye in the plot too ?"

" I know of no plot," said Mr Scott. " It is a fair question, whether you remember that your watch was an hour before the time on Thursday last ?"

" Ay, just the auld sang," replied the doctor ; " but, by my faith, ye 'll get nae chorus out o' me."

" I want no chorus," said Mr Scott, perfectly amazed at the conduct of a man so generally respected for *bonhomie* and politeness of a rough kind. "Will you not, Dr Wood," continued he, " allow yourself to be precognosced ?"

" Ay," shouted the doctor, who had by this time got the door in his hand, within which he partly stood,—" Ay, but no *cog*-nosced."

Whereupon he banged the door in the face of the astonished writer, who was thus forced to depart with a clean sheet of paper and wondering eyes.

It is comfortable for us to have to say that for that evening and night Dr Wood was free from any further questions on this now, to him, sore point ; and we wish we could add that he was equally free from questions put to himself by himself. This we cannot do, for it is of verity that he precognosced himself with an asperity to which his generous spirit was little accustomed, to the effect of ascertaining whether it could be possible that a man of his repute could be set up by the people of Edinburgh, to whom he had done so much good in a professional way, as a laughing-stock or public merry-andrew, for people to point their finger at and say, "There goes Lang Sandy Wood, and his watch that was never wrong." It might, he said to himself, be deemed a very small matter that the tail of his wig should be pulled by a few roistering friends ; but he knew human nature too well not to be certain that dignity, nay, even respectability, is utterly incompatible with public laughter, if indeed it is not so fine and brittle an article that the slightest touch of ridicule will begin the process of its destruction. Even in the morning he was impressed with these feelings, all tending to an apprehension that even his professional success and utility might be endangered by a decay of public respect. He could only hope that the new day would bring immunity from an evil which he probably exaggerated, and with this expectation he went forth again to his duties.

As a veritable chronicler, we are here in some difficulty, or rather fear, lest we may be subjected to the suspicion of having recourse to the rhetorical figure of accumulation; but we cannot help the danger, and must therefore aver that Sandy had not been on the street for a full quarter of an hour, when one of the gentlemen who had been present at the expurgator's dinner party came up to him and said, in a laughing way,—

"I hope, doctor, the trick played upon you by Hamilton did not put you out of time in paying your visits yesterday?"

"Again, and aince mair," muttered Sandy. "Really, really, this *is* ower muckle. What *can* be the meaning o' a' this?"

And so overcome was he that he did not even condescend to give his old friend, a very respectable man, a word in reply. On again he strode, a process which easily enough carried him away from one man, especially as that man was thunderstruck, and therefore unable to follow for an explanation; but we are to remember that Edinburgh at that time was more like a village, where every one knows the story of the hour within that hour, than a city with dimensions offering physical obstructions to the spread of petty scandal—the reason whereof being, that it was one long street, where every one might be seen at some hour or other of the twenty-four, and there is therefore nothing strange in the fact we dare to aver, that in half an hour afterwards another of the dinner party came in contact with our doctor, but with this difference, that Sandy accosted him with the question how he had got home that night, the said question being connected in the doctor's mind with a certain inability to walk straight exhibited by the jolly diner-out.

"Pretty well, after some surging and rocking," replied he; "but, O man," he added, "it was a pity Hamilton put your watch an hour back, (I knew you had purposely put it forward to get home early,) for I would have escaped sober, and got to bed an hour sooner. I fancy you would discover the trick next morning?"

"I discovered nae sic thing," cried Sandy, in a loud voice; "for the gude reason, that my watch next morning was just as correct as my head; and, sir, if you have naething to do but play the part of a confederate in a general plot to make me ridiculous, you had better have kept your bed and sent for me to physic you."

So, growling like an angry bear, away again he stalked, leaving his friend much in the same state of mind as the prior one, that is, utter bewilderment. Nor had he got well away from this tormentor when he began muttering to himself, "This is indeed awfu';" and a little afterwards, "Did ony mortal man ever think that I, after raising myself to the very tap of my profession, should have a pan tied to my tail amidst the laughter of a town full of idiots?" What more of monologue he indulged in we cannot say; but certain it is, if he had been judged by the hanging head and dejected look and moving lips, a great many more thoughts on this very subject passed through his mind than he was ever willing to admit. For two hours or more he fortunately met no more of the *bons vivans*, and he was gradually recovering himself—certainly it must be admitted without great reason, inasmuch as it is almost undoubted that if he had encountered any others of them he would have been thrown back into that very despondency from which he was getting free. A slap on his shoulder about the end of this time justifies our remark. The slap was from the ruffled hand of no less a personage than Dr James Hamilton, who, always brusque, attacked him instantly.

"Ah, Sandy," said he, laughing, "you are clever, and your watch carries authority."

"The muckle deil's in Auld Reekie," muttered Sandy. "What, in God's name, man, do ye a' mean? Is it the intention o' my best friends to drive me mad?"

"Mad!" ejaculated his friend. "What do *you* mean? If you had allowed me to finish my sentence, I would have said, as I now do, that though you are a clever fellow, and wished to send us all home an hour too soon, you would find in the morning that we were too much for you. Wasn't your watch quite right when you got up?"

"Weel," replied Sandy, "that may be a' very gude. You are just taking a roundabout way to get to the auld subject; but I'll tell you what, Jamie—it's my opinion that you are in the plot too. Now I gie ye fair warning, to this effect, that the first man who insults me again on this subject will kiss the causeway, by the mere pith of this right arm and this stick."

And he brandished the weapon with such force, rolling meanwhile such fiery eyes, that his friend became afraid and made off, with some sad thoughts in his mind, that his good and jolly companion was on the verge of insanity.

Even during that day a strange "sough" was going through Edinburgh, involving a story of some mystery connected with the time of night at which Mrs Gillespie had departed this life. The rumour had not reached the ears of Dr Wood, and we mention it at present only to shew that when Mr Scott, with Mr David Williamson the advocate by his side, knocked at Dr Wood's door next forenoon at lunching-time, he had some reason for an act which otherwise might be taken for a determined purpose of driving things to an extremity. On being admitted and introduced to the doctor, who at the time was chewing the bitter cud of resentment against an ungrateful public, they were received with that desperate coolness which can be assumed by certain people, even when the heart is leaping under the influence of fury. We do not say that Sandy was in that state, but it is certain that he was greatly moved, and there was consequently an irony in his politeness, which could not fail to be observed by the cautious, if not apprehensive, visitors.

" *Be* seated, gentlemen," he said, with a bow, which, taking into account the length of his person and his desperation, was equal at least to two common obeisances.

" I believe," said Mr Williamson, " that Mr Scott called upon you before, doctor."

" He did, and wi' a vengeance, to my certain knowledge," was the reply.

" And I believe there is some mistake," continued the advocate, " because I understand that when, probably too abruptly, he introduced a certain subject "—

" Certain subject," muttered Sandy.

" A certain subject," resumed Mr Williamson, " you would not, for some reason that I am ignorant of, give him any answer."

" No answer," again muttered the doctor between his teeth, set for grinding something harder than muffins.

" Yet," continued the advocate, " I assure you that it was only for the ends of justice that Mr Scott called upon you and "—

" You're no in the secret?" said Sandy grimly, interrupting the speaker. " You are brought here only as a cat's-paw to work the plot, because Mr Scott hasna courage to work it farther himself; but, Mr David, I'm prepared for you."

" Prepared for resenting a simple question, whether on a certain day you found a discrepancy between your watch and the clock of St Giles's?"

" Ay, even for that," roared the doctor,—" even for that seemingly simple question, which I'll be d——d if I answer to you or the best advocate that ever added twenty lees to a brief where there were twenty already."

"Why, my dear doctor," said the lawyer, in some wonder, " you have lost your temper."

"Na," rejoined Sandy, " it's you wha have lost your decorum. I'll tell you what, David,—just turn your battery against Mr Scott after ye are outwith my house, and if ye canna extract from him that he is in the plot of a parcel of vagabonds, who are determined to make me ridiculous, you needna wonder ye can make naething of me. I winna hear another word."

And, rising, he opened the door.

" There," he continued, bowing again with the humility of desperation ; " gude morning."

The gentlemen were thus genteelly turned out, leaving Sandy in greater astonishment than he had yet been, the proof of which might have been found in the fact that, although it was time for him to resume his professional rounds, he lay back upon his chair in serious and solemn reverie. " It's getting beyond a' bounds," he said to himself. " It maun be stopt, ay, even by the strong arm of the law. There's such a thing in Scotland as a law-borrows, and, by the powers above, as weel as below, a law-borrows I'll swear, or my name's no Sandy Wood."

What farther communings took place between the doctor's tongue and his ear, the records from which we draw do not shew, neither can we tell how further he comforted himself on that day, while still under the conviction that every urchin upon the street was ready to salute his ear as a common kenspeckle, with the cry of " Lang Sandy Wood's watch !" We have more authority for continuing our statement in regard to the report about the death of Mr Gillespie's wife. It appears that this gentleman had married a young lady of the name of Græme, with a tocher of some four or five thousand pounds. Though a writer, the husband had taken no precaution to have a marriage-contract, or rather he was precluded from having recourse to that mode of fixing conjugal rights, which the law could, on a certain event, annul, by having been under the necessity of making a runaway match, by reason of some disinclination to the marriage on the part of Mr Arnot and Mr Edgar, her trustees. A rather strange consequence was the result —no other, in short, than that if the marriage came to an end by the death of the wife within a year and a day of the ceremony, without a child (who had been heard to cry) having been born of the same, the money brought by the wife reverted to her relations, and the husband was left precisely, as to funds, in the condition which he occupied before the union took place. Such is the law of Scotland; and however strange or irrational it may appear, there will be found, upon examination, strong reasons for its justification, arising out of the view which the law takes of the nature and intention of wedlock, if it may not be said that almost all our old legal maxims and rules derived from the Roman jurisprudence have at their foundation a principle of justice and equity which, to the superficial thinker, may almost be said to be entirely concealed. Against this law Mr Gillespie could do nothing to defend himself; and, as fate would have it, there was not only no child, but Mrs Gillespie came to be *in articulo mortis* on the very last evening of the year and the day, so that if before twelve o'clock at midnight of the 29th of April she died, the husband would lose the tocher.

So far the story was clear enough; no one disputed these facts, the mystery, if any such existed, surrounded the actual period of the lady's death. It was alleged, on the part of the trustees, that the time of the death was half-past eleven, and not half-past twelve, as set forth in the certificate which Mr

Gillespie got Dr Wood to sign ; and the evidence of this consisted of the testimony of the sister, Miss Græme, and that of the nurse, both of whom declared that immediately after Mrs Gillespie's breath was out they heard the watchman call half-past eleven. In addition to this, one of the servants declared that having looked at the house clock immediately before Dr Wood's entry, and immediately again after his departure, she found, to her astonishment, that the hands had been put forward by some one an entire hour, while next morning they were in perfect harmony with St Giles's. To add to all this, there was the admitted fact that Dr Wood's watch was laid upon the side-table in the bed-room while he was occupied in hanging over the dying patient. On the other side, Mr Gillespie stoutly denied that he touched the hands of the famous repeater.

This extraordinary story very soon found its way to the ears of Dr Wood, and nearly as soon opened his eyes to the consolatory fact that the supposed persecution to which he had been exposed had had its foundation in motives very far from an intention to make him ridiculous. It explained even the attacks on the part of the parties present at Dr Hamilton's dinner, as well as the trick of the host, and the motive of that transaction ; nor did his satisfaction end with the mere conviction that he was free from the suspicion of having been made public game of, for he had upon the occasion a dinner party himself, to which he invited every one of the innocent individuals whom he had in his wrath snubbed so unmercifully, and where, as we may well fancy, no little fun commemorated the installation of the host into his old position of respectability and public affection. Sometime afterwards an action of declarator, at the suit of the trustees, was brought against Mr Gillespie, to have it declared that he had feloniously altered the doctor's watch, by putting the hands an hour forward, that the true period of the death was half-past eleven, and that the tocher reverted to Mrs Gillespie's relatives. In the proof which was led the doctor was himself examined, an occasion which brought out the peculiarity of his character. He stoutly denied that his watch had ever been wrong, and as there was no witness to say that either he or she saw Mr Gillespie forward the hands of the repeater, the evidence would have been scrimp enough. But the adroitness of David Williamson saved the pursuers' case. He pretended to sympathise with the doctor in his worship of his watch, and by getting him in good humour, extracted from him the admission that on the 30th of the month his watch was an hour before St Giles's. There was no necessity for proving whether the saint was right or wrong. The judges assumed that the town clock was the best, and so Sandy's watch was put out of court as a testimony that had been tampered with. The pursuers gained the day, and Mr Gillespie lost both the tocher and his character.

Deacon Macgillivray's Disappearance.

STRANGE book might be made out of those con-
curring events called coincidences. We generally
find them set forth in connexion with circumstan-
tial evidence; but thousands of them, and perhaps
the most striking, are lost, much to the regret of those who are
fond of direct interpositions of Providence. As the pegs upon
which superstition hangs her *pseudo-doxia*, we might expect they
would have been better preserved, at least in those cases where
they point, as they often do, to the preservation of life. A
curious example was told me by a Mr Robie, who stood in the
relation to me of gerund-grinder, and who used to relieve the
burden of his dry work by telling me and the others who were
taught by him at the same time, portions of his experience.
In the example I am about to offer, I shall adhere as nearly as
possible to his own words.

Many years ago, said he, that is, when I first came to Edinburgh, and was attending the university, I became acquainted
with the family of Mr Duncan Macgillivray, who lived in Borthwick's Close. He occupied the dignified position in those days
of a deacon, his craft being that of the hammermen, and therefore may be supposed to have been pretty well to do in the
world,—a fact of some importance to me, who was steeped in
the blessings of a ten pound-bursary, supplemented by an
occasional bag of meal and a junket of salt beef, not the very
best kind of food for the muses, then worshipped by me. So
it was that I had a great love for Mrs Macgillivray's tea-table,

and by consequence, a respect for the mistress herself, who
with much good sense repaid the honour by suiting plentifully
the supply to the demand, in consideration of which I fed the
two elder boys with the food of the mind, with this difference,
that the demand was not suited to the supply. This comfortable state of the domestic elysium in Borthwick's Close was
destined to be interrupted by that law of the gods, whereby all
mundane things undergo change, as if—so I have often thought
—variety in any form, and at any expense, were paramount to
all other counsels in Olympus. One afternoon, when I resorted
to my old haunt, expecting to find the hearth gods all in good
humour as usual, I was surprised to meet Mrs Macgillivray in
the lobby, with a face wherefrom the accustomed smile was
totally banished, and its place occupied by pale fear. I could
read it as I could have done a penny broadsheet of the time,
with a dreadful wood-engraving drawn in conformity with the
equally dreadful letter-press.

"What has happened?" inquired I, as I took her trembling
hand.

"Oh, have you not heard?" replied she.

"Nothing," added I with increased apprehension.

"I have neither seen nor heard o' the deacon since yesterday morning after breakfast," was the announcement.

"A mere case of absence," said I, with an effort at cheerfulness; "it is not a case of missing."

"Ye may gie it ony name ye please," said she, "but the
like has never happened since the day o' our marriage, and ye
know that the deacon was aye punctual, aye to a very minute."

I was forced to admit that that was true, yet I could see no
great reason for fear, and proceeding with her to the parlour,
I took a seat alongside of her, with a view to get some
further information. I saw that as a friend of the family I had
something to do, and my first effort was to procure all the information she could give me, preparatory to my undertaking a

search for so important a personage as the deacon of the hammermen of Edinburgh. There was, however, wonderfully little to be got. She could tell me of no reason for his absence; there was no journey he had intended to undertake; he had no habits of intemperance which might have laid him up in a tavern : nor any loose inclinations that could have wiled him into any of the dens of the dissolute; neither, so far as she could say, had he any money upon him, to tempt the robber and the murderer. Then, inquiries had already been made in almost every quarter where he was known to frequent, so that if I had started upon the instant, I might have found it difficult to know in what direction to turn myself: our conversation was getting exhausted, as every suggestion fell away, leaving only an addition to the prevailing gloom, when I started, more by chance than good guidance, the question whether the deacon had any enemies.

To this I got an answer which surprised me; for of all the men in the world, the deacon might have been supposed to possess an immunity from the incursions of revenge.

" I had forgotten," said she, as she seemed to revert to some idea which startled her; " yes, there is one man I fear: strange I never thought of it till ye put the question; yes, his own brother, o' the same blood, born o' the same mother—Angus Macgillivray, flesher in the Fleshmarket Close; that man has been the very curse o' our family ; he was a sweetheart o' mine before I got acquainted with the deacon, but I never liked him so that I could have married him, or rather I aye feared him for his passions, let alone his trade o' killing lambs ; he never forgave our marriage, and I'm no sure if he didna hate me as much as he did his brother; he never came to see us, though the deacon often invited him, prayed him to let byganes be byganes, nor even after he married a wife o' his ain did he forget and forgive, just as if he felt dissatisfied that he hadna got some revenge; and then, to make things waur, the deacon got rich as he got poor, a change that never could be forgiven ; so things went on for years, nae reconciliation, but as their ways lay different and they seldom met, there were few opportunities for quarrels. Now a' thae things come up upon me ; and mair, for it is only about six months syne that Angus, having met the deacon in a tavern, got into wrath, and made threats which forced the deacon to swear a lawborrows against him."

These words, uttered in the peculiar tone of grief and fear, made an impression upon me which I tried to conceal, and it was aggravated by that involuntary action of the nerves which doctors call "working up,"—an effect consequent upon a process of reasoning where all the ideas are led by the feelings. I sat for some time without speaking, for I felt that it would have made matters worse to admit what I thought, and an effort to cheer does not do much good unless it is backed by some indisputable fact of a favourable kind. I did not even know what to suggest in aid of further inquiry, but I endeavoured to ascertain whether any one had called at Angus's flesh-booth, to know whether he was at home, and having got something like a negative from her, I resolved within my own mind to find out what I could in this direction. It was now about six o'clock in the evening, and so great had been the solicitude, or I should rather say fear, that there had been no thought of the stated meals. It seemed to be my presence, which bringing up the instincts of hospitality, suggested what otherwise was so regular to the household, so true it is that amid all trials, not excluding the final one, we are still in some way bound to the duties of life. She urged me to stop; but·I had got so interested in this extraordinary case of absence, and was so especially occupied by the thoughts and expedients which were revolving in my mind, that I declined to tax a kindness when selfishness was a virtue.

I accordingly left her with some words calculated to assure

her, and bending my steps to the Fleshmarket, I met several friends of the well-known deacon, all of whom had heard of his unaccountable disappearance without being able to suggest any mode of accounting for him. On arriving at the market, I made at once for Angus Macgillivray's booth. He was not there, and a boy who served the customers answered to my irquiry, that he had not seen his master since the morning of the previous day. This was, no doubt, very strange intelligence, insomuch as it conveyed one of these phenomena called coincidences, which play such tricks in questions of evidence. I tried to view it philosophically ; but as there are states of mind where one little fact outweighs a bushel of reasons, so I felt myself under a still stronger obligation to trace the steps of the flesher. I got accordingly from the boy the place of his master's residence, and though in the chance of finding him there I might have hesitated as to the propriety of a direct call, what I resolved was to see his wife in his (by me) supposed absence. Angus, I found, lived at the corner of the turn which the Cowgate makes into the Grassmarket, and thither I bent my steps ; nor was it many minutes before I was in the presence of Mrs Angus Macgillivray ; but what was my wonderment to find this woman very much in the same condition as that in which I found the wife of the deacon. Her husband had left the house the previous day after breakfast without saying a word that he was to be otherwise engaged than at his stall ; and as it was his invariable habit to tell her when he was to go to the country (which he often did) for cattle, she could not account for his absence in any way. So far there was a difference between the conditions of the sisters-in-law, that Mrs Angus Macgillivray did not entertain any apprehension that any violence had overtaken her husband, yet it was clear enough, even from the suspicious eye she cast upon me while making my inquiries, that she was not free from the fear of some untoward accident. She even questioned me as to my motive for calling, as if she thought I had something to tell, and was afraid to tell it; and I had some difficulty in satisfying her that my object was not in any way connected with the circumstance of his disappearance. At all hazards, it was my especial care to avoid any reference to the deacon, and especially *his* absence; for as she doubtless knew that the enmity was all on one side, that of her husband, she might have drawn, with very different feelings, the same conclusion to which her sister-in-law had arrived.

Having left this woman also in a very unhappy condition, I wandered about without there being any special direction claiming my steps, but rather from a disinclination to go home without making further effort in a case which, even in its beginning, was so mysterious. Meanwhile my mind began to work upon the coincidence. So fertile is the mind of suspicions, that one would be inclined to think that as there is apparently a stock of pleasurable and painful feeling in us from which any paramount idea draws to make itself, as it were, bright or dark, so also is there ever ready the pabulum of suspicion ready to be appropriated by excited curiosity. It seemed that it had fallen upon me to clear up a mystery; and as the mind relucts against a state of suspended doubt, I found myself ready to rush to the conclusion that Angus Macgillivray had murdered his brother, and run off for fear of capture. The non-discovery of the body did not appear to me to militate against the notion, as the power of secretion, in cases of this kind, is not of difficult execution, at least for a time. The longer I pondered the more paramount the idea became till—such is the effect of brooding—I came to be *certain* that such would be found to be the real cause of the absence of the two men. In my goings to and fro, I met a good many people, who put the same question, " Has Deacon Macgillivray cast up yet?" but no one seemed to be aware of the absence of the brother, otherwise, so I thought, they must have adopted the same supposition, seeing they all knew what was indeed all but notorious, though I was strangely an exception, that the hammerman had sworn a lawborrows against the flesher. None of these people, however, viewed the affair in the serious light in which it appeared to me; if it was not, indeed, that they tried to make light of it, as one of those seemingly inexplicable knots which, resisting the fingers for a time, come all out, as it were, at once when the proper turn is given to one of the involutions. All this was without effect upon me, who knew what I thought the fatal circumstance of the absence of Angus. So I stept up to the bailies' office and inquired there whether any search had been made by any of the officers or constables; but here again I was met by the remark, that a day-and-a-half's absence did not form even a ground for such a fear of any occurrence, either disastrous or fatal, as would authorise any search by the authorities of the city. I had my reason for a different conclusion, but I was necessarily restrained from telling my story, from a fear of throwing suspicion upon a man vindictive enough to take revenge upon me.

On going towards Borthwick's Close, with the intention of again seeing the deaconess—for so these great dignitaries were sometimes called at that time when corporations were a species of dominions or powers—I met Andrew Girvan, her brother, a currier, who lived in Niddry's Wynd. A sensible man, not prone to fancies, he took a very different view.

"I have been everywhere I could think of," said he, "but I can find no trace."

"Everywhere but the house of his brother," said I, fixing my eyes on him.

"The house of his brother!" rejoined he; "what on earth would take me there—the place of all others he would avoid?"

"Very true; but what would you think were you to find that Angus is also amissing, having left his house about the

same time?" said I, with a view to sound him, and thereby
test my own suspicions.

"Think!" replied he, "why, was not I present at Glennie's
tavern that night when the villain drew his knife against his
own brother, and I hurried the deacon away; and was it not I
who recommended the lawborrows? Think, why if I were to
find it true that Angus Macgillivray was away, I would con-
clude at the instant that he had repaid the lawborrows by a
secret stab."

"Yes; but there are difficulties," said I, with that straining for evidence of a conviction which is so natural to us.
"Where could such stab have been given in broad day; and it
must have been in the forenoon, seeing the deacon did not
come home to dinner. Then any secret den or out-of-the-way
place is scarcely to be thought of, insomuch as the deacon
could not have been wiled there by one whom he feared."

"Nothing in all that," replied he; "for we all know that
the deacon's business led him down dark closes and out-of-the-
way places, where there are dens for all customers, dead or
alive. And besides, he was so simple and generous a man,
that if Angus had met him and proffered the open hand of
reconciliation, he might have led him anywhere."

"Well," said I, getting more confident, "I may tell you, as
his brother-in-law, that I have ascertained from Angus's wife
herself that he too has been amissing for the same time."

"Then by all that is good," cried he, as his eye flashed,
from the suddenness of the impression upon the ear of these
words, "the mystery is all but cleared up. The villain has
murdered his own brother, and run the country."

Nor was I much astonished at this ejaculation, for the original suspicion had gradually been becoming a conviction
with me, and my mind was almost eager to have any remaining
doubts removed.

"But," said I, "what is to be done?"

" Go to the city authorities," replied he on the instant, "and get them to issue a warrant for the apprehension of Angus Macgillivray."

" I have been at the bailies' office," said I, " and found that the officers there do not consider the affair as sufficiently alarming to induce even an official search."

" Because," replied he, " they don't know the facts,"—adding satirically, " It is generally believed that those who are blind don't see."

" But even if they were put in possession of the facts, no warrant would be issued without a signed information ; and would you take that responsibility?" was my question.

" No," replied he ; " but you might, because you have made the proper inquiry, and found Angus fled."

" I would not like to take that responsibility either," rejoined I. " Besides, the time is not far enough gone for any very serious apprehension. We must wait another day. There is an old saying something to the effect, 'that if you want to keep your friends, don't prolong your visit beyond three days ; and if you want to be thought not dead, don't be unaccountably absent from home beyond three nights.' "

To this Mr Girvan agreed, and both of us saw the propriety of visiting the deaconess, who was hour by hour losing hope. We found her in the same position in which I had left her. I noticed that as we entered she turned a wistful eye upon us, with an expression that seemed to speak and say, Is he not with you? and there followed that blank look in which the orb seems dead. There was silence everywhere, as if Angerona had there set up her temple, and the votaries were mute. The children, ignorant of the cause of change in the mother, had been put to bed. The servant whom we saw as we passed the kitchen sat at the fireside hanging her head, as if she mourned the death of a kind master, and no neighbours dared to intrude where they could carry no comfort—a species of kindness this in the people of Scotland which results from a delicacy they get small credit for from those who judge from a rude speech and homely, if not coarse, manners. We sat down quietly and gravely—a clear enough indication to her that we brought no hopeful intelligence; nor had we sat many minutes when we came to understand what was the direction of the current of her thoughts. They had been all running towards the conclusion that Angus Macgillivray was in some way connected with the mysterious affair.

" Have ye inquired," she asked, as she cast her eye over us, "if Angus has been at hame syn yesterday. I could wad my marriage ring he 's awa, and nae suner than he should be. Will ye no answer?" she continued, in a wailing way. " Is he in Edinburgh? when was he seen? Can naebody tell?"

I looked to Girvan—for I could not answer without false-hood—and he understood me.

" I have made no inquiry, Margaret," said he; "nor did I think it necessary to go there—the suspicion seems so un-natural, so unlikely. Besides, are you not taking on too heavily? This is only the second day."

" The second day!" she burst forth, " and Deacon Macgil-livray hasna seen his wife or his bairns, nor sent a letter or a message to tell whaur he is. The second day!" she continued in the same wailing strain. " When was it that he was half an hour behind his dinner? And this has taen place in Edin-burgh, which is just a lang street, whaur everybody kens everything about everybody."

" Many a longer absence has had as happy an explanation," replied her brother. " We have only as yet one fact, and it will just look as you view it. You know peats will build the side of a house as well as make a fire that will burn you."

" But there 's nae use buttering peats," cried she impatiently. " I tell you Deacon Macgillivray is dead, and Angus is the man who has made me a widow, and my bairns fatherless."

M

And then came a fit of hysterical sobbing, which we had no means of alleviating. While I looked at her, and of course pitied her, I could not help thinking how completely her suspicion was confirmed by the information I had got, and which I dared not communicate to her. There was enough of sorrow for the hour. And as we saw we could be of no further service that night, we left her to that kind of consolation which the heart seeks for itself, and sometimes the more readily and successfully that it is left to itself and to Him who is master of the heart and the issues thereof.

Next forenoon I repaired to Girvan's, as arranged between us, in order that together we might make a more thorough search to the effect at least of ascertaining whether the missing man had been seen, and when and where, during the forenoon of his disappearance. On going along I found that the affair had spread, insomuch, indeed, that the question, "What has become of Deacon Macgillivray?" belonged now to the public. Every one put it to another with just the usual amount of success, and as usual in all such cases, the ingenious took advantage of the general curiosity to interpolate the proper amount of romance. The lawborrows was without hesitation a part of the terrible tragedy, no less than the cruel murder of one brother by another, perpetrated in Angus Macgillivray's shambles, and no doubt was entertained that if the clay floor of that place were turned up the body would be found. Both Girvan and myself entertained as much suspicion as the circumstances warranted. We had, moreover, the power of regulating it so as to keep us from the infection of a belief due to the proclivity towards the horrible, and that accelerated by sympathy, we had therefore before us a process of sifting. We traced reports to the supposed authors, and always found the origin of the black crow. The story about the shambles soon vanished, and others equally extravagant came in the end to nothing. The inexplicable fact of the absence of the two brothers at the same time of course remained—dark enough and ominous, even to the satisfaction of the sensation quidnuncs—and at the bottom of the heap of chaff which lay over it, there was only one solitary grain. It appeared that a person of the name of Peter M'Glashan, a labourer, who resided in the Cowgate, and whom we saw and interrogated, had been the involuntary cause of some of the theories, but all that could be extracted from him amounted to this, that he had seen Deacon Macgillivray that forenoon hurrying up the High Street, and that, having occasion to return, he had met, about ten minutes after, Angus Macgillivray coming up the Bow, the top of which he doubled as if he were going down the High Street ; one or two others spoke to having seen the brothers respectively on the same route.

Such was the result of our investigations continued throughout the entire day. It confirmed so far the original suspicion, and it must be confessed that, after abstracting the superinduced fiction, the mystery was a very good one as it stood. Only one thing was to be regretted by the philosophers who have so much to regret in the doings of mankind—that the public will not let good alone. Enjoying a dark story as all men do, even in the midst of their pity for those who are the victims, we might wonder that they do not prolong the pleasure by retarding the denouement; but then we are to recollect that the fruition which ends enjoyment is the necessary step from which commences another turn in the play of life, and to this fruition impatient nature is continually driving her children with such hurry that they try to anticipate it by mock representations. All this we found very well illustrated by our day's search. Towards evening the ferment had increased ; politics were suspended in the taverns ; even scandal, always a great personage in Edinburgh, lost her charms. The tragic fate, in whatever form, the more hazy and indefinite the better, of the deacon of the hammermen, was the universal theme of conversation ; a tribute to that wonderful power by which the fate of one man, however obscure, if involved in her folds, demands more of human interest than is accomplished by the incidents of a battle where thousands lie slain or wounded on either side.

And so it was with minds very ill prepared for a meeting with the deaconess, that we betook ourselves about eight o'clock in the evening to Borthwick's Close: we found the same house of gloom, with the shadows increased in the darkness of these hours, and all appearances betokening utter hopelessness. Even on the previous day, Mrs Macgillivray had all but renounced the pleadings of the goddess of the lamp, and the brooding night with its abnormal figures and frowning shapes was not favourable to any return in the morning to a more rational mode of consideration. It cannot be said that she was more miserable when we entered than she had been at our last meeting ; probably even less, in so far as her grief had arrived at that state where, from diminishing the action of the heart, and consequently, as the doctors say, the circulation in the small vessels of the brain, the nerves of thought lose their irritability and become torpid. Yet as we entered she opened her half-shut eyelids with a start, as if some association between the creak of the door and the usual incoming of her husband had vindicated a power over the apathy of despair ; a glance satisfied her that we had no favourable intelligence for her, and it seemed vain to us to have recourse to expedients for removing a depression which might, in God's kindly providence, be a preparation for the final intimation. We therefore fairly admitted that the mystery remained as dark as ever, but that we ourselves had not given up all hope of an agreeable surprise. Even these words sufficiently indicated the low condition of our hopes, and the return was accordingly merely a shake of the head ; thenceforth the meeting became every moment more painful : the long periods of silence seemed to have a weight in them, our looks were sym-

pathetic, carrying a moral gloom in the physical light of the eye; no one was at the trouble to remove the long charred wick of the candle : we sat with bent heads, and seemed to be afraid to allow to the body its ordinary movements, as if we considered all natural action as a desecration of an occasion where God's hand lay heavy on the wife and the mother.

Nor did we think it proper to put an end to this scene by parting : we felt that there would be something cruel in leaving the stricken sufferer to thoughts that were all but unbearable, and this at the very time we were conscious we could yield her no comfort; so the hours passed without any better reckoning than the increasing silence in the street, and the gathering gloom of the unsnuffed candle, till it might be about eleven, when a slight knock was heard at the door. Mrs Macgillivray again started, and we were not less surprised; nay, I have no doubt that all of us had some notion that the visitor might be no other than the deacon himself; the door was opened by the servant, we listened to the step on the passage—tramp— tramp—so like one well known, that Girvan ejaculated with a kind of spasm, "It's the deacon!" The words were electric, we started up, and even Mrs Macgillivray sat upright in her chair gazing at the door : it opened, and before us stood one of the town officers with the red neck on his blue coat.

"Here is a bit of paper," said he, "which was brought up to the office about an hour ago."

And Girvan taking it out of his hand, fixed his eyes upon it as if he were charmed, yet he did not seem to comprehend what he was reading; for although I asked him what it contained, he could not utter a word. Mrs Macgillivray's eye was fixed upon him; and I myself sat with open mouth, wondering what ailed the man.

"Can ye no read?" said the officer.

"Read," added I, impatiently.

And the same word trembled on the lips of the deaconess.

Out it came at length; and the effect was certainly proportioned to the cause. I took the paper out of his hand, and read for myself the following words, disposed in lines in this manner—

      " Deacon Macgillivray,
            Borthwick's Close, Edinburgh,
Killed on the 19th."

The paper was much crumpled, as if it had met with rough usage; and what added to the effect of the direful words, it was besmeared with blood to such an extent that some of the letters were scarcely legible. I would willingly have kept it from the eyes of the deaconess, but she held out her hand tremblingly to get possession of it, and it was too late to attempt concealment. She read it at a glance; and, as if it had been on fire, threw it from her, unable to utter a word.

"Stay a little," said Girvan, as he rose and took his hat. "I will be back in ten minutes."

He hurriedly left the room. And I, taking up the paper, began to question the officer as to the person who left it at the bailies' office. I ascertained that his name was Hugh M'Pherson, a cobbler, who resided in the Cowgate; and that his account of the manner of obtaining it was, that he found it among some straw on the street right opposite to the coach-office in the High Street, from which the coach to Galashiels started twice a week. It was further stated by M'Pherson, that his opinion was, that the paper had fallen from the coach along with the straw among which it was found.

Before I had time to form any opinion as to the real purport and meaning of this sibylline scrap, Girvan came again hurriedly into the room, breathing hard, as if he had been running—an effect, no doubt, due more to his excitement than to his bodily exertion. Laying down his hat, he resumed his seat, and putting his hand into his pocket, he drew out another paper some thing like an account.

"Look at that," said he, as he handed it to me.

Glancing over it, I found it to be an account for skins, due by Girvan to Angus Macgillivray, duly discharged.

"What of this?" said I, utterly at a loss to know the meaning of it all.

"Examine the handwriting of the two papers," said he.

I did so, and immediately ejaculated, "Why, that blood-stained scrap is written by Angus Macgillivray."

"No doubt of it," said Girvan. "I knew it the moment I saw it, but I wanted to make sure work."

"And sure enough it is," replied I; "but what conclusion do you draw from it?"

"I am afraid to mention it," was the reply.

"But I'm no," cried the deaconess in a wild way. "It is just as I thought," she continued, as she moved her arms as if to enable her to utter the words, "Angus Macgillivray has murdered my husband "

"But why should he publish the act in his own handwriting?" I rejoined.

"Because the awfu' man glories in his revenge," she cried again hysterically.

"That hardly squares with human nature," said Girvan. •

To this I assented, adding that "Angus was not so mad as not only to write his own condemnation, but give the officers of the law a direction to go in pursuit of him."

With all these qualifications, it was impossible to get rid of the direct effect of the words of the paper clearly enough indicating that the deacon had been killed by some one, whether Angus or not. The officer himself seemed to have no doubt; and as for Mrs Macgillivray, her former conclusion was only rendered more certain, and the calmness into which she quickly relapsed appeared to be the consequence of resignation to the will of God.

Meanwhile, the officer had intimated that the paper was to

be preserved and taken up to the office in the morning, with any explanations that could be given of it. He then went away; and late as the hour was, we resolved upon seeking out M'Pherson, to ascertain from his own mouth the true circumstances connected with the finding of the extraordinary paper. We accordingly went to the Cowgate, and having found the man, who was on the eve of going to bed, proceeded with our examination. He adhered strictly to what he had stated in the bailies' office, nor had he any more to communicate; but we derived thus much from our visit, that we became satisfied the man was honest, and was not accessory to any trick or deception whereby some one might have been supposed to have taken advantage of the public fermentation to infuse a new interest into what was already sufficiently engrossing. Girvan took the paper home with him; and we parted with the hope of getting some more light next day.

That light certainly did not come; but there was now more official inquiry as well as energy. Girvan, at an early hour of the forenoon, took the blood-stained paper to the bailies' office, and found that the assessor was so much impressed with the strangeness of the whole story, that he had resolved upon handing it over to the fiscal. Nor did he fail in this, as soon appeared by a wall-bill which, about one o'clock, glared in various parts of the city, to the effect that, whereas, a paper, on which was written the following words, (quoted,) had been found on the High Street of Edinburgh, a reward of £5 would be given to the person who had written the contents of the said paper, (assuming it doubtful whether Angus Macgillivray was the man,) if he would come forward and give testimony as to the object or meaning thereof; or to any person who would give information tending to shew where the person of Duncan Macgillivray, deacon of the hammermen, could be found, whether dead or alive. Nor did the fiscal limit his official duties by this proclamation; for about two o'clock he commenced a precognition of all parties who knew anything regarding the affair, among whom were the deaconess, (who was, in consequence of her weakness, taken to the office in a sedan chair,) Mrs Angus Macgillivray, M'Pherson, Girvan, myself, and the individuals who had seen the missing men on the day of their disappearance.

These precognitions were, according to the custom of the office, kept a secret, a circumstance in itself of no great importance, as the public were pretty well aware that no very important information had really been communicated in addition to that which they already knew. The new interest in the minds of the people was concentrated on the blood-stained paper, the real history whereof they were no more able to comprehend than they could translate as many words of Greek. The fact set forth, that Duncan Macgillivray had been murdered, was not doubted except by a few wiseacres, who saw further than other people; but after this was conceded, there remained a field for the ingenious quidnuncs and mystery-mongers sufficient to keep them in delightful operation for a week. The questions, Who wrote it? The murderer himself or another? Why was it written? How did it come to be where it was found? and so forth, were in all mouths, and all these mouths were ready with answers, every one of which was as certainly true as sacred Writ, and yet scarcely two of them could be found to agree in all points. As for the wiseacres, few in number, and (as usual) with brains quantitively and qualitively in the inverse ratio of their conceit, they looked upon the paper as a hoax; but when asked to explain the absence of the deacon, their wisdom receded into a direct ratio of the said brains.

But busy as the lady of many tongues was, nothing came out of the bill or the precognitions tending towards any theory sufficient to stay the mind, or induce belief, if we except a statement made by a young man, a clerk in the coach-office, opposite which the blood-stained paper had been found. He went forward in the afternoon, and was precognosced by the fiscal, to the effect that on the day of the disappearance he saw two men, whom he did not know, mount the coach just when it had begun to move, and without having time to pay their fares, which they probably calculated upon settling at the other end of their journey. One of the men, who was stouter and fatter than the other, got inside, and the other immediately, upon perceiving the movement, sprang up behind. He observed no concert between the two, yet he felt satisfied that the one had resolved to go after he saw the other about to take his seat. It was only after he heard a description of the two Macgillivrays that he began to think they were the men whom he had observed. When this story came to be known, it was conveniently found to agree in some respects with the history of the paper. Assuming that the men seen by the clerk were really the two brothers, it seemed probable that the deacon was he who went inside, probably called upon to undertake the journey on short notice by some business emergency, and that Angus, who was prowling about, and had seen his brother in the act of entering the coach, had suddenly formed a resolution to dog him into the country, and there wreak his revenge at a distance from Edinburgh. This sudden purpose seemed probable, because if there had been any concert between the two to travel together, Angus would have gone inside also, where, according to the clerk's statement, there was plenty of room for him. So far ingenious, and certainly in the circumstances not improbable. Then as to the paper, what more likely than that it should have come with the returned coach, having been sent by Angus when upon the eve of his flight after committing the deed, and bearing the marks of his bloody fingers. As for the motive for thus proclaiming his own villany, the most difficult element in the whole story, it might have been (What might not be when the mind is predisposed to find that it *is?*) the wild act of a bravado, glorying, as Mrs Macgillivray herself expressed it, in his revenge at a time when he knew he would be far away before the paper reached its destination.

With this last and, by consequence, the newest view of the subject which obtained anything like a wide assent, the people went to bed, probably to rise in the morning and find the many-tongued goddess blowing word-bubbles of an entirely different hue, aftei which they would run with renewed alacrity, to find them end in a little liberated air, as all the others had done. Another day dawned, bringing with it of course further confirmation in the mere passage of time, of the universal conviction that whatever might be the speculations as to the when, how, or wherefore, there could be little doubt of the fate of Deacon Macgillivray. And with the same increase of effect the day passed. I had not been at Borthwick's Close for a considerable time ; indeed, I found that with no power of being of any service, I was subjected to the severe necessity of being a silent witness of irremediable misery. Yet I found a pressure upon me, partly from the charge I made against myself of inconsistency, if not ingratitude ; and taking Girvan along with me, I called at the house a out five o'clock. We found there Mrs Girvan, and another, of all in the world the most unexpected, the wife of Angus Macgillivray herself. Nor was this woman's visit without a cause, and one, too, calculated to give a new turn altogether to our speculations. She had, of course, heard of the charge against her husband, and after overcoming much reluctance, in consequence of the alienation of the two families, had determined to vindicate her husband, even in the presence of the widow of the murdered deacon. Her story was extraordinary enough. She said that ever since the taking out of the lawborrows, Angus Macgillivray had been a changed man. He read his Bible in the morning, and shewed other indications of penitence for the enmity he had entertained towards his brother; "And now," continued the woman, as she took from her pocket a Bible, which she had probably brought

with her for the very purpose; "I swear by this holy book,
which I hope to be the means of the salvation of my soul and that
of my husband, that Angus Macgillivray, on that morning when
he so strangely disappeared, stated to me, ay, with tears in his
eyes, that he mourned continually over the separation of himself and his brother; that he was determined to throw himself in
his way, to confess his contrition and sorrow for what had
passed, to offer him his hand, and swear a renewed friendship,
which he would keep true to the day of his death."

This remarkable statement, which was confirmed by the manner as well as the honest character of the woman, was, I think,
believed by all of us excepting the deaconess, who had been
so completely wedded to the old theory of the murder by
Angus, that it seemed as impossible to move her from this
conviction as it was to raise her out of the great depth of her
sorrows.

"The news has been lang o' coming, woman," said she
" I will believe 'it when Angus proves himsel' to be innocent
o' a brother's bluid."

"But you forget, sister," said the other, "that I have nothing
to expect from coming here and telling you a lie.   I am here
for your comfort; to satisfy you that whatever has become of
your husband, he has received no injury from the hands of
mine."

"That looks like reason," said I; "and I think I now see
some light breaking through all this darkness."

"Whaur?" ejaculated Mrs Macgillivray. "There is nae light
to me except the light of heaven.   Nae earthly light will ever
shew me again the living face o' Duncan Macgillivray.   He is
dead—dead !"

"And I may say the same of my husband," said the brother's
wife.   "Is he not amissing as well as Duncan? and who has a
right to say that the one killed the other, or that other the
one ?"

I was struck with the reasoning of the woman, who was better educated than the deaconess, and with a greater power of penetration, and the mystery was about to take another turn. I was about to enlarge upon what had been last said, when Mrs Girvan laid her hand on my arm and said, " Hush!" We had no notion of what she meant. Every one looked at her now. I saw plainly that she was busy listening.

"I hear Deacon Macgillivray's voice on the stair," she said.

And the words were scarcely spoken when a confused shuffling of footsteps was heard in the lobby. The door opened, and in there came the deacon and his brother Angus.

" What is the meaning o' a' this?" cried the cast-up dignitary. " A dozen of people have met me, and told me I have been dead and buried for five days."

"And that I murdered my ain brother," cried Angus.

"And surely I am dead," added the deacon, with a laugh, " for my ain wife is feared at me, and winna even offer me her hand. Peggy, woman," he continued, as he went round and took his wife in his arms, " what ails ye?"

During all which the deaconess was in a vertigo, with nothing in her brain fixed except the image of her husband, received through a pair of staring eyes

" And Johnny Gow didna tell you?" continued he, as he looked round upon us all still in amazement.

" No," responded the wife, as she began to recover herself. " What had he to tell?"

" Just that Angus and I had gane down to Blackha' to see our brother Andrew," said he; " but I see now how it is. Johnny was half drunk when I gave him the message, and the sixpence had helped him to mair drink, and the drink had driven him stupid."

" Why, deacon," said I, " it has been a serious affair. The whole city has been in the belief that you were murdered, and

Angus was suspected of the deed. Nor is it to be wondered at, for even yet we want explanations."

"Explanations!" replied the deacon. "What mair do ye need than just that as I was going up the High Street I met Angus, who came up to me and said he was a changed man, that he wanted the past to be forgotten, and that he would gie the world to be friends wi' me. I couldna refuse the offered hand of a brother ; and, after a', I was as anxious to be friends again as he. So maybe our hearts got big, and there might have been something in baith our een that belangs mair to women than men. When we were in this saft mood, the coach for Galashiels was on the very point of starting, and Angus said that he had intended to go to Blackha' to buy sheep the next forenoon, but that if I were agreeable, he would take his trip that day, and we might go together. I have no objections, said I, but we maun send notice to our wives. I beckoned Gow, because I thought I could trust him, gave him a sixpence, and got a promise. Next moment we were on the coach, and by my troth I never enjoyed a jaunt better in my life. Andrew was delighted to see us friends again, and maybe there was a sowther o' kind that gaes mair to the heart than words. But what though the cadie deceived us, didna ye get," he continued, as he looked into the face of the deaconess, " *didna ye get the salmon that Angus sent you on the day it was killed, the* 19*th ?*"

The secret was all but out. What was wanting was afterwards ascertained. The driver had appropriated the fish because he saw no ticket of address upon it ; that ticket was found by Hugh M'Pherson. And thus was explained a mystery which occupied the metropolis of Scotland for nearly a week ; in other words, which are less or more applicable to most mysteries, the worsted was rolled off—and, behold, the cork !

Lord Braxfield's Case of the Red Nightcap.

HOWEVER true it is that nothing is absolutely lost in the world either of matter or mind, it is just as true that much is lost to the memory of the short-lived creature man. Nor is this inconsistent with very evident final caus.. insomuch as every generation has enough to do with itself, its anguish and pleasure, without going back to the actions of those who have performed their parts in the old tragedy or farce of life. Every year of increasing civilisation helps this oblivion, in proportion to the increased and increasing bodily and mental activities of the age ; and while many think we are laying up stores of books, which will by and by be incalculable, it is certain that the *papier-mache* manufacturers swallow up more than we dream of. These observations are suggested by the fact that the story I am about to relate derives its foundation from what I found set forth in a Session paper ('Turnbull *v.* Gemmel) which was on its way through Mr Adcock's paper-rooms, direct to be made part of a tea-tray. In which circumstance you may trace a fanciful retribution, in that my story may contribute to the enjoyment cf some circle of very pious ladies, seated round a beautiful specimen of the said art, composed, it may be, of the literary remains of Thomas Payne and Bishop Colenso.

In exchange for opening up to you, my reader, so curious a chapter of human life, I ask no more than that you should, for a minute or two, fancy yourself in Blackfriars' Wynd some time about the end of last century. You will ascend a stair on the east side, which leads to several flats, occupied by different tenants, the first of those being the only one claiming our attention. It is divided by a long lobby, with doors on each side; and though at one time it was occupied by one family, a part, consisting of two rooms nearest the outer door, is occupied by John Grant, a house-painter, his wife and daughter; the rest, consisting of several rooms further ben, being the residence of David Turnbull and a certain Mrs Gemmel, who stood in relation to him as a servant, yet using an authority which does not often belong to menials. On a certain night, —I cannot even give the year, far less the month, but the night is not the less certain for all that,—the painter and his family are engaged taking their "four hours"—that is, simply their tea. All is very quiet in that small parlour, by reason, it would seem, of some solemnity throwing a shadow over minds otherwise healthy and cheerful; and if we were curious about the cause, which we really are, we would find it in some way connected with the state of the domestic *lares* in the other end, where a dark angel is dealing sternly and unrelentingly with honest David—even that power

> " Whose short five-letter'd name
> Is but a syllable, yet carries fear
> When whisper'd stealthily from man to man,
> And makes him shudder, and cry out, Alas!
> Whence do I come, and whither do I go ?"

Yes, so it was; and Mrs Grant, breaking the silence, only added to the gloom.

"It's nearly ower wi' him," said she. "A look o' death is ill to bide in ony case, but I never saw a deathbed like David's, so gruesome. Mrs Gemmel never mentions a word o' religion, and nae friend is allowed to come near him. His face, which is a' ye see o' him, is by a' the warld just as if ye had brought a whitening-brush owre it ; and the only other thing ye can see is a fiery red nightcap on his bald head."

A description which, in other circumstances, might have produced a smile, but Mrs Grant's face was long and serious.

"It signifies little for the nightcap," said John, " if his sins are no red as weel."

" True," replied the wife " And if they were as red as scarlet, they may be made even as the driven snaw ; but Mrs Gemmel allows nae minister to come near him, only the doctor, who comes but seldom, where he sees no hope, and the writer, who comes often, because he thinks there is much. The twa hopes, ye see, have different things to look at."

"I haven't heard the doctor's foot to-day," rejoined the husband.

" Nor I," added the wife ; " but Wilson has been twice in, by token, nae doubt, that his nose is as sharp as a blue-bottle's; but here will be Mrs Gemmel," she added, as a gentle knock sounded on the door.

This remark soon proved to be wrong, as the daughter, a fine young woman of eighteen, rose and opened the door, and let in a youth of somewhere about twenty.

"William Turnbull," cried the mistress, " what hole o' the earth have you come out o' at the very time your father's brother is preparing to enter ane ?"

" It is just because my uncle is going in that direction that I am come in." This was the reply.

"Ay," continued she, " you have heard the corbies cawing round the sick heifer, and ye're come to fleg them awa, but I fear ye canna."

" I know I cannot," said he, "nor do I much care. He made his money by his own industry, and if he chooses fairly and legally to leave it to Mrs Gemmel and her daughter, we have no right to complain ; but it is our duty to inquire after so near a relative, and seeing we and his other relatives have been so

N

long banished from his presence, I have come to you to know how he is."

"Just as Mrs Gemmel would wish, I fancy," replied she. "The old man is posting to death; I fear the deed is done,—I mean the will is made,—and what can you do?"

"Perhaps nothing," said William; "but the law has a leaning to relatives, and when it is in their favour they are not in the habit of casting it over their shoulder. We can, at least, see that the will is all right; and with that view, I have a favour to beg of you, which you will the more readily grant, that" (turning to the daughter) "you know that Maggy and I have been long friends, and may, with God's blessing and your consent, be more than that."

A reference which changed the colour of Margaret's face more into that of David's red nightcap, than that of the face which it partly covered.

"That is right, Margaret," said the mother. "There's nae use for blushing, lass, except it be to tell you're willing before you're asked; and, mairower, there's naething wrang, merely because death is next door; for death and marriage have aye been gude friends, if the ane doesna live by the other: but what's the favour ye ask, William?"

"Just this," replied he; "if any turn takes place ben the house, you'll send over to Mr Allan the notary, who will come and lock up repositories. He can do this in spite of Mrs Gemmel, Wilson the writer, and all the other corbies."

"Wha'll no care a bodle," said the shrewd wife; "for dinna ye see that Mr Allan would just be taking care o' the will that's to cut you out."

"We may have two words about that," rejoined he, "at least we cannot be worse by being prepared. Then Margaret will perhaps take a ride to Musselburgh, to tell me when the change takes place."

"He's a willing horse whose head is turned to his ain farmyard," said she, laughing. "Margaret says naething; but I'll answer for this, that the breath is nae sooner out o' his body, than she is out o' this house, and on her way to Musselburgh."

"Then all is right," added he, as he rose and shook hands; "I will trust you."

And the young man departed, leaving Mrs Grant to execute a commission, not in itself perhaps very easy, insomuch as the said Mrs Gemmel, though not in the proper sense a *vir-ago*,— one who can play the part of a rough man,—was one not easily turned or put off her purpose; resembling, perhaps, the tiger's paw when the talons are retracted, soft as velvet, but ready on the instant to become a formidable weapon. But then Mrs Grant knew her, and she had the greater heart for performing her promise, that her daughter stood in a relation to the nephew, which made the business somewhat her own; for if it should happen that David Turnbull's property should by any chance escape the hands of the schemers, and come to William, it might go down in the line of her own flesh and blood. During the evening, accordingly, she paid particular attention to any footfalls in the passage, as indicating visitors; for occasionally cronies of Mrs Gemmel were heard to pass, no doubt to ascertain how her hopes pointed, and perhaps with the distant view of some secondary benefit to themselves, if it should amount to no more than the never-failing "dram"— that wonderful agent in the economy of low life, which, however apparently insignificant, works greater wonders on hearts and livers and tongues than we wot of. All was very quiet that evening, not even the doctor's foot had been heard, and David's cough, which might sometimes be heard in more than ordinary stillness, was, as it came now and then, the only sound of living action thereben, and even that did not seem so strong as it used to be.

So at the hour of nine, Mrs Grant, more intent upon personal interest now than influenced by sympathy, though per-

haps she had just as much of that as sick-bed visitors often
have, ventured to tirl at the door of her neighbour. It was
almost instantly opened, and by the help of a lamp which was
in her hand, the face of Mrs Gemmel herself appeared. She
was serious, of course, as became the nurse of a patient so very
ill, but there was a hopefulness about her which was pleasant
to see, if not a kind of satisfaction which could come of nothing
else than a change in honest David for " the better "—leaving
these words to be construed according to her own view of what
was good, and to whom it was good. But, indeed, she did not
wish to leave that doubtful, for she immediately saluted Mrs
Grant with the intelligence that David had got a turn.

"A turn," echoed the visitor, in a dry tone, as if she did not
understand exactly whether the turn was backward or forward.

"Ay, even a turn," continued the soft nurse. "He has
supped a bowl o' strong beef-tea ; and, Heaven be mercifu',
woman, you would almost think the blood was coming to his
face again."

"Which it has muckle need to do," replied Mrs Grant, in
the same dry way, as no doubt she thought of the gruesome
contrast between that face and the red nightcap.

And the two women having by this time got into the bedroom, the nurse resumed her half whispers.

"We maun speak low ye see, Mrs Grant, as you may hear by
his snoring that he is sleeping."

"Snoring," echoed the other, all but involuntarily, for somehow or another the thought came into her head that the sound
was the death-rattle.

And whether she had very foolishly allowed her lips to move
so that Mrs Gemmel might "read" them, certain it is that the
latter immediately rejoined—

"Dinna be feared, woman ; it's no the death-rattle."

"I didna say it was," rejoined the other, as if she felt that she had committed herself; " I never heard o't coming so soon after a hale bowl of beef-tea."

A remark this which brought a grim smile over the face of Mrs Gemmel.

" Ay, and a pipe," added she, with an increase of the pleasant expression.

" A pipe!" echoed Mrs Grant again.

" Just a pipe, cummer," repeated the other. " He had nae sooner ta'en the beef- ea, than he asked for a whiff, and ye may be sure he wouldna want it lang, for I was ower happy to think that he could take it."

" And so ye might," said the astonished Mrs Grant; " for yesterday, when I saw him, I thought him as far from a pipe as he was from a bowl o' punch."

" Ay, but where there's life there's hope," was the reply. " We ken little about the spirit; it comes and it gangs, and it comes again, when ye would think it was awa on its journey to heaven. Woman, I wouldna wonder to see David Turnbull sitting again in his easy-chair, with " (and she almost laughed) " the tail o' his red nightcap hanging ower the back o' 't; wouldna that be a gay sight ?"

" And sure it would," said Mrs Grant; " but, Mrs Gemmel, are ye serious, woman ?" she added, as the gurgling sound still came from the bed.

" 'Deed and I am," replied the nurse; " and I just wonder what makes ye ask it."

" There's nae harm anyhow," said Mrs Grant.

And here the conversation for the time ended. Mrs Grant returned to her parlour, where she related to her husband the import of what she had heard and what she had seen. Neither the one nor the other could reconcile the apparent contradiction, and there was even a wonderment expressed by both as to what could have induced so shrewd a woman as Mrs Gemmel was known to be to assert what, especially as regarded the tobacco, not a trace of which was in the room, appeared to be utterly ridiculous, if not impossible. And then the matter appeared the more perplexing, that all along during the illness of the invalid she had generally expressed her absolute hopelessness that he would ever rise from the bed again; the change in her words, her manner, and her looks having come on in the course of a day, and being, moreover, in full contradiction to the actual state of the patient. There was clearly something to be explained, and that something they could not get at. At one moment they thought Mrs Gemmel was belying her true sentiments, with a view to keep off a suspicion that she expected soon to be the mistress of certain tenements; at another they glided into the more chari-table construction, that the woman's hopes had become a little hysterical from the sympathy of an old love which had revived in its cinders from the influence of a conviction that their long connexion was on the eve of being ended. But no solution would suit the conditions of the case, and rather than be ungenerous they left the secret, if secret there was, to the development of the passing hours, knowing, as they both did, that Time is a great babbler.

Notwithstanding of this somewhat unsatisfactory conclusion, Mrs Grant was as fully determined as ever to attend to the interests of the man whom she had begun to think of as a son-in-law. Vague suspicions haunted her—as vague as those generally are which arise from some conviction that the con-nexion between appearances and what *ought* to be realities will not hold the two together. She would, being a woman, and therefore by instinct an eavesdropper, have listened at the door; but being in some respects an exception from the normal character of her sex, she considered that mode of getting at a secret to a certain extent unseemly, and therefore she con-tented herself with listening a-bed—perceiving a clear difference between the two acts by means of her conscience, which is, as

we all know, endowed with a microscopical refinement unknown even to mathematicians, who admit they cannot see
infinitesimals. Nor was this safe and honourable eavesdrop-
ping, away from the eaves altogether, without fruits. Something was going on thereben, and something was not going on.
The cough of honest David, for instance, had not been heard
even in the sound of that "kigh," as we call it, in contradiction
to the "hoast," even as the latter is distinguished by an irreve-
verent writer from "the Lord of hoasts"—the whoop; and
Mrs Grant suspected that it had passed into the rattle. Then
she heard, about two in the morning, some footfalls, as like
those of Mrs Gemmel's as it was necessary for them to be to
suit her watchful ear; they were those of a person going out
and in. About half an hour afterwards there were steps in the
lobby, as if two persons had come in; nay, she could hear
that the door was opened stealthily, and shut again in the same
furtive manner. What could all this mean? Was David dead,
and had Mrs Gemmel gone and brought Wilson the writer to
help her to lay him out? or had he grown worse, in spite of the
beaf-tea and the pipe, and she had gone for Dr Henderson to
administer to him? In either supposition, why had the woman
not called her, Mrs Grant, who had often before been applied
to in David's domestic emergencies? She was puzzled, as all
people who syllogise upon suspicions generally are, but still
the preponderance of her favour was extended to the first
theory, insomuch as it harmonised best with the stealthy
operation of opening and shutting the door; and so she
veritably came to the conclusion that David was dead. Meanwhile her husband was busy snoring by her side, and as that
peculiar sound of the vocal chords is often not less catching
than yawning, she acknowledged the power and straightway
fell sound asleep.

In the morning she consulted her husband as to what she
ought to do, in reference principally to sending or not send-

ing for Mr Allan ; but Mr Grant not being under the fervour of suspicion, made short work of the question by stating that it was impossible that the old man could be dead and no intimation made to the nearest neighbour — a fair enough statement, no doubt, yet no better than a supposition after all. On one point they both agreed—viz., that they ought to wait and see what sign should be made by Mrs Gemmel. If she did not make some intimation by ten o'clock, then Mrs Grant would go ben and judge from what she saw ; but all this wisdom was rendered vain by the entrance of Margaret Grant, who, having set the breakfast, had gone out for some eatables, and thus encountered her father and mother for the first time this morning. She had something to say on the mysterious subject, and, what is more to be noted, that which she had to say was rather to add to the mystery than throw light upon it. Her information was to the effect that, wanting a light, she had gone ben to get one from Mrs Gemmel. In passing David's bedroom to get to the kitchen, she looked in and saw the bed with nobody in it. Wondering at this, she took another glance in coming out, and saw David himself, with his bright-coloured Kilmarnock, sitting as he used to do in his old armchair by the fireside ; but, strange to say, there was no fire in the grate, and she got so alarmed by what she thought was an utter impossibility in nature, that she had no power to put any question to Mrs Gemmel, hurrying away as fast as she could. In giving this narrative, the girl appeared excited in no ordinary degree ; and, as might have been expected, the father and mother look on from sympathy. Yet this effect, in so far as regarded Mrs Grant, was short-lived.

" Margaret Grant," said she, as she began to recover herself, " I have brought ye up in the fear o' God and a reverence for truth, and now ye tell me what is impossible and against common sense. The man has been confined to his bed for months ; I have seen him from day to day, getting every day waur and waur, till his flesh is worn aff his banes, the colour gane frae his cheeks, at last, even yestreen, the death-rattle was in his throat, and now he is sitting by the fire ; I canna, I winna believe it !"

" I cannot help that," replied Margaret, gently ; " I have told you what I saw, and you can go ben and judge for yourself."

" And that I will, Margaret," cried the mother, " even for your sake ; that if ye are right, I may like you the better ; but that if wrang, I will ken what kind o' a dochter I have."

And under the influence of a roused motive, very different from that which was actuating her towards the same object, she hurried out of the room. The tap on the door was soon answered. Mrs Grant entered, and even as before she was met by the same hopeful if not smiling countenance.

" Did I no tell you," said Mrs Gemmel, before any question was put to her, " that David had gotten the turn, and you was na very willing to believe me ? Just look you in there."

And as she edged up the bedroom door, Mrs Grant put in her face, with a pair of eyes sufficiently determined to judge for themselves ; at least they did their part in looking, whatever her reason might afterwards do in any opposition offered to the report of these soothsaying witnesses. There was the bed, just as Margaret had said, quite empty, but with the appearance of having been vacated by the tenant who had occupied it so long. The fire was now lighted, and by it stood the old armchair, wherein was, of a certainty, the good old man, David —his arm leaning on the left side of it, his left leg extended, the top of the well-known nightcap appearing over the back ; all vividly enough visible, in spite of the gloomy atmosphere of the room, caused by a dark green window-blind, through which the light could scarcely penetrate.

" You see how it is," said Mrs Gemmel, as she drew the door to her. " I am just making his breakfast ; you see where there's life there's hope."

"A turn indeed," ejaculated the other, after she had recovered herself; " and the cough he has had for years "——
"Clean gone."

"And the—the rattle ?"

" You mean the snoring," was the answer. "You forget he
is wide awake, and, though you dinna see his face, with a pair
o' een as gleg as a hawk's. But," continued Mrs Gemmel, "I 'll
no keep you, for I fancy you have na got breakfast, and as for
David, I am thinking he 's as hungry as you."

And Mrs Grant, able to take a hint even in the midst of her
confusion and amazement, returned to her room, where she re-
ported what she had seen without a ray of glamour having
been thrown over her eyes ; nor did any scepticism on the part
of her husband diminish either his amazement or the expression
of it, for he had the testimony of Margaret in addition to that
of his wife, and he could recur, for a justification of her wonderment, to his own experience of only two or three days old,
when he saw David lying in the bed, as one worn out with
years and disease, as near death as any one could be with any
life in him at all.   It might be all very well to wonder at what
looked so like a miracle; but wonder expiscates no truth, it
only leaves, after it has abated, a desire to bring the laws of
nature again into the harmony of consistent experience ; and so
Mrs Grant had misgivings which she could not justify, and no
less a desire for further insight, which she did not know very
well how to gratify.   She knew that in Mrs Gemmel she
had the soft tiger's claw to manage, and she had to fear the
extension of the talons ; yet she felt that she would encounter
some risk, just to ascertain the real circumstances of David's
recovery and the exact state of his health,—not that she wanted
him dead for the sake of her daughter, but simply that, woman-
like, she had a craving of curiosity requiring to be fed.

The affair had, indeed, become something like a romance to
her, and so she continued during the day to watch all the pro-

ceedings that came within earshot. She noticed that the doctor did not call as he was wont ; but, what was also unusual, she ascertained that one or two of the neighbours, who had scarcely ever entered within the limits of Mrs Gemmel's sacred charge, had actually been invited ben to witness the great and marvellous recovery. These individuals Mrs Grant took special occasion to see and speak to, and no doubt they all concurred in the conclusion that the affair was very marvellous, but then they knew that God's arm is never shortened ; and were there not examples of people having been brought back from death to life, yea, of buried corpses having turned in their coffins, no doubt from a desire to lie more easily on one side than another ? All this was very consonant to women's ways of accounting for marvels, but Mrs Grant ventured little till she knew more. So in the evening, again, she made a call at a time when David *ought* to be in his bed, and sure enough she found he was ; but then, again, he was unfortunately dead asleep, and could not be approached ; while as regarded the snoring, the cough, or the rattle, they could not be heard by reason of their having been "clean gane," or at least sopited in sweet slumber. His face was to the wall, and all she could see was that redoubted red Kilmarnock, and the shape of the body under the clothes.

But was not all that sufficient for any one not a very Pyrrhonian ? It might seem so, but what can a woman do with a crave when curiosity is a-hungered ? We all know the answer, and accordingly we will not be surprised to learn that next day Margaret Grant was commissioned to call and see what she could see ; but the result only tended to stimulate what it was intended to satisfy. David was again snugly seated by the fire, nay. she was given to understand that he had been indulging in a pipe of tobacco, the fumes of which were perceptible enough—more so indeed than the objects, for the room was as dark and dismal looking as ever, just as if all movement had been stilled by enchantment, and all sound frozen in the very midst of the warm atmosphere, a phenomenon only known to Sancho Panza and the spasmodic poets. So also in the evening again the usual change took place, and though Mrs Grant exhibited a sympathetic desire to see the restored colour on the face of the invalid, which was becoming in a Christian, yet somehow or other she could succeed in her praiseworthy effort no better than before. If she was kind, Mrs Gemmel was more so, and David could not in any event be disturbed. Nor did the next day change this fine regular programme in the sick-room, if that term could now be applied to one so far convalescent as to be able to take a bowlful of beef-tea and smoke a pipe after the same.

Yet, withal, this most unreasonable woman, Mrs Grant, would still be on the watch; and what would she not have given just for "a handling" of her old friend David, and a few words from a throat where the death-rattle had been rumbling (as she thought) so short a time before? Patience has her triumphs, because she is often so like wisdom; nor does even grimalkin sit all day, and sometimes all night to boot, at a hole, without having had recourse to an argument—that if a mouse has entered there, so it is likely it will some time or other come out again. Then Mrs Grant's patience was the more wonderful, that everything tended to strengthen the very enemy of that virtue. The doctor had given up calling, and the writer had more interviews with Mrs Gemmel than ever. An abnormal condition of matters reigned everywhere ; nay, on the fifth night, what could induce Mrs Gemmel to go out and lock her door at the hour of eleven at night? Mrs Grant did not even try to answer. She was at the moment lying quietly in bed, with her husband asleep alongside of her, and no better opportunity could offer itself for rewarding her patience and satisfying her crave at the same time ; she accordingly rose as quietly as possible, for fear of awakening her husband, who she was sure would set his face against her project, and striking a light

in the lobby, she took from her own door the key,—an act to
which she was directed by a remembrance that Mr Grant had
long before remarked how singular it was that all the locks on
the flat were of the same make ;—that key she appl ed to David
Turnbull's door, and that door opened with due obedience.
So far she was bold ; but when the way was clear before
her into the house of which, and its inmates and strange ways,
she had been dreaming night and day for so long a time, her
foot faltered, the candle shook in her hand, and she hesitated ;
she stood for a moment, with her ear sharpened by fear, to hear
if there were any sounds. David might be awake, and see her ;
Mrs Gemmel might in the meantime return, and thus she ran
a risk of being caught in the act of entering an honest burgess's
house with a false key, and no doubt with the object of plun-
der. But, O Curiosity ! thou

> " Who erst did disregard
> Divine command, and though forewarn'd
> That knowledge hath two sides, or good or ill,
> Didst yet, midst flaming swords of seraphim,
> Elect *to know*,"

we find thee not yet unleavened of the old leaven. Even
though the nerves of the eye twittered behind the candle, the
balls looked forward, and the tremulous limb was no hindrance
to the step. She saw the light of the kitchen cruise, but it was
not in that direction the object of her curiosity lay. It was to
David's bedroom she directed herself, the shut door of which
only tempted her the more ; nor even when she perceived that
all was dark there, was she moved otherwise than to push forward her small light, that she might drive the shadows that
came between her and what she wanted to know from the
remote corners. First, the bed. Was he there ? No. She
even passed her hand over it, lest her eye might escape some
shrunken body under the clothes. The old armchair next.
Was he there ? Most surely not. It was truly the empty

chair so much made of by poetic fancies. In the room anywhere? No. Her eye flashed round and round, as the light
threw its beam obedient to her trembling hand, but no David
Turnbull could be seen. Thus discomfited, or rather more
and more awakened by the increasing mystery, she was about to
depart, when she thought of the dark pantry, where Mrs Gemmel used to stow away trunks and clothes, and thereto she
directed herself, pulling open the door hurriedly, for she was
getting more and more nervous by the additional fear of the
return of Mrs Gemmel. But what was that, or any other fear,
to that which shot through her entire body, making her "very
een reel," when she saw honest David hanging, with his face to
the wall, from a cleik in the roof! She could be under no
error of vision, for the light of the candle discovered the object
to her eye, with the tails of his old coat she had seen him wear,
the red nightcap in full crimson, and all the rest of the habili-
ments that go to make up the covering of man's body. Of a
kindly spirit as she was, she would have rushed forward and
tried to bring him down ; but where would have been the use,
when the man was clearly dead and motionless, and then,
moreover, time was pressing her. Yet all this did not prevent
her from calling out, by way of hysterical effort, "David! David
Turnbull!" words to which David made no reply, for a reason
which is much too evident to mention. Her curiosity was so
far satisfied, though not in the way she had expected, and
wishing to remove any sign of her having been there, she
threw the door of the closet to in its old position—a disastrous
act in this her monodrame, for the wind of the movement blew
out her weak light ; and, oh strange coincidence ! she heard at
the same moment a rap from within the closet, as if the supposed dead man had at length made a sign !

Even if the state of her nerves had enabled her to respond
to that knock, with whatever intention made, the want of a
light was enough in itself to have prevented her ; and the fear

of Mrs Gemmel returned upon her in the dark with so much
force that she immediately resolved upon a retreat. But this,
in her state of mind, became a difficult affair ; for having made
a mistake in her first turn, she lost her topography, and went
groping about, trying to identify wh itever object she encountered ; nor was even this difficulty left with its own entangle-
ments. She heard the sound of a foot, and by and by some
one moving in the room ; nay, she even heard a mortal breathing not far from her very side. Her first thought was—and
surely it could not be said to have been unnatural in the circumstances ?—that the closet door had been opened, and that
it was David Turnbull in person who had disengaged himself,
and come forth ; nor was this a mere suspicion. It became,
as she still kept groping with spasmodic efforts, a conviction ;
and now she had not only the door to seek, but this resusci-
tated being to avoid. Neither the one object nor the other
could she accomplish. She had gone two or three times round
the room, and how many more times she might have gone,
with David trying to follow her, no one, however versed in
windings in the dark, might say, if it had not been that she felt
a hand upon her shoulder. The melodrama was now to be
completed, by the required scream ; and scream she did, with
so shrill a sound that David, even from his suspended position,
if he still maintained it, and was not verily the owner of that
imposed hand, might have been recalled to consciousness by
it. At the same moment she retreated, but with no improved
sense of her local position, till, having found the bed, she got
upon the right track.

Confused as she was, she had, on getting out of the bedroom,
enough of thought and prudence left to her to enable her to
shut the door as she had found it. It was comparatively easy
for her to get to the outer door—that, too, she closed and
locked, and hurrying along the passage, she got at last into
her own room, and then to bed. Her husband, she suspected,

was awake, and she wondered why he did not put a question to her, where and what she had been about. If so put to it, in all likelihood she would have told the extraordinary circumstances of her midnight adventure ; but knowing that he was a man who would have condemned strongly the mode she had adopted of satisfying her curiosity, she rather inclined to holding her secret. Meanwhile her chief thought regarded the person who had been in the bedroom with her. When now somewhat composed, she would rather have recurred to the suspicion that it was Mrs Gemmel herself, than entertained the extravagant opinion that David could, after a period of suspension by the neck, have been able to move about in the manner she had clearly experienced ; but this alternative, to which the question seemed to be limited, was soon deprived of one of its terms, by the fact that as she lay in this meditation she heard Mrs Gemmel come stealthily in, open her door by her key, shut it after her, and relock it from the inside. She had now, therefore, no second theory as to the identity of the living being who had been along with her in the bedroom,—unless, indeed, she might have conceived that Wilson the writer, so clearly in league with the housekeeper, and who, it was even whispered, intended to marry her after the spoil to come by the will had been realised, had been in the house. But then Wilson was not the kind of man—a pettifogger and savage poinder of the poor—to have been contented with such mute, if not pantomimic action ; and, above all, she was deeply impressed by the conviction that the noise she heard from the inside of the closet came from the same person who had moved alongside of her, had breathed near her, and who had his hand upon her shoulder.

The excitement which keeps off sleep precipitates it in the end, by the exhaustion which itself undergoes. So Mrs Grant fell over when the time came ; nor did she awake till it was pretty far gone in the morning, nay, till the breakfast, by the early ministrations of Margaret, was upon the table, and the husband returned from his morning's work. On sitting down to the morning meal, it seemed clear to each of them that there was something to be said by one to another; and it is not unlikely that each thought his or her own story the most interesting—that is, assuming that Mrs Grant could be induced to get over the fear of her husband's condemnation, for the sake of easing her heart of what she thought a terrible secret, involving attempted suicide or murder. The mystery of the prior night's evolutions had culminated without yielding a hope of a revelation; and we may fancy Mrs Grant's astonishment to hear Margaret declare, that having been ben again for a light at a pretty early hour, she had seen David again in his bed.

" In his bed !" echoed Mrs Grant.

" In his bed !" ejaculated Mr Grant. " Why, I have been waiting till we all sat down, so that we might help each other to some rational explanation, to tell you that David Turnbull is lying in the back bedroom dead, and streeked upon the bed, where, for aught I know, he has lain for days. I tell you this from my own observation. About eight o'clock I was up putting a first coat of paint upon the windows of the third flat, and on coming down the ladder I saw the corpse. Nor was it a slight look of it I took—I stood and gazed at it for several minutes ; I could even recognise the features, for there was nothing over it, nor anything on the head, not even the red nightcap about which you have spoken so much."

" Eight o'clock !" rejoined the daughter. " That was just half an hour after the time I saw him lying in the other bed-room. So," added the simple Margaret, " Mrs Gemmel had just removed the body from the one room to the other in the meantime."

" Weel," cried Mrs Grant, holding the while her hands up, as a very inadequate expression of her admiration, " the

o

murder's out at last! I saw last night, at eleven o clock, David Turnbull hanging by the neck in the dark closet off the bedroom ; and now, when ye tell me that he is lying dead, it must have been his spirit seeking for vengeance that laid its hand "——

" Laid its hand !" interrupted the husband. " Why, woman, ghosts have no weight in their forms, so that the laying of a hand could be felt by a mortal. Besides," he added, with a smile playing through the gravity demanded from the terrible story of his wife, " it was a hand you have felt before."

" Sae, sae ; and it was your own ?" rejoined she.

" I admit nothing," was the reply. " You were deceiving me when you opened another man's door by what may be called a false key, and I had a right to deceive you ; but we have something else to do than to account for small deceptions. If you saw the dead body suspended from the roof, then you saw what we are bound to communicate to the authorities of the law. We have to look to the interests, also, of William Turnbull, the nephew."

There thus seemed to be something certain and fixed amidst all these fleeting appearances and contradictions, but the words of Mr Grant's wisdom had no sooner fallen where they might germinate into conviction and action, than the door opened, and who should make her appearance but Mrs Gemmel herself.

" The bearer o' guid news is aye welcome," said she. " I am happy to tell ye that Mr Turnbull is still improving. I have just left him at the fire, taking his smoke after his breakfast."

A communication this which was surely calculated to reduce all these certainties to the old doubt. Every one looked to another, but no one seemed to have the power to speak, and Mrs Gemmel, having added a few words to break the painful silence, left and returned to her own house.

" What is the meaning o' a' this ?" was the first ejaculation from Mrs Grant. "I have heard o' folk being deceived by glamour thrown ower their een ; has ony o' the devil's agents been busy wi' mine ? I 'm at my wits' end."

" And what if I have been deceived too ?" added the husband. "It is certainly possible that David might have been laid in the bed where I saw him merely to rest a little. You say that the last time you saw him his face was as white as if a whitening-brush had been brought over it, and I confess I have had but little experience of the dead."

And, strange as it may seem, so tortuous, contradictory, mutable, and ridiculous were the circumstances of the whole story, that they could not refrain from a laugh—a phenomenon which, to a student of human nature, might appear as inexplicable as any of the appearances in this extraordinary play. Yet, amidst all these apparent contradictions,—absurdities we cannot call them, for the reason that they were sufficient to produce convictions and emotions in the human heart,—there appeared to Mrs Grant quite, and more than enough to require inquiry and investigation. If David Turnbull was not dead, either as a consequence of the wearing out of the silver chord, or the breaking of the same by a hempen, it was clear that he was the victim of some mercenary motive, dictated by Wilson and acted upon by Mrs Gemmel ; and so the painter took up his hat with the intention of going to Mr Allan. Nor was it long before he found that gentleman. The story, with all its changing aspects, took some time and pains to tell ; but the narrator was repaid by the intelligence of the writer, who informed him that, by some means he was not at liberty to declare, he suspected where the key would be found that would pass all the complicated guards of the operose lock, constructed though it was by one of the shrewdest pettifogging heads in the city,—a remark which he chose to accompany by a laugh. The first thing to be done was to see the doctor, to whose residence accordingly they bent their way. From him they learned that he had attended David up to a period when it might be expected he would not live another day, and that then, to his surprise, he was told by Mrs Gemmel that he need not take the trouble of calling again,—a hint he had acted upon, with a due regard to the honour of his profession. This information confirmed Mr Allan in the view he had taken of the key to the mystery; and thereupon, with Mr Grant still accompanying him, he proceeded to the office of the pro-curator-fiscal for the city. To that gentleman Mr Grant again told his story, at hearing which, the man of prosecutions, pains, and penalties shook his head, though it may be easily conceived he saw no further into the mystery than an owl does into sunshine. There was indeed too much light or too little concentration, and it required Mr Allan to collect the rays and direct them to a point; so the two conversed apart, and as they say that the duller the brain the greater is the joy of an idea, so it appeared that as the fiscal commenced to comprehend Mr Allan's view he began to laugh, so boisterously too, that the painter wondered how so serious an affair, involving the mortal fate of a fellow-being, could ever be enlivened by so much hilarity, forgetting, no doubt, at the moment, that he and his wife had been forced, by the ridiculous incidents of the story, to do something of the same kind themselves.

Notwithstanding of all this hilarity, the affair was serious enough to require instant action, as appeared from the fiscal calling for an officer and a concurrent to accompany him to the scene of the operations to be. So all being prepared, they proceeded in a body down the High Street towards Blackfriars' Wynd, on their arrival whereat they ascended the stair, and now they are all at the door of David Turnbull. A knock from the fiscal's cane was responded to by a man's voice requiring to know the object of the visit, to which the fiscal replied that he was there by authority to seek for the body of the said David, who was said to have been hanged by some person or persons resident within. Upon hearing this, Wilson (for it was he) set up an ironical laugh ; but he refused still to open, upon the ground that the fiscal had no right to enter the house of a citizen without exhibiting a written information from some respectable burgher ; at all which the officer laughed in his turn, nor did he deign further reply than to take the key from Mrs Grant's hand and apply it to the lock. The party thereupon entered, and, amidst the growling of the writer and Mrs Gemmel, proceeded to. David's room, where the key of the secret, whatever it might be, was no doubt to be found. The room was, as usual, darkened by the means of the drawn-down blind, but there was light enough and to spare to enable them to see, in the first place, that the bed was empty. They next went to the armchair, where they were more successful, for there sat David Turnbull, all dressed, even to the red nightcap, the tail of which was carefully hung over the back of his seat ; his corporation made up of dried hay, yet so well stuffed that, if you had not been too inquisitive about the face, you would have taken the figure for the genuine David. There was here a partial clearing up, and to make the *éclaircissement* more evident, the fiscal, who had an official humour of his own, took up the figure, and, proceeding to the pantry, hung it up by the neck-cloth to the cleik in the roof, whereat Mrs Grant at least was so moved that she got into a fit of hysterical laughter ; nor did this suffice for the humour of the party, for Mr Grant having set the figure on the swing, shut the door, and Mrs Grant was again gratified by hearing, from the impulse of the pendulous legs upon the back of the door, the very same sound which had so terrified her on the former occasion. Mr Grant now led the way to the other bedroom where he had seen the corpse, and there of a surety they found the dead body of David stretched out on the bed, and of such a colour as might have led any one to the conclusion that he had been dead for a week.

All these acts were just parts of the winding up of a dark story, and what followed contained the *dénouement.* Next day the corpse was interred, William Turnbull acting as chief mourner. After the funeral, the repositories, which had, we forgot to say, been sealed up by Mr Allan, were opened. No will was found, but to make amends for this want, Wilson came forward, and, with a look of triumph, read a settlement, executed by David exactly fifty-seven days before, conveying all his houses and property to Mrs Gemmel. On hearing *the date,* Mr Allan indulged in that same kind of laugh he had been moved by on that day when Mr Grant narrated to him the story, for he had been told of the date by one of the witnesses, and his shrewd mind at once pointed to Wilson's device, aided by Mrs Gemmel, to make it appear that David had lived out the full sixty days required by the law to make the will good. Wilson stoutly asserted that David had been dead only for a day, or at most two, but that same afternoon two doctors certified, from having seen the body, that he must have been dead six or seven days before the discovery. It afterwards turned out that Wilson's project was not to trust to David outliving the sixty days, but to get him to "kirk and market," as the law language goes, whereby the will would have been saved from challenge, but this was found impossible, in consequence of the increasing feebleness of the invalid, and the next scheme was resorted to of apparently prolonging the old man's life.

However clear all this, it was not possible to get Wilson and Mrs Gemmel to give in, so that the law-plea of Turnbull *v.* Gemmel, to which we have alluded, was the consequence. The scheme of the stuffed effigy made a great noise in the Parliament-house at the time, but the difficulty lay in the question when David actually died. The doctors' certificate went so far, and was supplemented by witnesses who could speak to the beginning of the deception. Nor was the mere act of the deception itself without its weight, so that the issue was in favour of the heir-at-law. Legal justice was thus triumphant, and there was also something like poetical justice, for William took Margaret for his wife, and from that day the family of the Grants rose in the world. We may add, that David Turnbull's ghost was long a by-word in the Wynd, as an ironical allusion to doubtful speeches. We have given the title which is at the top of our story in consequence of an incident in court. One of the lawyers, on some time afterwards referring to the case of Turnbull against Gemmel, happened to say that the court would "recollect the case." Whereupon cried Braxfield, "Wha could ever forget the case o' the red nightcap, man?"

The Strange Story of Sarah Gowanlock.

AMONGST the various definitions of man, we think there might have been placed this one—viz., that man is a credulous animal; at least we are pretty safe in hazarding the opinion, that no faculty or quality of our nature sets us apart from the lower animals with a broader line of demarcation than our tendencies towards belief in things merely imagined; nay, we might almost say, that the lower tribes are so true to their instincts, that they are the only " positivists" in the very sense of Compté; and surely it was among them that the Frenchman ought to have looked ·for his happy condition of animated beings. At any rate, it must be admitted that if our fancies add to our plea-sures, they also add to our pains. And, alas, for the old truth, that our very mean of knowing and relishing the pleasant, consists in our experience of the painful; so that without the one the other cannot be. An old Court of Session summons, now in our hands, suggests the reflection we have here made. The case never went further than the summons, because the counsel saw that there were no grounds of action; but the nar-rative is altogether so curious, and, like all our legends, so extraordinary, that we think it proper to put it in a storied form for the benefit of our readers.

The pursuer's name was Sarah Gowanlock, the daughter of a leather-merchant in the High Street, who, dying long after his wife, left his only child, the said Sarah, the heiress of all he had contrived to make out of a calling—to him a goodly proof that there is "nothing like leather." In truth, John Gowanlock had had his victims skinned to some purpose, for goodness knows the thousands of merks he had realised thereby; and Sarah, the heiress of the whole, lived in Laurie's Land at the top of the Canongate; all, too, by herself, (with the exception of honest Maudge, her maid-of-all-work;) a spinster not under any necessity to spin, but extremely desirous of being the cause of that spinning, which is in another, and no other, than Clotho, that lady who weaves the destinies of all of us, and particularly the destiny of those who want to be married. And surely in thus premising, we might assume, even had we not the veritable fact, that these two females, living thus together from one year's end to another, knew each other's thoughts and sentiments pretty well ; and sure enough also, if there was one thought or sentiment on the part of Sarah which was *not* known to Maudge, it was not one on the subject of love, for the young lady was so exuberantly confidential to her handmaiden on the engrossing affairs of her heart, that there was not a throb in that organ that was not made as patent to the favourite servant as if a piece of crown glass had been the only medium between it and Maudge's eye. Nor less surely was that eye *not* unobservant, if it was not true that, having given up all hope herself, Maudge, like all other women in her condition, felt so much interest in the love affairs of her young mistress, that it almost seemed as if she realised, by proxy, her own old flames.

But coming to particulars, we find from the said writ that on a certain Sunday Sarah and her maid resorted, according to their custom,—for Maudge, although with her hook-nose, from the sides of which shone a pair of most "speculative eyes," betokened more of the witch to be than a sanctified child of grace, made great pretensions to holiness,—to the good old church of the Tron. They had got into their seat, and had sung the psalm and heard the prayer, and got the text and coughed, the usual herald of silence, when Sarah observed that a young man, in a seat very convenient for the purpose, was very busy fixing his eyes upon her, not in that stealthy way had recourse to by bashful lovers, but with a determination indicating that he had made his calculations to follow the Diogenian rule of staring a woman into love. Conduct this, appearing to the simple-minded Sarah very strange, but merely because she was simple-minded ; for if she had had the worldly wisdom of old Maudge, she might have known that the number of merks of which she was possessed were, or at least ought to have been, in the consideration of all true-minded Scotsmen, so many marks of matrimonial excellence ; and that that number was so great, that it was almost impossible to suppose that any prudent young man could contemplate them without loving their fair mistress and custodier to absolute distraction. Of which motives being perfec ly ignorant, Sarah contented herself with blushing—the very result, probably, the young man wanted to produce ; but one cannot blush for hours, neither can one hold the neck awry for more time than nature permits, and so she was in the end obliged to give in, and bear the searching look in the best way she could.

If we keep in view the modest character of Miss Sarah Gowanlock, we will be forced to the conclusion that she had not repeated her look at *him* after she had fairly satisfied herself that she had become the object of his attention ; but however this might have been, we are certiorated of the fact, that his countenance was so vividly imprinted on the retina of her eye, that she carried it home with her, even as if it had been a physical mark, with this difference, that there was something in the image that enabled it to intensify itself; and so, to be sure, it did, and that so effectually, that even if she had wished to banish it from her mind, or attenuate its lines, the effort would have resulted (as such efforts generally do) in adding, as the dyers say, a mordaunt to bite in the lineaments. But there was even more appertaining to this apparently simple, if not frivolous affair, for in the evening it became the subject of conversation between her and Maudge, in such a form as to evolve consequences not at all proportioned to the ostensible cause. The question was put by Sarah, whether Maudge had observed the youth. The answer was in the affirmative, with the anticipative addition that she, the said Maudge, did not know who he was ; but the old woman was not content with this, for she made the subject a peg whereon to hang such weirdly rags as were sufficient to make a " bogie " for such grown-up children as our poor Sarah Gowanlock. All which was done, too, with such great apparent innocence on the part of honest Maudge, that Sarah's ear was taken as if by a grip. " Be the young man who he may, Miss Sarah," said she, "ye 'll no get past him if he is to be yours." Words delivered with such a solemn shake of the head, and its trolloping gear, the low deep voice, and all the rest of the accidents of mystery, that they struck Sarah much in the way of a conviction of destiny, and all the more that the night was that of Sunday, and the hour near midnight, when the candle was within an inch of its termination. Nor was honest Maudge satisfied with one form of her oracular saying, for she repeated it in other set terms, " Ay, Miss Sarah, it is true. Nae woman can escape her ain ;" with an effect directly proportioned to Sarah's credulity; the capabilities of which, perhaps, Maudge knew very well from the experience she had had of her impressible mistress.

So the parties separated to go to bed; and while they are taking off their clothes, we may remark, to help the modern reader, that this notion about a destiny peculiarly appertaining to marriage, was then very much more a conviction than it is in our day, especially among the common people, of whom the existing form of religion made a kind of coarse homespun metaphysicians. Yet the notion is only a part of a great scheme of philosophy which attracts those puzzle-pates who are much given to the unfortunate habit of ultimate thinking. Nor, perhaps, is that scheme more true than another which asserts that a great portion of our religion, with all our ideal poetry, is composed of a web, the working whereof is effected by the waft being mere sentiment, straining after images, and the warp mere words, and which woof is the unavoidable drapery of the human spirit, just as woven wool, cotton, or silk, go to form the covering of the body. None of all which speculations could have helped our heiress of the many merks, as after lying down in her bed she thought of the words of Maudge. Another young woman would have, perhaps, made the bed posts quiver under a repressed shaking of the diaphragm, but then, as we have indicated, Sarah Gowanlock was under bond— (and who is out of bond to some unseen power?) first, to the susceptibility of a credulous nature ; and, secondly, to the dictates of an old woman, perhaps though not a witch in times when witches were, yet certainly not a whit better than she should have been. So Sarah could not by any means at all shake the thought away that Patrick Ruthven, her own true lover, might not, after all, be the man " she couldna get past;" a thought that seemed terrible to the poor soul, and the more that it brought along with it the image of the church-worshipper who had been so strangely associated with the dictum of necessity so ominously enunciated by the sybil. A very vain thing we consider it to be to try to account for motives—these subtle agents that draw the very marrow of their power from unseen things belonging to both worlds, as we see plants living, apparently, upon nothing, and winged creatures, with beautiful wings, arise out of worms which feed on substances destitute of a particle of sap. So we will be wiser if we take the fact for granted, that Miss Sarah Gowanlock was kept awake for hours meditating upon the question, whether she could escape "*her own,*" and trembling at the thought of some unseen power having in its hands the destiny of her condition, so far that, perhaps, she had not yet seen the man who was to make her happy or miserable.

Nor did some supervening days free her from the disturbing thoughts; nay, they were busy with her even on the following Thursday, when Patrick Ruthven came to visit her—a great occasion those visits, for Sarah loved the young man with all the ardour of an ardent, confiding, and guileless heart; and Patrick was not unworthy of her, honest and true, as he was well-favoured and manly, and every way calculated to make a young woman happy, barring those accidents which the hope of the virgin reduces to impossibilities, and the experience of the married elevates into unavoidabilities. Even the ardour of their meeting was calculated to bring out Sarah's bit of philosophy; so she told Patrick, not with a smile, but a real serious expression of countenance, how she had been troubled with the thought that no one can get past " her own."

" No more she can, my dear girl," said Patrick with a laugh, "and I am glad of it, for it proves that you cannot get past *me;* for," he added, as he took her kindly in his arms and kissed her modestly, " am not I *your own ?*"

And so he tried to shake her out of her notion; and, perhaps, the more that he saw these indications of seriousness, for which he could not very well account, on the mere adoption on her part of a common sentiment, at which even the utterers of it generally laughed. But the whole truth had not been told to him; and, no doubt, if he had known of the church-starer and the authority of honest Maudge, his good sense would have enabled him to do battle against the prejudice otherwise than in the jocular way he had adopted. As it was, Patrick had little doubt when he left her, that he had banished the prejudice, nor did he expect to hear of it again.

But Sunday came round, and Miss Gowanlock was not to be scared from the Tron by her unknown admirer any more than others of her sex would have resolved to stay at home for the same reason. So she and Maudge were, at the proper time, in their seats ; and no sooner had they gone through those peculiar preliminaries resorted to by the sex, and the sex alone —not unlike the turns and wheelings of a certain mute creature before he lies down—of rising and sitting, and rising only to sit again, than they beheld their old friend of the prior Sunday, all ready, as it seemed, to resume the old process ; but what was Miss Sarah's astonishment to find, sitting along- side of him, her own sweetheart, Patrick Ruthven, who, no doubt, was supremely ignorant of the secret thoughts and intentions of his friend and companion. It was just to be polite, and a little more perhaps, that Sarah nodded graciously to Patrick ; and he returned the compliment so graciously that she was placed in a state of comfort for the whole of the service; the more, too, that she could, with what is called "the tail of her eye," discover that the unknown youth now purposely, as she thought, avoided looking at her—a circum- stance this latter which satisfied her that Maudge's wisdom .was not to be justified by any such upturn as finding her destined "own" in any other individual than her own dear Patrick. Nor did matters even rest here, for upon the skailing of the church Patrick introduced to her the said youth, by the Welsh name of Mr Tobias Jones, in that free and easy way which satisfied her that he had no fears of a rival to prove that "her own" in present and prospective love was to be super- seded by another in future destiny.

All things waxed thus again pleasant for Sarah ; yea, so far that she wondered why she had been troubled by the image of one who was as nothing to her, merely because it had been associated in her mind with a foolish old saw. But perhaps Sarah had yet to learn that earthly wonders any more than miracles have no ultimate or final climax. Honest Maudge was, as usual, creeping about, saying little or nothing, till the time came when the Bible was to be read—a duty pleasant to Sarah, who was a good soul for other reasons than that she was a devout one, and very pleasant to Maudge also, though she was not a good soul to any one for any reason, even that reason of reasons that she was superlatively holy. The only exception was Sarah herself, who looked upon the old woman as a saint, merely because, having an exuberance of goodness mixed with her simplicity, she was able to allow a surplus as a covering to her domestic; in which fashion we work every day without knowing it; yea, every one of us. And so, as Maudge proceeded with her reading, she was merely projecting upon Sarah the goodness she had got from her mistress, and which the latter thought belonged to her maid. But, as the saying is, you may dress the devil in the white robe of the saint, but, as saints do not wear high crowned hats, what are you to make of the horns? No sooner had the Bible been shut than the devout Maudge suggested to her young mistress that she should have her "lot" cast by the holy Book. Now, Miss Sarah Gowanlock became curious to know the meaning of this, whereupon the devout Maudge laughed, of course in a holy way.

"Ken ye na the lot by the Bible, Miss Sarah?" said she. "Why ye see, my dear young lady, you just do as the gude-man who wrote that holy book, 'The Life of God in the Soul of Man,' did when he was at sair loss what kind of fortune he should dree: open the Bible, even as the seals were opened, and read the first words your look rests on."

"Oh, I would be afraid!" said the simple Sarah.

"Of what?" rejoined Maudge. "Have ye forgot that ye canna pass by your ain?"

Words which again struck the ear of Sarah like hot needles, though she could not have told why, even for the value of all her merks. Then a dreary feeling came over her as if she felt conscious that she was to be called upon to part with her will and motives of action. She would read the lot, and she wouldn't; curiosity suggested compliance, and hope backed curiosity, but fear whispered of something to interfere with her love. All which signs seemed only the opportunity of the devout sortileger, who put her hand upon the Bible even as Sarah repeated, "Oh, I 'm so terrified!"

"We put the Book on its back, in this way, ye see," continued Maudge, so like a Sybil, "and let the twa sides fa', and when it is open the lot is the first thing ye read."

All which Maudge acted as she was speaking, while Sarah was looking fearfully on, her cheeks pale, her eye fugitive and nervous, and a shiver running over her from the head to the heel. Yet, as if charmed, she could not resist the temptation to see into the future. And surely it is no less than a charm in the very wisest of us, for are we not for ever divining, building up imaginary elysiums on earth and above the earth, with ministering creatures formed for no other purpose than to feed us with nectared sweets; yea, all the time that perhaps the sordid flesh of our wretched bodies, so exquisitely capable of anguish, is quivering under lancinating pains? No! Sarah could not resist the instinctive impulse, and her eye following, without being conscious of the leading of the long wrinkled finger, fell upon a passage. She glanced hurriedly at it. Her own name was there, and another's as well; they burned into the very texture of her brain. Yet she *would* read, even without the power of gathering up the words into meaning; but Maudge took up the task, and with her cracked screechy voice, she read :—

"'Then he called his daughter Sarah, and she came to her father; and he took her by the hand and gave her to be wife to Tobias, saying: Behold, take her after the law of Moses, and lead her away to thy father; and he blessed them."

"A false lot," said Maudge, "and tells naething, unless the young man's name is Tobias, and we have few Tobys in our day."

"But his name *is* Tobias," cried Sarah, with a gasping effort to articulate.

A communication apparently so entirely new to Maudge, that she could not have been more surprised if she had read, *ad aperturam Bibliorum,* that at her years—not much younger than another Sarah—she was to bear a child, to be called Toby. Meanwhile, as regards our Sarah, it might be pronounced impossible to describe the effect of the words upon one who was facile enough, in obedience to a vulgar opinion, to look upon them not only as divine, but as divinely intended to shadow forth her earthly fortunes. What was she to think, if she had not the knowledge or the energy to baffle those subtle things called mysteries? Nay, even if she had been possessed of logical acumen beyond the generality of her sex, what could she make of such questions? Why did that young man's face impress itself so strongly upon her brain? how did it happen that the image of that face became so strangely associated with the metaphysical or supernatural notion of a prevision of matrimonial matches? but above all, how did it come that the cast of the Bible lot brought up her name and that of the young man as linked together in the relation of marriage? Was she such an adept in the doctrine of chances as to be able to discard the whole affair as a series of effects in the chain of natural wishings? Wiser heads than that of poor Sarah have been baffled by such strange occurrences; nay, in reference to the Bible part of the illusion, how could she hold fast by the faith of a thousand miraculous violations of nature's laws, recorded in the holy Book, and let go one, even that of the lot, not more wonderful or impossible than the others?

How vain all these things, yet not vain, as regards us poor

P

creatures who, tossed between faith and reason, hold by the one as the other gives way, till, often engulfed by despair, many die in a relapse of sullenness, at war with God and themselves; yet not vain as regards our happiness or unhappiness, as we may well declare of Sarah, who that night again retired to her bed to be as miserable as one whose love is, by inevitable signs, crossed by the decrees of God. Nor, in the morning, was she to be relieved from her misery, for about eleven o'clock of the forenoon she was visited by Patrick Ruthven, who was accompanied by no other of all men in the world than the said wonderful being, that very individual with the Bible name, of whom she had been in terror all the prior night, and whose face scared her eye as if it had been flared upon by the light of a spectre. Then, to add to her confusion, if not dismay, Patrick told her that his father (a merchant, with shipping connexion in Leith) had resolved upon sending him as supercargo of the brig *Diana*, on a voyage to the West Indies. The communication in any circumstances would have been ill to bear by the young woman, but it was aggravated by the strange position in which he stood, and more by the statement that while he was absent he would commit her to the care of his companion.

"Jones will give you my letters, Sarah," said he, "and any that you may wish to send me—and I know you will lose no opportunity—will be forwarded by him to me."

"And are you to be so long away, Patrick?" said she, with a despairing look.

"I am not sure what may be my destiny," replied he. "If we take the vessel to South America, of which we have some intention, it may be a considerable time before I return, but cheer up, 'my bonny may,' as the old song says," and singing cheerfully the three other lines, he took her in his arms.

All which time Sarah imagined that the eye of Jones was fixed upon her, though as for testing the truth of her convic-

tion by looking him straight in the face, she had no more
power than she would have had to peer into the visage of the
ghost of her mother. And so the young men departed, leaving
Sarah in one of those states of mind of which almost all have
some experience when the thoughts, unwilling to concentrate
themselves into a motive, career through the brain as moral
meteors, lighting up dark recesses and burning wherever they
flash—all the while the individual feels himself the slave of a
power which he can neither overrule nor comprehend. If any
reasoning could find room amidst these automatic thoughts,
she might wonder, in the midst of so many wonders, how it
should come about that the absence of Patrick should be, as
an event apparently so well fitting in with the others, that it
seemed a part of the scheme so mysteriously illustrated by the
Bible lot. So that there was really, after all, a little more than
the mere waft and warp of feeling and words—some facts
entered into the texture of her thoughts, but these facts were
as mysterious as her very fancies, and thus she was bewildered,
even as a traveller seeking his home in a night of darkness and
storm, wherein fitful flashes of light only tell him that he is
now in a place that he does not know, and then that he is in
another which, he has reason to fear, is one of danger.

Nor did the days that passed bring any amelioration. Jones
was left as a solace—the very man she shuddered to look at!
And he came, as in duty bound. Nor could any one have
said, that he did not act the part of a lover's proxy, for if he
had known the old song, which describes the feelings of the
mistress for him who comes to her to praise her absent lover—

> "He spoke such pretty words of love
> Of him she loved so true and dear,
> That she loved him because he spoke
> The pretty words she loved to hear"—

he could not have been more true to the nature of woman; nor
did a look pass from his eyes, a word from his lips, to indi-

cate that he had any mission to discharge but that confided to him by the absent friend. So far Sarah could find no offence ; nay, the offence was in her own mind, for really there appeared nothing about Jones's conduct, with the exception, perhaps, of the somewhat ardent gaze on the eventful Sunday, the beginning of the divination, if we should call it so, which could be construed into a notion that he was included in the fate of a sortilege. Yet his visits were repeated oftener than his commission required, and, what escaped the eye of Sarah, it became clear that honest Maudge, whether actuated by the sortilege or not, looked upon the visitor as having some better right to visit the heiress than that which he derived from Patrick Ruthven ; nay, might we not venture a suspicion that Maudge considered that his right was derived from heaven? So far, at least, we may be certain that Sarah, though still remaining under the awe of that cloud of mystery, was beginning to think that, even in the event of the sortilege being to be realised by some new turn in her destiny, such as the death of her lover, to prepare her for it, she would not consider the result so terrible as at an earlier period she thought.

But he who looks into individual natures will find that no general laws will prepare him for developments which mark the individual by the workings of that more general law which insists upon variety. We might suppose that the terror which resulted from the gambling with fate would have scared her from the very mention of the prior circumstances. Yet it was not so, and neither was Maudge averse from the old topic ; nay, the desire to look into futurity seemed so far like the passion of the gambler, it fed and increased upon its losses. The conversations between the two were still engrossed with the wonderful topic, and so consistent with female nature when acted upon by curiosity was the result, that if they had not thought it inconsistent with the reverence due to what they reckoned the words of divinity, they would have cast up another lot to see how far it agreed with or differed from the other ; but even amidst the workings of the credulity of both, or at least one of them, they could not but see that it was a tempting of the Divine wrath to make a dice-box of the Bible, whereby they might set one oracle from its sacred leaves against another, and thereby render the divination a thing of no faith, or rather a subject of ridicule.

But was there no other mode of ascertaining the intentions of Heaven? Yes, there was. The old temples were in ruins, and the priests and priestesses dead ; the gods and goddesses, who served as mediums between Jove and man, were gone, of course to Olympus ; but for all that, human beings were not consigned to the darkness of secondary causes. Besides the Bible lot, which was in the power of all, was there not famous Girzel Jeffrey in the Cowgate, who for a fee of a shilling was able and willing to draw the slide between the two worlds, and give the disconsolate maidens of the time an opportunity of peering into the future, even so far as to be able to know who were to be their husbands? Of this modern Dodona, Sarah Gowanlock knew—as who did not in Edinburgh at that time? —and as for Maudge, she not only knew the priestess, she was even so far favoured that she was permitted to speak to her, if not to sit upon the very tripod. So there was nothing extraordinary in the fact that she who had suggested the Bible sortilege should recommend to her mistress another attempt to penetrate the vail, were it for no other object than to confirm the Bible lot ; for as to reducing its authority by a contrary oracle, that could not be supposed possible so long as the holy Book was looked upon as divine, and its soothsaying by the chance opening viewed as certain and irrefragable. The recommendation was listened to by Sarah with a shudder of fear, yet with no diminution of curiosity, which, indeed, as we all very well know, waxes even stronger in proportion to the perils through which it is gratified. We now treat these vulgar oracles lightly, at the very hour when we are substituting for the old hags refined ladies and gentlemen, whose gentility does not unfit them for communication with spirits, and whose education does not enable them to resist the delusion. So it is; the faith of one age is the mockery of the next, and ours may be subjected to the contempt which we throw upon that which has gone before us. Yet, is not every feeling true for the moment? Yes, true insomuch as it is the most real of all things, because next the heart, and the mistress of our motives; and yet, too, the most unreal, as being furthest from the head, and the very slave of our reason.

Accordingly our Sarah and her maid were ready for the strange adventure by the hour of nine, when all was dark; for Miss Sarah Gowanlock would not for the world have been seen going into a witch's cave for the purpose of getting her fortune read,—a fear on her part not at all inconsistent with another fear which darkened her spirit, even that superstitious one which makes the believing diviner hold her breath. They hurried along, threading their way among the crowd of street-loiterers, and secure by their muffling cloaks from any recognition, till they came to the close, which at its foot opened upon that part of the Cowgate where " the wise woman " held her levees. Even in the short space they had to pass over after issuing from the dark entry, Maudge had some part to play which separated her from her mistress for a minute or two, her excuse being that she had made a detour to avoid some one whom she knew, and who might possibly follow her to the door; but though Maudge was perhaps as inexplicable a being as Girzy Jeffrey herself, that was no reason why Sarah should not believe her when she explicated herself. And so without further impediment they got, by a gentle rap, into the very adytum of mysteries.

And who need be told now of what kind of place that was, and what kind of being occupied it? The little dark room,

with a few old sticks of furniture, the cruse on the wall giving
forth the merest glimmer, which, if not helped by the convenient adaptation of the residenter's eye, could scarcely shew
her the faces of her votaries—the four or five upright ribs of
iron built in for a grate ; and she, the priestess of Fate, a
smoke-dried old beldame, in a crazy chair, with her eye twink-
ling in the internal light of her own cunning, her scraggy palm
itching for the fee, and her tongue not less "yeuky" for "the
fiery nectar by damned-devils brewed." But familiar as these
characteristics of the place, of an old trade, and of its mistress
may be, there was something exceptional in what might have
been taken for a small looking-glass, which hung on the partition wall dividing the room from either the lobby or the
adjoining room of another lodger. We require to be particular about this ornamental bit of furniture, so little in keeping
with the other plenishing of the dingy cave, for we have misgivings in using the word room ; and we have further to say
of it, that being placed on the same wall where the cruse was
hung, it could scarcely be observed, except when a flicker
from the red embers was sent from the fire to the opposite
side. So much for the place and the residenter; as for the
visitors, Sarah and Maudge, they behoved to occupy a couple
of stools placed opposite Girzy, so that from the *multa in medio*
she might catch the hints whereof she manufactured her truly
wind-woven oracles. Nor were they seated for a minute, when
the inspiration began to work.

"The auld story, I fancy," said she.

"Yes," replied Sarah, as she placed twice the ordinary fee
in the outstretched hand. "I have at present very particular
reasons"—— And she hesitated from pure fear to proceed,
as if she thought she was like her of old, even Aglaonice, who
prayed the moon to come down, courting her own ruin.

Whereat the wrinkled creature laughed within her chest, as
if she thought the laugh sat more pleasantly there than up

among the vocal chords; and as she laughed, she vocabulised
something to this effect :—

" Particular! Miss; and was there ever a young heart here
that hadna very, ay, just very particular reasons to ken something? But maybe ye will see as weel as hear, though I'm no
in the custom o' that."

" But that is just what we want," said Maudge. " We want
to see the shadow o' the man wha is to be the husband of my
mistress."

" Shadow!" muttered Sarah, as a gruing (to use an old
Scotch word) produced that effect upon her so like the shiver
of an accession of cold, yet the curiosity deepened upon her,
according to the primeval law of the female mind.

Whereupon our mistress of incantations began to enact her
antics and weird motions, all in the usual way of her kind ;
for these strange beings that work upon the credulity of mankind have ever, since the days of Apollo, kept up their stage-
tricks, not from any inheritance of knowledge, but rather from
an intuitive consciousness that the miraculous must be impressed by gibberish and forms, which are as complete a violation of all usual laws of human intercourse, as it itself is a
violation of the laws of nature; and that the sorceress did
not undervalue her efforts might have been apparent from the
pale face of the charmed votary who sat fearing lest the sight
she was to see was something other than the form of Patrick
Ruthven. Whereupon the incantations began to take effect
in reversing of all natural phenomena; for although there was
no light from the cruse, and far less from the red embers of
the fire sufficient for the optical illusion, there—most wonderful
no doubt to behold!— the mirror on the partition wall, with
its gilded frame, was lighted up so vividly that it seemed even
to cast a glare through the dark room. Even Sarah, simple as
she was, and certainly not versed in optics, wondered mightily
where the light could come from, for she had never seen or

heard—no more she could—of a mere looking-glass possessing the power of illuminating itself; and as for Maudge, she looked wonderment too, only qualified by a devout smile, which seemed to correspond with a similar impression on the face of the old "she incarnate."

"Now he will come," said the old witch. " Him thou'lt see will be thy husband, will ye or nill ye."

Words surely sufficient to fix Sarah's eyes on the glass still more intensely, as to be sure they did. Nay, it would have formed a subject for an artist of the chiaro-oscuro school, that poor simple soul, with the hood of her cloak thrown back, her sweet yet pensive face looking out of the head-folds, her eyes fixed on the glass even as by a strain of the muscles of the orbs, her mouth open, even to the extent of shewing the most beautiful teeth in the world, and the whole body fixed immovably, as if rigid by a general spasm, standing between these women, who might seem as incarnations of evil on either side of the personification of goodness and virtue. Nor had this attitude lasted longer than a minute, or perhaps two—the light from the mirror being still as bright as ever—when there appeared in the glass, surrounded, and made vividly apparent by that light, *the very face of that man* which Sarah knew so well, yet trembled to behold, even him of the Bible sortilege, Toby Jones himself. Yes, and the face remained there until a scream from Sarah shewed more than sufficiently that the charm had wrought its worst or best. Then the light in the mirror disappeared, and with it the face, and nothing was to be seen but the glass as flickered on externally by the glimmerings of the fire.

No sooner was all this accomplished than Maudge took the torpid Sarah by the arm, and having drawn over her head the hood of the cloak, led her out, and the two were soon again threading their way among the people of the Cowgate, as mute as the fourth person in the old comedies. Not a word was spoken by either, the more by reason, we fancy, that the one was unable to utter a syllable, and the other was unwilling. Upon arriving at home, Sarah, even in the very absence of all practical thoughts, looked to the locking of the door as if she felt that some power menaced her from without ; a suspicion or conviction common to all mankind, with the exception of a few who, defying the power of external circumstances, contrive to knock their brains out in the great cause of the nobility of the human soul. Of these few no woman could surely ever be included ; at least our Sarah proved herself as being signally one of the many, for from that night she was so entirely changed from the happy, hopeful soul, rejoicing in love, and the sun the most beautiful and cheering respectively of internal and external things, that she was thenceforth—alas ! how long to be ?—a creature oppressed with a grief which she could scarcely tell to God, because He had set His face against, and doomed her to one of the cruelest of decrees. Seldom going out, solitude increased the gloom of her spirit, while within her appetite for melancholy was fed by the woman who had, whether wilfully or not, led her into all this evil. Meanwhile, as quadrating with all these circumstances, Jones's visits were unremitting ; and what was viewed by her as a working out of the will of Heaven, he began to bear upon her thoughts and try to wear them away from her first and only lover, even him who was now away. At first she recoiled, like a victim from the sacrificial blow, but the recoil was brought up by the sharp strain of the fatal rope that bound her. Even when her face was turned fearfully from him, she listened to his words as if she had been bound to hear them, nay, to admit their truth— even to consent to the sentiments they conveyed, not yet of love, but something as nearly approaching to it as he found courage or occasion to utter. Nor when he departed was she restored to peace, for Maudge had begun to harp on the merits of Jones as a lover superior to those of Patrick Ruthven.

Alas! for the religion and philosophy of our enlightened days, involving us in a darkness unknown to the ancient world, where the plays of Fate were founded on the crime of the victim. We have in our domestic story the inevitable coils of the serpent; but in place of the priest of the Thymbræan Apollo we have a young and innocent maiden, whose only crime was a pure love, the very essence of the virtues of Olympus.

Nor were the coils of the serpent exhausted by mere tortuous windings. There were energies within ready to add their forces to those without. Our Sarah came to be arrayed in conflict against herself. Some duty she owed to the authority of Heaven came to be opposed to that love which first emanated from the fountain of love, so that she felt the beginnings of a conviction that her love to Patrick was neither less nor more than *a sin;* and as our sentiments are at best but feelings of pain or pleasure wound round objects, or words representing objects, his image came to partake of the darker hues connected with her notions of rebellion against superior decrees. Here, also, the natural laws, so far as merely retributive, were at work; for the feelings which hung round the notions of obedience clustered about the image of the rival Jones, and even clung to his words. The indications were, indeed, soon too apparent to escape the new lover himself, who, taking advantage of the growing favour—not ultraneous love, but mere obedience simulating it—made his court with such effect as even to be a wonder unto himself. The case we here portray bears no analogy to those instances where the stern commands of parents come in opposition to the dictates of the heart; in these there may be obedience without the effort to love, if, indeed, there be any such that ever succeed, and custom may take the place of instinct; but here the duty was so far higher that it was associated with devotion, and a religious feeling was transferred to the object which it favoured.

That the sense of calamity is ameliorated by custom is not so true as Homer with his *assuetudo malorum* would have us to suppose, but we cannot refuse to go along with the ancients, when they speak of that strange conduplication of evil which is observed in the mysteries of Providence. Nay, it would seem as if some calamitous event were first postulated in fate, and then wrought out by forces expressly called up—at least, twisted out of their natural direction, in order to bring about the foregone conclusion. Mark the occasion of our reflection : No other than that Jones called one day, and, with a face lengthened by the weight of grief, told Sarah that Patrick's father had got intelligence that the *Diana* was wrecked, and his son lost in a fearful storm. This intelligence at another and foregone time would have struck a moral paralysis through her entire frame ; nor even now could she bear it without a cold shiver ; but the mind, when under the supernatural cloud, which reflects sometimes the hues of the many-coloured arc, sees everything as tinged by its shadow. The strange reflection occurred to her that Heaven had thus taken away her lover—that the sortilege and incanta tion might be fulfilled with less pain to her than otherwise it could have been. So it is. Heaven is always viewed as kindly by man in adversity, merely because things might have been worse, and we shudder to ask why that worse should ever have been made possible. Then if grief for the afflicted is not love in tears, it is at least its opportunity ; and surely no love could be supposed more acceptable than that which is conveyed through the medium of sympathy. All which was apparently known to the Heaven-favoured suitor, for he straightway acted as if he had been an adept in the knowledge of the female heart. Yet we do not say that that love of his was accepted ; it was only borne for the sake of the duty she owed to the Author of the inevitable decree. But then again it was borne as a thing to be tolerated, and it was tolerated as a thing which had a preparation made for it even in the heart which was being, by the mind, moulded into love as a duty.

Thus, in conflict with herself, she turned to the devout Maudge ; but as well might· an old Greek devotee have applied to the priestess for reasons to disprove the delivered oracle. Maudge was true to her craft, and denounced the hesitating obedience of her mistress to the will of Heaven as a rebellion which could only stave off the inevitable marriage with him who was decreed as '' her ain," and whom she could not get past.

" Ye see how it works," said the oracle, pointing her finger up, whereas, perhaps, it should have been down ; " Patrick Ruthven was swallowed up in the storm, because it was neces· sary he should be ta'en out o' the way."

The very idea that had occurred to Sarah herself; and she shook as she heard a response, as it were, to her own questionings.

" But what although," she said, " if my heart cannot love Mr Jones ?"

Whereupon Maudge laughed in a screechy way, just as if she had wanted to shake that heart ; but the meaning whereof Sarah could not for the life of her understand, nor did her words which followed her laugh make it more plain.

" Ye may argue," said she ; " but you canna argue yoursel' out o' the loops, nae mair than the bird can whistle itsel' out o' the net o' the fowler."

" But still if I cannot love him," repeated Sarah, " how can I marry him ?"

" Just by lettin' the minister say the words," replied Maudge. " And as for what the warld ca's love, it will come when it canna help itsel'. You 've to learn, Miss Sarah—and ye *will* learn whether ye will or winna—that the love which marriage makes is better than the love that makes marriage."

"And is there such a thing, Maudge?" inquired the simple maiden.

"I trow there be," was the answer; and with another laugh which was to be a prelude surely to an adequate idea. And so it was : "If marriage, as the Bible says, makes o' man and woman one flesh, may it no' make o' them as weel one spirit? Ye will come to love him as he loves you ; and surely never man loved a woman as Mr Jones loves you."

"Yes, yes," said Sarah ; "that's true!"

"And see ye no the holy wark there too?" added the devout Maudge. "How could the lot hae been wrought but through his love? Even the dead paper leaf o' the Bible, wi' letters printed in it by the hands o' man, sees better than you."

"Yes, but it is so strange!" added Sarah.

"Strange to be married to your ain!" continued Maudge. "Then strange, and mair strange, it would be to be married to ain who is anither's."

And Maudge laughed again, so that Sarah could make nothing of the oracle, except it was that she felt that the old woman was simply backing the judgment of Heaven. All tended to the foregone conclusion ; and meanwhile Jones continued his suit—a fact itself in harmony with the facts, apparently unknown to him, which had so clearly shewn the intention of Providence. Then we are to remember that strange law of moral forces, whereby persistiveness draws, as it were, a power from the wearing out of resistiveness. We know it in the daily triumphs of perseverance. But Sarah was not able for this kind of reflection. She only felt herself under the influence of a devotional obedience on the one side, and subjected to the allurements of good looks, youth, an eloquent tongue, and ardent solicitations on the other,—all which in time produced their natural effects. Yes, as our summons sets forth, Sarah Gowanlock, spinster, was not long after verily married to Tobias Jones by the minister of the Tron, who, if he had known the history of this strange wooing, might have thought there was more dust to be brought out of the Bible by very devout people than he could accomplish even by the pretty forceful application of his palms on a Sunday.

And now comes the pity of our too true story. This Tobias Jones soon began to shew that poor Sarah Gowanlock's merks were in his eyes more beautiful than her personal or mental qualities, though these were enough to have made her a paragon of a wife. He began early to get her money into his hands—an article exquisitely suited to his dissolute habits; and the gentle remonstrances of the young wife raised quarrels, which, if there had been love on his side, would soon have been quelled, but which, in the absence of that most wonderful of all conciliators, became every day worse. Nor could the devout Maudge reconcile this strange denouement with the Bible lot; far less could she console her unfortunate mistress by telling her still that he was "her own," which she could not by any means have got past. Sarah only sighed, and applied the handkerchief, often enough now too wet, to her red eyes; and even in all this suffering she could see nothing but the fulfilment of the intentions of Heaven, though what she had in the wide world done to merit such a punishment she could no more see than could a dogmatic theologian perceive the secret of the covenant of redemption. But why dwell on what Homer calls the domestic evil? for does he not tell us that it is so irremediable—nay, so much of a despair to those outside the place of the Lares, whose mother is Mania—that it must be hushed up as a thing which concerns none but the sufferers themselves? Yet, uniform in its workings as it is, there was one extraordinary event in this domestic tragedy which we cannot but mention. One night Sarah, left to the intensity of her grief, was sobbing out her sorrows to herself. Jones had been upon the ramble for days, at the end to return and renew the scenes of internal strife; even the inevitable Maudge was not present with her peculiar comforts. The hour was comparatively late, and the quietness in the streets suggested the contrast between the peace without and the grief within. All the issues of her mind, which were once the outgoings of the spirit, charmed with the attractive power of one she truly loved, were now the sighs and sobs of unavailing, irremediable woe. In this state of moral stupor she was roused to listening by a movement of the outer door, as if by one who had been accustomed to open it ; then it did not appear to be the act of Jones, whose return was usually announced by the noisy demonstrations of the drunkard. There was a foot in the room adjoining, which opened into that where she sat. She thought she knew that sound, and her heart trembled, yet only with the recollection of what had been, and what would be no more for ever. Her eye was fixed on the door, which she expected every moment to be opened ; and it was opened, but by whom? Patrick Ruthven stood before her.

> " Whence come ye? What Neptunian power
> Hath oped the sea and spued thee into air?"

Not that Sarah put such a question, for she was speechless ; nor less he ; and the two looked at each other as two statues so formed that the eyes only spoke by the light which seemed to have the motive energy of turning the orbs of the one upon those of the other. But these fixed eyes spoke more than the mere fixedness of a charm. Sarah's were filled with sorrow; his with pity, as if he had known the story of her misery before he came. We suspect the scene in the old ballad was not so true to history as that which we here relate ; but we would only overstrain our efforts, and weaken the effect by that very overstraint, were we to try to put into description what is claimed by fancy as something to be treated in her own fine way.

Let it work on, and when it has finished, we may be per-

mitted to state that after nature had gone through her part of
the scene, there was enough to justify us in saying that the two
came to understand each other.   Sarah explained the strange
manner whereby she had come to be the wife of Jones—an
explanation which struck Patrick mute by the very force of a
conviction that there had been some devil's work in all the
affair from the beginning.   He remembered how Jones had
sought his company, and almost forced him to introduce him
to her.   By and by he discovered that Jones was the nephew
of Maudge, a fact which the latter had kept a secret.   Nay, by
visiting Girzel Jeffrey, he got at the secret of the mirror, which
was only a pane of glass in a partition, behind which Jones
had secreted himself with a light which shewed his face.   The
whole scheme, including the Bible sortilege, had been the product of the brain of the devout Maudge, aided by the cunning
of her relatives.

We have spoke of a summons, and the facts were these.   It
was thought by good lawyers at that time that the acts of
witchcraft were not only a crime for which the party might with
the Bible's licence, or rather command, be punished, but that
whatever might be caused by them was illegal ; and so it came
to be a question whether Sarah Gowanlock's marriage was good
in law.   A summons of reduction of the voluntary contract was
accordingly written out by Mr Lawson, Sarah's agent ; but when
it came to be known that the supposed witchcraft was mere
chicane, the aspect of the case underwent a change ; for it had
long been fixed law that a marriage brought about by deceit
was still good, except in the case where the *person* was changed,
so that, while the party thought she or he was marrying a
certain individual, another was superinduced by stealth.   So
the summons was given up, and the evil remained,—how long
we have no means of knowing.   *Insperabilis vita !*

John Cameron's Life Policy.

IT is not often in these palmy days of ours, when drawing-rooms, pianos, Italian music, illustrated albums, and parties, form a goodly portion of the domestic economy of well-to-do tradesmen, that we read or hear much of a certain class of people who, not so very long ago yet, had a hearty contempt for what they called the seductions of Satan. Nay, we are not sure if the latter great personage has not a good right to charge us with ingratitude, insomuch as, although we owe him a great deal for the "sweet sins" he bestows upon civilised people—and the more, we fear, the more advanced the civilisation—we have almost pushed him out of our Christian mythology. Nor is the reason very far to seek, for while not very long ago yet we were proud of being much infected by sin, if not altogether *ex capite ad calcem*, unclean and corrupt, we have got into the civilised notion that we are not so very bad after all; if we have not as much free will about us as to enable us to choose to be very fine ladies and gentlemen, as clean outside as the Bavarian princess, and as pure within as a new-born Wesleyan.

A great contrast all this to the views and feelings of even many who lived only half a century ago. The genuine Cameronian of the north is now nearly an extinct species, to be recognised only in books ; and the few individuals who may, perchance, linger in some of the out-o'-the-way places, do not appear to be of the proper type. They have degenerated from the historical picture. The blue bonnet and plaid, the rigg-and-fur stockings, the snuff-mull and spoon, have given way before the inroads of modern fashion ; and as for their religion, especially those grand and yet terrible ideas of the covenants, including that of redemption, with the wonderful " election," and that mystic scroll of the unhappy reprobates, (in which no genuine Cameronian lamb could be included ;) these deep convictions, too, and the stern and honest preju- dices that would hold no parley with sin though arrayed in silk, and smelling of *millefleurs*, all which made them the pride of Scotland, the boast of Calvinism, and the terror of the English cavaliers, they have all suffered equally from the polite conformity, and, we fear, slip-shod religion of our modern days. Yet, withal, it is not long since we had, even in these parts, some fine examples of the more ancient type; and one of these in the person of a certain John Cameron, a worthy whom, with some curious incidents in his life and conversation, we are anxious to bring to the acquaintanceship of the readers of our legends.

Now, this special John Cameron of ours resided in the Fountain Close of Edinburgh,—a circumstance to be carefully remembered, for the reason that the numbers of the name are so many, albeit their remaining characteristics be so few, that otherwise we would run a risk of an inconvenient identification. And with this worthy son of worthy sires lived his wife Janet, a Cameronian as well; yea, as true-blue a specimen of the hard-featured yet noble-hearted sect as honest John himself. Nor were these two, though the Lord had denied to them children, the solitary occupants of the dwelling in the said close of the Fountain ; for there was still another residenter who, in some respects, bore a closer relation to the heads of the house than even children themselves sometimes, especially in our day of governors and hopefuls, do to their parents. This was Jenny Cameron, who rejoiced in the character of half-companion, half-servant; and whose name, though the diminutive of that of her mistress, will sufficiently distinguish her for our purpose.

But speaking of Cameronians, with their broad lines of demarcation, we need hardly say, that Jenny was well supplied with other marks of distinction besides her name; nay, she was as peculiar as her master or mistress; the chief peculiarity being an all but worshipful feeling of respect for, if not a downright adoration of, John Cameron, whom she considered to be not only a perfect man, but, to speak more correctly, a perfect Cameronian; for it behoves us to keep in view, that in Jenny's estimation, as well as in that of all the privileged sect, a Cameronian was considerably greater and better than a man. So strong, indeed, was this feeling on the part of Jenny, that it was of very small importance what John Cameron said or what John Cameron did, the saying or deed was not only not wrong—it could not by any actual potentiality under heaven be wrong. Yea, if John Cameron had worn a mortar-hat, like the old Pharisees, or stood for a week singing psalms on the top of the Fountain well at the head of the close, or put out the life-candle in a new-light saint, or said a prayer with Laud's service in the one hand and Clavers' sword in the other, or anything else wonderful or *outré* in the estimation of ordinary people, Jenny Cameron would have approved it and upheld it, not only as right, but something worthy of being imitated by all men who had a grain of sense in their brains. And may we not say with some regret that the race of Jenny Camerons is pretty nearly extinct? but whether to the advantage or disadvantage of masters and mistresses, we leave to the decision of those aged judges whose period of life having comprehended the real Jenny and the modern Abigail, may be able to form an estimate.

Meanwhile it is necessary, in obedience to the requirements of history, that we should inform the reader that John Cameron enjoyed only a very small portion of the good things of this life, and that portion came to him in a peculiar way, insomuch as, having been a small trader, and laid past a small sum of money, he had, as he saw years coming upon him, laid his earnings out on an annuity which was barely sufficient, with the blessing of Heaven, to keep up even a household of three Cameronians—making all due allowance for the economy of certain Scotch dishes, not well qualified by their names to bring water to the mouth of an Englishman, but at the cooking whereof Jenny was an adept, and thus securing verge for a small joint or savoury stew on very set days.

No doubt, to very scrupulous people it may be matter of surprise why a man so grave and sensible, and so fond of his helpmate, as John Cameron was everywhere acknowledged to be, should have thought of limiting his small annuity to the period of his own earthly pilgrimage in this wearyful world of accidents, mishaps, and all manner of misfortunes, and not extending the same to Janet as well, who, independently of being in the fold of the lambs, could eat and drink (of course, after a suitable grace) just as copiously, and with as much of the zest of the flesh in that corrupt corporation of hers, as John himself. Nor is this wonder at all unnatural; but, nevertheless, like all other wonders beyond the sphere of miracles, it will shrink at the touch of its own sufficient reason, or, we should rather say, reasons; whereof the first was, that John Cameron was much the younger of the two partners, and though he knew very well, independently of the Northampton Tables, that women, and especially Cameronian women, wear better, and live longer than men, he was not dead to the suspicion that his beloved helpmate had so much of a tendency to dropsy, or, to sacrifice to the ruling euphuism, aqueousness, as to indicate serious uncertainty of life, even to the extent of tapping itself, which he considered to be nothing better than a death-warrant. Yet, to do him perfect justice, as he lived to see those symptoms wear off, he was delighted,

as became a Christian, a Cameronian, and a loving husband—
yea, even at the same time, so nicely are woven the threads of
good and evil, that he felt serious apprehensions of the consequences of Janet's good health enabling her to outlive him;
for no man was less selfish than John Cameron, in saying
which we intend no more than to mention that, even the best
Cameronian that ever sent a bullet through the heart of a
Clavers' lamb for a noble cause, was not an angel. But the
second of John Cameron's reasons for so limiting his annuity
was, if possible, still more curious, if it did not smack (to
appearance) of that very vice of selfishness of which we have,
even at this moment, exonerated him. A far-seeing man as
he was, and well versed in the lore of human nature, he knew
that annuitants, upon whom others depend for their subsistence, are the most loveable, the best beloved, and the most
daintily cared for of all the people in the world; so much so,
indeed, that a policy (exquisitely named in this respect) has
been known to do that which some ill-natured people deem
impossible, *videlicet*, to change a woman's temper. Yea, as
the old saying goes, to transform "a shrew into a doo," or, as
a certain quaint punster said, a "wo-man into a woo-man."
Vulgar and well known as this may be now—and yet how
seldom insurance offices take notice of so charming a reason
for stimulating their customers!—it was the great merit of John
Cameron that he knew it early, and not only knew it, but
acted upon it; yet not selfishly, as we take upon ourselves to
declare, only prudentially: in the first place to provide against
certain changes which, without any observable cause, are known
often to make terrible inroads upon the domestic happiness of
married people after the first love, (usually fugacious,) if not,
perhaps, a second, (always feeble,) has died out, and requires to
be replaced by another sentiment—not always so ready as it
should be to take its place; and, secondly, to benefit Janet

herself by that curious. chemistry of the feelings, whereby our love for others becomes a happiness to ourselves.

> " The hearts of those we love are but as banks,
> Wherein we treasure up our loves, and draw
> Our happiness as interest."

Very good reasons these at one time; but then, unfortunately, such is the mutability of the human heart, and head too, just as if we changed morally, as we do physically, every seven years, no opinion or motive will suit every period of a man's life, and every position of his circumstances. So John Cameron, as he came by and by to see Janet getting into excellent health, began to take blame to himself for not extending the annuity to the two, and the longest liver; and what in his case made his regret the more ingeniously severe, the affliction fed and got stronger upon the very means adopted for reducing it; insomuch as the love and attention of Janet, all quickened by sympathy for his secret sorrow, just went to increase his remorse the more, and he felt, and groaned as he felt, that the Lord was laying His hand upon him for his backslidings from the virtue of his forbears, who wrapped their shivering wives with their plaids, when hunted on the hills and exposed to the mountain storm.

But, bad as all this was, matters grew worse from another cause, which was in some degree extraordinary,—no other than the fact, that John began to have a presentiment strongly and painfully borne in upon him that he was soon *to die.* Not that there was any disease about him, for no pathological symptom, nor any premonitory signs of any kind importing a bodily change as impending over him, could be discovered even by himself. "The spirit sometimes previseth death before the body feels any premonition of his being near;" so writes an old wiseacre. Certain it is, at least, that even Jenny's keen eye could detect nothing to cause any apprehension that her saintly master was in any degree changed, except in being older, from what he was. His appetite was still adequate to the big cog, filled by Jenny's own hands, nay, as "yape" as ever it had been. He could walk as well and as far as formerly; and as for his spiritual exercises, formidable as they were in his wrestlings with the Evil one, they evinced no want of fervour, unction, intonation, or action. Neither could he himself attribute the presentiment to the regret he felt in having taken advantage of his wife in the matter of the policy, for he could trace no connexion between a moral feeling, even with so good a cause for it, and any threatening of a physical change in his bodily economy, naturally tending to suggest any such extraordinary notion as that he would not be long an inhabitant of this sinful world.

Yet so it was; he *felt* this connexion, yea, his selfish act was, he thought—no doubt superstitiously, but still not the less really—about to fructify far sooner than at one time he had any fear of, and that, too, in a manner secret and mysterious, without bodily sign or note. Is it not true that there are secret retributions that work within us, and are known only to ourselves? Certain at least it is, that John kept all this to himself; not wrestling with the enemy as his forefathers did with Satan, but rather giving in to the conviction, as if it were a punishment imposed by God which he was doomed to bear all the while, that the thought of leaving Janet penniless was terrible to him.

But, as all of us who have any experience know, there is often a something in the affairs of life that turns up for our weal or woe in the very heart of occurrences apparently altogether independent of these occurrences, and which we might justly call a phenomenon. And so it was here; in explanation whereof we require to state that the house occupied by our Cameronian family consisted of three rooms—one for the master and mistress, one for Jenny, and a kitchen. Now, it so happened that the last of these apartments and the second stood in the relation to each other of many couples in the world—the one of which having more light, and the other less, than is needed. In which cases in the moral world nature provides an accommodation whereby the less illuminated party gets some light from the other; and the builder of this domicile, following the good example, had made a partition window whereby Jenny's room got a portion of what it so much required from the kitchen, where the worthy trio more generally sat. All which being understood, we go on to say that on a certain evening Jenny had gone out—not, we are authorised to say, on the errand of another old-light Jenny, known in song, to bring home a " strapping youth "—only to purchase some of that simple fare, at the time called " friends of the people," for the supper of the homely, and, but for the state of John's conscience, happy family. Meanwhile Mrs Janet Cameron was in Jenny's room, with a candle, having of course, in John's hearing, carefully shut the door when she entered. To all this John had paid wonderfully little attention, the more by reason that he was at the time trying, with all his powers of dialectic subtlety, to elaborate and bring forth a conclusion whether Jenny Geddes or Clavers was the greater warrior ; and feeling inclined to put a question to Mrs Cameron on the subject, he naturally recurred to the sound of the closing door as an impediment to the gratification of his purpose. So he turned naturally enough round to the partition window — *hui ! quantam fenestram ad nequitiam patefeceris*—and looking through, saw Mrs Cameron on her knees before the muckle kist, busy counting what John could easily see were real gowden guineas. Acute man as John Cameron was, he could not fail to detect that Janet kept a little bank, that is, a purse, made, according to the fashion of saving housewives of the time, out of the leg of an old stocking, deprived of the foot and tied at both ends with a garter—a

peculiar form of hoarding or laying up for an evil day much in
favour in Scotland, and so far, we are bound to say, different
from the act of the miser, that it has been known many a time
to be the means of rescuing a poor family from the ruin
brought on by paternal improvidence.   Nor is the custom, so
creditable to the economical prevision and provision of our
good Scotch dames, done away, for it is only the form that is
changed, the modern savings banks being well known to be
more resorted to by wives and mothers than by husbands and
fathers.

Struck, as he well might be, by so strange an apparition,
John sat for a time with his brain at a dead stand ; but no
sooner did his thoughts begin to work than he felt himself
precipitated into a monologue :—"She that is married careth
for the things of the world, but verily, had she been a Philis-
tine, she couldna mair effectually have been delivered into
my hands."   Beyond which words the stern Cameronian said
nothing ; nay, to have seen him afterwards when Janet and
Jenny fell to settling the change, one would have been assured
that he had not an idea in his head in addition to the one or
two that usually found so much space in that capacious organ
to swell into the enthusiasm of religious metaphysics.   Enough,
surely, for the time, that he saw it was his concern to inquire
into how this secret affair stood—for was not the money his
own *jure mariti* ? (the only bit of Roman law that ever, in
Roman words, got down into the understandings of the common people.)   And however well pleased he might be to think
that Janet had been so considerate as to take care of herself,
he could not view with any satisfaction the idolatry, in his own
house, of a Cameronian Rachel sitting upon the images—
reflections which, however sincere, did not by any means
interfere with his resolution to see those images with his own
eyes, to handle the same, yea, to count their number.

Nor was it long before he procured for himself satisfaction

on this point, for Janet one day left her keys by mistake on the mantel-piece of their own room, and Jenny having been fortunately at the same time out, he got access to the little bank, and counted with his own hands no fewer than fifty-eight of these golden pieces. That he looked at them both "amazed and curious" we need not doubt, nor if we had said that he actually "glowered," would we have used a word unfitting the extraordinary state of feeling in which he found himself. But we are to keep in view that Mr Cameron was not the kind of man to be satisfied with the mere sight of a glittering bawble, or with the satisfaction which gold contrives to vindicate amidst the religious reflections of vanity. He could, like other good Christians, hold a Bible in the one hand and a purse of gold in the other; and why not, if that other hand is otherwise unoccupied? and if nature did not intend that a man might hold by two things at the same moment, why should he have two hands? Good enough logic, as the world goes; and so it was felt by John Cameron to be necessary as well as decorous to turn this wonderful discovery to some practical account, connected with the prevailing tendency of his thoughts and feelings. In reference to which latter, we are to remember that he was, at the very moment, under the presentiment that he was soon to die—an idea or feeling which had become a ruler in the kingdom of his mind, conducting all its workings, and regulating all its desires, even as an engrossing passion which absorbs and turns into its element every mental act and aspiration. Nor could he get quit of that as part of the contemplated event, which shewed him, every hour more painfully, the situation in which he had placed his wife, to whom he stood as a debtor, unable to pay even a penny in the pound. And then the contemplated years of her privations when he was gone! why, they were perfect agonies to him. Against all which thoughts it mattered but little that Mrs Cameron stood to him also in the relation of debtor, even in the said fifty-eight guineas, constituting the hoard she had laid up for an evil day. No doubt that money was his; but who knew that Janet did not intend it for him in the event of her predecease?—a thought that went sharp to his heart and aggravated his remorse for the manner in which he had treated her in the matter of the annuity.

But man's ingenuity is never so good as when he is under an obligation to ameliorate his pains; and so, amidst his meditations, it occurred to him that he might appropriate the hoarded sum and apply it as a premium for an insurance on his own life, (so soon, according to his presentiment, to clos·) whereby he might leave his beloved Janet six hundred pounds, or even eight hundred pounds, to support her and Jenny after he was gone. No sooner had he examined the merits of this expedient than he brought his hand down upon his knee with a slap, which implied a Cameronian purpose. Difficulties there were, no doubt, in the way; nay, one of the most formidable that could be conceived,—no other, indeed, than a stern, ingrained hatred on the part of Janet Cameron herself against all forms of life assurance—a subject on which the two had had arguments only a week before, and which may be supposed was rendered desperate when it is known that Janet's objections were affiliated to religion.

"Man's life," as Mrs Cameron said, "is the gift of the Lord. He gives it as an awfu' mystery, and He taks it again as nae less a fearfu' thing. The dry bones lay in the valley, but even the prophet couldna blaw into them the breath of life. And will man," she said, "chaffer and huckster and bargain with his fellow-creature, as if his life were his ain, and he could settle it just as if it were a bit of auld furniture?"

To which strange speech Mr Cameron replied—

"They dinna chaffer about men's lives," said he. "They say only that if it should be the will of the Lord to remove us out of this evil world, men will, for a consideration, help to relieve the sorrows of the bereaved, be they widows or be they orphans."

"Ay," rejoined Janet, briskly, "but it plays right into the hands o' the auld enemy the deevil. It is a temptation, John, to the unbelieving spirit, which is ever ready to jump at the clink o' siller. But," she continued, "it's mair than even that, for it is a mistrusting o' God's providence and mercies, as if you should say to me, I have nae faith in His providence, and can provide for my widow better than He can."

And Janet paused to see what effect she had produced; and finding John's eye a little more vivacious than it should have been in so serious an affair, she resumed with increased fervour:—

"Did Methuselah insure his life, think ye? or Mahalaleel, or Enoch, or Lameth? Ay did they, but it was in the office o' God's mercy, and the only premium they paid was faith." Then getting a little screamy, "Were there ony insurance offices mentioned in the covenant o' works? I trow no; and whaur in this wicked world will ye find a real saving assurance but in the covenant o' grace?"

At which stage Janet seemed to have got so deep that she could not drag out her foot for another step, and so she paused while John sat meditating a reply. In the meantime Jenny, who had heard the argument, evidently wished to have a share, but then it was only to bring out her no small wonderment that there were no women mentioned in the Bible as having liv l a thousand years or so. Whereupon John, who was somewhat nettled at being beaten in dogmatic orthodoxy by a woman, muttered, in reply to Jenny, that a woman's tongue could not, unless it had been made of iron, have held out for a thousand years; whereby he got quit of that old question of the matriarchs, which has gravelled pretty deep thinkers. An interlude this which enabled Janet to resume the argument.

"Besides, it's a lottery," said she; "and lotteries are the temptations o' Satan."

"The Israelites divided the land of Moab by lot," cried John, with an inward chuckle of triumph at finding Janet at fault in her Bible knowledge.

All which John remembered; but he was satisfied that though he got a partial advantage he did not conquer, and he behoved to have recourse to some other reason to justify the scheme he had propounded to himself. Nor was he here under any difficulty, because nature, being as prolific of reasons as of maggots, was not slow to help him, and that too by a weapon taken out of Janet's own armoury. Why, was it not plain, from Mrs Cameron's own tied stocking, that she was in favour of assurances, insomuch as that very article was an insurance in a small way? And so Mr Cameron might surely have no great difficulty at least in the propriety of doing that very kindly thing for Janet, to the extent of six or eight hundred pounds, that she had done for herself or him, to the extent of fifty-eight guineas.

The main objections, viz., Janet's scriptural scruples, were thus easily disposed of; and as for the right of appropriating the hoard, he felt no difficulty whatever, because it was his own by fact and law; and then, to crown all, was he not to lay it out for her advantage after his presentiment had wrought out the prophetic feeling by his death? All which sounded with the true ring of honesty and benevolence. But there remained the fact of this very presentiment as a deception if he concealed it from the office, and a barrier if he made it known. Why, was not John Cameron an honest man? To be sure he was, and so away he went on a certain day to Mr Henderson, the agent of the only insurance company in the city at that period.

"I am come on business," said he to that gentleman as he entered the office.

"It's not pay day, Mr Cameron," replied Mr Henderson.

"I know that, sir," rejoined Mr Cameron. "You are in

the habit o' paying me for *living*, but I am come to bargain with you to pay me for *deeing*. In short, sir, I want to get my life insured for the sake o' Mrs Cameron."

"And little objection there can be to that," replied the agent. "You are hale in constitution, and that is all we look to. But are you sure you can manage the premium, which, at your age, will be heavy?"

"I dinna intend to pay it lang," was the dry answer.

Whereat the agent opened very widely his eyes, and seemed as much puzzled as ever he had been by a calculation of chances.

"Yes, for I'm an honest man," resumed John; "and I tell ye right plain and down-plump that though I am as hale and healthy as ever I was in my life, I feel a strong presentiment that I am no to be lang on this side o' Jordan. Yea, sir, it is as true in this case as it is in the other—' He that believeth hath the witness within himself.' And what's mair, sir," he added, "this is the very reason o' my being here this day."

Whereat, to John's great wonderment, the agent laughed right heartily the while he looked at the square-built son of the old hillmen, who disdained deception even in the midst of their sore persecutions. And having finished his laugh—

"We put no value on presentiments," said he, "unless the doctors can trace them to disease of the liver or hypochondria, and I see nothing of that kind about you. But you will be examined by the medical men, and unless they can see more than I can, I have little doubt you will pass muster."

"Very well," replied John; and having appointed a day whereon to undergo an examination, he returned home, ruminating as he went as to what might be the consequences of all this rebellion against the authority of his wife.

But as ruminations, whether physical or moral, generally end in the detrition of what is objected to them, so John's resulted in his being more stanch than ever in his purpose

Thereafter, at his examination, he persisted doggedly in adhering to his statement of the presentiment, and was again surprised to find, as in the case of the agent, the doctors were not moved by it, if, indeed, they were not very much pleased, both with the robust state of his health and the equally robust constitution of his honesty.

" Weel, weel," said Mr Cameron, still determined to make sure work, " ye may pass me if ye please; but I just tell you again, as I told Mr Henderson, that I hae little chance o' paying the company mair than a premium or twa at the furthest.   At the same time, I offer ye my heartiest assurance that I will live as lang as I can, yea, I will remain on this side o' the vail as long as the shewbread of Janet's weekly stews will enable me to cling to life and the comforts o' the bodily tabernacle."

" But you may eat too much, Mr Cameron," rejoined one of the doctors, laughing, " and that would be as bad as eating too little."

" ' For meat thou shalt not destroy the work o' the Lord,' " replied John; " yea, ' all things are pure, but it is evil in that man who eateth with offence.' "

And with these assurances Mr Cameron was passed.   All easy enough; but the next step of his progress, to carry off the contents of the stocking, did not seem so very easy, if it was not extremely formidable, for he had scarcely ever before known Janet leave the keys of her treasure behind her.   Indeed, to all appearance, it was vain to think of waiting for any such chance as he had enjoyed on the former occasion; and as for forcing the kist, it was one of those old sturdy safes which seemed to have been made and clasped to defy the fingers of Clavers and his troopers.

It is surely good to know the worst of a thing before you measure your resolution; and John, taking the advantage of the *c nsilium in nocte*, even when he was lying alongside of the unconscious Janet, came to the conclusion that he must fail in his grand enterprise altogether unless he could stealthily extract the keys from under the pillow of his wife, and furtively entering the room where Jenny slept, might trust to the chance of escaping her observation, or, in the event of being discovered, bind the neophyte over to religious secresy. So, resolved at last on this only alternative, Mr Cameron waited for a moonlight night, as ever did the Border children of Laverna in the good old times of black-mail and quey-harrying. And the silvery queen, so propitious to love and theft, having come round to that part of the heavens wherefrom she could send a beam into the window that supplied light at second-hand, as we have said, to the room where Jenny slept, John got up quietly, albeit it was in the dead of the night, leaving Janet in all the luxury of a snore, as deep (if not so musical) as if she had been engaged in singing the "Auld Hunder," secretly removed the keys, groped out of the room—listening attentively as he moved; and at length, and after some false turns, got to the kist, which stood nearly opposite Jenny's bed. He then listened to catch the deep breathing of the other sleeper, and having satisfied himself that she was as sound as her mistress, he applied the key, opened the chest, abstracted the gold, and—fatal backsliding!—stuffed an old napkin into the stocking to give it the appearance of being unrifled. But, ah! John Cameron, "the security of the wicked is even as a reed that breaketh under the hand." No sooner had he finished his operations by locking the chest, than a voice saluted his anxious ear.

" Is that you, Maister Cameron ?"

" Ay, Jenny lass," replied he, in something of a loud whisper, " ken ye onything ?"

" Brawly, maister," said Jenny, clearly enough indicating that she had been awake all the time, and that her deep

R

breathing had not been exclusive either of deep hearing or deep thinking.

"Weel, then," said John, "tak ye that," (putting one of the guineas into Jenny's hand,) "and say ye naething, lass, but just think o' the text, 'Lay not up for yourselves treasures upon earth, where moth and rust doth corrupt, and where thieves break through and steal.'"

"Amen," replied Jenny.

"Hush, nae mair," rejoined John. "Read the morn the chapter on the eight talents."

"There's nae fear o' me," replied Jenny.

And thus certified, Mr Cameron sought his bed, deposited the gold in a safe pocket of his clothes that lay on the chair, replaced the keys below the pillow of his wife, lay down, and long before he fell asleep began (we are sorry to say) to snore so immoderately that Janet awakened in a fright, which, on going off, left her well pleased to think that her dear and well beloved John was not going to forfeit his annuity by a fit of apoplexy.

Thus far successful in his "nefarious virtue," Mr Cameron on the subsequent day, but not before he had studied Jenny's face, and found the muscles delicately poised into exquisite negativeness—even into that expression of seriousness which, with the exception of those necessary cases where defensive virtue must resist the aggressions of unjust suspicions, is, we fear, the great sham of our present world—repaired soberly and resolutely to the office of Mr Henderson, paid down in Janet's gold the first premium of an insurance for the sum of six hundred pounds upon his life, presentiment notwithstanding, got his policy, and laid it past in an old cabinet of which he kept the key, and where his bond of annuity had been for a good many years.—All which thou, John Cameron, hast done from a royal sense of what is honest, just, and prudent; but thou shouldst have known that the right which is just demands more than the motive which is honest—more than the uprightness of the action, even the *manner* of action, in the face of man, that nothing shall be hidden, nothing secret, nothing to take the good by surprise, nothing to gift the wicked with an opportunity.

But John Cameron did not so apostrophise, however useful it might have been for him, while as yet there was good time and to spare for him to have redeemed the sterling honour of his sect. Then, as we all very well know, the want of sun-illumined openness is the very opportunity of fear—that power which has made more than gods, insomuch as it has made self-tormenting devils. And so our Cameronian began to take on painful apprehensions more and more as the days passed, till it became, hour by hour, and minute by minute, more probable that Janet Cameron would wish to delight her eyes with a look of that "treasure upon earth" which she had so industriously and with so much self-denial laid up, not for the moth and the rust, not surely for such a thief as her own husband, but for the evil day which comes to the improvident. So it came to be that he was engaged every moment in watching the faces bo'h of Janet and Jenny, in the latter of which there was a gravity approaching to terror, in the former the calm repose of a conscience "void of offence to God and man." Yet all this watching was mere supererogation, and none know this better than they who are under fear, for the discovery he so much dreaded would assuredly be known by signs and tokens requiring more for their adequate conveyance than the motion of eyes or the evolution of looks. But, however all this may be, certain it is that his restlessness increased to such a degree, that, in order to procure for himself some temporary refuge and relief from this insufferable condition of anxiety and apprehension, he resolved on a visit to a brother Cameronian who lived at some distance in the country, and to whom so devout a man as John Cameron could not fail to be agreeable, were it for nothing else than the opportunity it afforded him of satisfying himself by the test of so genuine a Lydian stone that all the Cameronians were in the scroll of the Approbates. Nor could this be a lesser luxury to our member of the limited fraternity, whose still prevailing sentiment whispered to him that he was not far from heaven, while his fears told him he was not far from earth. And in so far as he might thus escape the first sounds of the great thunderburst, it was assuredly well for him that he had formed and executed his purpose; for no sooner had he put it into execution than Janet Cameron made the terrible discovery that her money was gone.

Yet we doubt if we have here used a proper expression, for of bursts in the ordinary sense of human passion Janet Cameron was altogether incapable, for the reason that her surprise ran right on into stern prudential energy. No doubt she was robbed; but she was not, nay, she could not, have been robbed by her husband; for how was it possible to suppose that John Cameron, a great shining light in a world of darkness, could snuff out his own candle, even though it had been a farthing one? But where was Jenny? Alas! poor Jenny, having heard the fearful sound of the keys, and the still more ominous creaking of the lid of the big kist, had fled into a neighbour's house to escape from the wrath to come. But was there not her own trunk at the side of her bed? an object which came as naturally into the red and searching eye of Janet as the image of its possessor did into her mind. Then it so happened that that trunk was open; for such innocence as Jenny's —even taking into account the small taint of resetting—feels only that fear which shudders before unjust reproof. And Janet, after a short search, found the very guinea which John had given to his handmaid. Yes, that guinea was laid neatly in a corner beneath a sacramental token, which, though made of lead, was more valuable to Jenny than even the guinea which was made of gold. But this superposition was in Janet's opinion a terrible aggravation, insomuch as the symbol of grace was made the cover of the wages of sin ; and Janet, having made this discovery, sat down upon the trunk in stern meditation.

" At length," she monologised, " the evil day o' the house o' John Cameron has come, when our handmaiden has done evil in the sight o' the Lord. Yea, she whom I trusted even as I would have put faith in the offspring o' my ain loins, has proved a Jezebel in the house o' her master. I will deliver her into the hands o' Midian seven years."

Which gravely delivered words were simply the expression of a relentless nature hardened by a peculiar theology, better understood in its threats than in its promises, in its punishments than in its mercies ; and, in place of relieving the heart of the utterer, they rather added to a firmness of purpose which was one of the characteristics of her race. Deliberately, if not slowly, she rose from her seat, put the fatal coin into her side-pocket, dressed herself in her mankey gown and red plaid, all as carefully, if not solemnly, as if she had been going to her special tabernacle. Thereafter she set out for the office of Mr John Gibson, the procurator-fiscal for the city. That gentleman she saw, and the consequence was, that on that same night Jenny Cameron was lodged in jail on a warrant which charged her with abstracting theftuously and feloniously a sum of money from a locked chest belonging to Mrs Janet Cameron, her mistress. We need hardly say that the news spread wherever there was one of the sect, for they were all well known to each other, and the espionage they exercised among themselves was more a fear of being touched in their tender part than a wish to detect an offender. But the case was such as to rouse peculiar fears where the prosecutor was the wife of a shining light in their congregation, besides being herself one of the special elect, and the supposed culprit was, in her humble way, a privileged daughter of the sanctuary, as much beyond the suspicion of evil as any spotless lamb of them all.   One thing was at least certain in the minds of all of them—that an impossibility had been set up even by the Evil one himself, as a thing that was not only possible, but real, and it behoved them to gird up their loins and take up the sword of Gideon ʳo defend themselves against the machinations of the enemy ; the consequence of all which again was, that the sympathy for the innocent prisoner was more a selfishness in themselves than a generosity towards their unfortunate sister.

All which could not stop the course of justice.   On the following day Jenny Cameron was put under examination, but, as might have been expected from a Cameronian maiden, all the ingenuity of the fiscal could extract nothing from the prisoner which could tend—not of course to criminate herself, for she had committed no crime, nor to implicate her master, for he was nearly as guiltless—but even to elicit the real circumstances of the transaction, or in any way to clear up what seemed to be a mystery.   She refused steadfastly to tell how she came to have the guinea in her trunk, denying firmly that she had taken it out of the chest belonging to her mistress. That trunk, she declared, she had never opened.   The prosecutor, as may easily be supposed, was not satisfied ; no more, as we may as easily conjecture, was Mrs Janet Cameron ; and the culprit, as she was so fairly, even by her so determined resistance to question, and her refusal to tell what she must to a certain extent have known, presumed to ʰe, was remanded for further examination.

In the meantime, John Cameron himself had been sent for by Janet to come to town instantly, for the purpose of vindicating the rights of his spouse, who had, as she said, been robbed of a large sum of money by no other than the saintly Jenny.   Nor did she fail to take especial care to let her husband know how she had accumulated the pose—how she haʳ guarded it all for his sake and her own—and how she had been so cruelly deprived of it. All which would, in all likelihood, have brought a smile into the face of honest John, if he had not by God's grace been a Cameronian ; but as it was, the result behoved to be very different. The affair, so much dreaded by him, had taken a turn even more critical, formidable, fearful than he had in his most apprehensive moments anticipated. He had committed himself; and even the self-imputed righteousness of the man rendering it impossible for him to make a clean breast of what, in the eyes of the world, even in those of his congregation, and surely in those of his wife, must have appeared rather a virtue than a crime, called up all the doggedness of his nature, and confirmed him in the historical obstinacy of his peculiar race. The climax to which matters had arrived claimed precedence over his apprehensions, and he came to town determined to fight out the cause which he had, for the sake of a consistency in religious character, espoused, even to the death. We are here describing a particular case, which is but a sample of a class consisting of many where a recedence of two steps back would save many successive plungings into pitfalls, nay, eventual destruction, and where a candid confession, with nothing to be ashamed of but a little inconsistency, would render impossible a complication of toils in which the victim perishes.

At the second examination of Jenny the master of the house accordingly appeared, and again Jenny displayed the same resolution to save the man whom she considered to be the chief of God's chosen ones of the earth. All which was just what Janet had reason to expect, and which, too, she could bear so long as she thought—and how could she doubt?— that her husband stood by her in defence of her rights and his own, yea, of God's justice and Cameronian purity ; but when she observed that John's manner, words, and looks were all in favour of Jenny, she began to fear that he was in a secret and unholy league with her servant,—a conclusion which seemed all but confirmed by the conversational eye of Jenny herself, as she looked at her master with all the confidence and kindliness due to a friend and protector. The consequence of all this would soon become apparent, nay, it emerged almost on the instant when the suspicion flashed through her mind; whereupon the unrelenting spirit which had prompted the harsh step whereby Jenny was laid hold of, and which might have been softened and ameliorated by a due and mediatorial participation taken by her natural protector in her defence, drew aliment and strength from the apparent concert. Her increased persistence was exhibited in the additional grimness of her hard, iron-bound countenance and grating voice, while terrible looks flared on the face of the male reprobate. On the other hand, John resisted, with the solemn gravity of his natural character, far as he was from any thoughs of retaliation, for he was conscious that Janet had a fair plea, and it is not improbable that he pitied her while he still loved her. But, alas! he had elected his course; and when was it that a true Cameronian made an acknowledgment that he had diverged a hair's-breadth from the direct path of duty? Meanwhile, Jenny was as impregnable as ever; and when the fiscal seemed weary of his efforts, John stood up.

"I have borne this ower lang," said he. "I am master o' my house; and, so far as law gaes, the money in that house is mine, and nane but mine. I needna tell ye that Janet Cameron's rights extend nae further than her weel-thumbed Bible, and her paraphernalia; and that, therefore, she has nae lawful presence in this room as a prosecutor of this innocent young woman, nae mair than she has to prosecute me, her lawful husband and protector. I now, therefore, solemnly avow, by all the pledges o' a standing covenant, that Jenny Cameron is as innocent o' this crime as was the bairn under the ju.'gment o' Solomon o' the lee o' its false mother. I bring nae charge against her; and I now demand, in the name o' eternal justice, that she be delivered frae her enemy."

"But the law must be satisfied," said the fiscal. "We have some evidence here, and some presumptions; money has been stolen, and a part of it has been found in the trunk of the prisoner."

Now was Janet's time, or, rather, her time had passed already, yet she shewed no precipitation as she rose solemnly from her chair.

"Presumptions, indeed," said she, in very grave and deep accents. "John Cameron, wha has lived with me for thirty years, and wha now pleads the cause o' my servant against his lawful wife, maun shew how Jenny Cameron came to possess this guinea, which I can prove to have been amang my money in that kist."

"And you *will* be satisfied," replied the husband, in words equally grave. "It was I, John Cameron, wha gave Jenny that guinea."

"And was it one of those in the woollen purse?" asked the fiscal, as he now begun to think that the ice was broken, and some clear, though very cold water was about to come.

"That nae man in this kingdom has a right to ask," replied John; "and to nae man will I answer, ay, were he as great and powerful as ane o' the judges of Israel."

Whereupon the light in Janet's eye, which had been increasing in intensity, flared more strongly than ever in the face of her husband, who, as he sat down, met the fiery gaze—well qualified to scorch and harden—with one equally stern, as if he had made up his mind to the last result, irrespective of the love that yearned in his heart. But, meanwhile, the fiscal was still after his duty.

"Your statement, Mr Cameron," said he, "is quite sufficient for us. Until you explained how the guinea came to be in the young woman's trunk, the law had its rights no less than Mrs

Cameron ; but you have explained the only available presumption which appeared against the girl, and we, as a matter of course, are bound to discharge her."

"And I," said Janet, as she again stood up, and again looked at her husband with the same expression of severe gravity—"and I discharge her too, and that for ever. For what communion is there between righteousness and unrighteousness, yea, the Spirit o' the Lord and the spirit o' Satan? From this time forth I declare that Jenny Cameron is nae servant o' mine."

" The which ye have nae power to do," added John, "nor will ye, sae lang as I have the rule o' my ain house. Janet Cameron," he continued, as the gloom gathered on his face, betokening an intention to rivet what he had to say with the hammer of Scripture, "you forget in what case Jenny Cameron stands. She has been taken up on suspicion o' a crime by the men o' the law, and she has been absolved. We maun abide the judgment. 'This is the covenant I will make with the house of Israel. I will put the laws into their mind, and write them in their hearts.' Were we denying the spirit o' mercy of which we ourselves stand so muckle in need, to cast off our handmaiden in this the hour o' her great need and utmost extremity, yea, even as if we had judged her and found her awanting, it would be imputed as a sin unto us, and, mairower, it would ruin the puir orphan for ever in this world. That canna be—that winna be. Jenny Cameron," he added, as he looked kindly, and you might almost say with the smallest portion of the moisture of pity suffusing his gray eyes, "ye gae hame with us, even as one who has regained her honest repute and guid name, and will keep it pure and unspotted, ay, as the snow that lay in the valley o' Salmon."

A screed this which seemed to make considerable inroads on the patience of the officials, by this time anxious to get quit of a case apparently of domestic disagreement; and so the fiscal interfered.

" You will settle this better yourselves," said he, " when you get home."

A remark which ran right against the grain of Mrs Cameron's resolution.

" It will never be settled there, sir," said she, without the slightest abatement of her sternness. " When Jenny Cameron gaes hame again to my house, at that same moment I leave it, never to return."

And thus the old hill-and-glen spirit was roused once again in the breasts of this once happy couple. So certainly as Mr Cameron had committed himself to the first false step, so truly was he now caught by the elastic cleft stick of his dogged obstinacy; nor from this did he seem to have any power to deliver himself. It seemed as if the sword of Clavers had been replaced by the sharper tongue of Janet Cameron, and while he was fortified by her opposition, so she was confirmed by his, even with bitterness.

" Come with me, Jenny," said he. " Mrs Cameron can come o' her ain motive, yea, when her ain deil bids her; ye canna."

Then leading Jenny out by the hand, he departed. And, to our great sorrow, we have to say that Mrs Cameron, equally determined, took the direction of a friend's house at the far end o. the city. Now, for the first time during thirty years were these two godly people separated—it might be for ever in this world.

And surely so strange an occurrence may excuse a remark, however little inclined we are to moralise in a general way in a story which should tell its own moral. We all know how often it happens that a transaction is to be regretted the more in its results that the alternative by which these might have been avoided comes to be considered as comparatively easy. Yet the explanation is not by any means difficult, for that which is done in passion might have been left undone in reason, and as reason sees, while passion is blind, she can easily discover the means whereby hosts of evils might have been avoided. But what use can we make of the observation so long as it is the law of our nature that the fountain of our emotions is the source of our actions, and while it is playing the reason seated above is darkened by the spray? There is no better definition of man than that which represents him as a regretful and remorseful animal, for no traces of these feelings can be found in the lower creatures, by reason that they have no reason. But it may be said that John Cameron did what he did in calm reason, and never could have been said to be blinded by passion. The remark is not, we suspect, very philosophical, insomuch as obstinacy is so far an emotion that it has been called by a quaint writer, and we think not improperly, a passion frozen *in situ.*

Speculations these which have drawn us away from our story at that point of the separation of the worthy couple, when Mr Cameron had the best opportunity yet remaining to him to have made the easy confession, whereby all would have been mended, and happiness and love and confidence been restored where these Heaven's blessings had so long been. But, unfortunately, even then, and when he had the set-off against Janet of her having, as it were, stolen his money, and been guilty of the deceit of concealing that she had it, he was still, in addition to his natural obstinacy, so deadly ashamed of the mean and furtive manner whereby he had effected his purpose—yea, even that of benefiting the wife of his affections —that he felt he could suffer all, nay, renounce life, rather than make the disclosure. So he let Mrs Cameron depart, without so much as a farewell, or even a kindly look, suggested as that was by the love which still reigned in his bosom, but which for the time was overlaid by the demon of his nature.

In which very unfortunate position, that is, a total separation between husband and wife, the domestic affairs of this couple now stood, without any interference on the part of friends being, even to a small extent, effectual. Nay, so strangely do misfortunes, when the unfavourable powers get fairly the advantage, drift into all imaginable aggravations, even such as cannot be predicated of them by any mortal prevision, that this interference was deemed unseemly, for the strange reason that the goddess of the many tongues sent it belling abroad that the true and secret cause of all this discord among the very darlings of heaven consisted in the fact that Jenny Cameron had superseded Janet in the affections of the holy man. So that it came to be considered a desecration of friendly offices to attempt a reconciliation where all was rotten at the heart. Nor could the church friends of the parties be blamed for this, seeing that Janet herself had taken up the notion. And who, again, could say that she was unjustified in a suspicion, the causes of which stood out in such relief as even to take you by the skirts of the coat, yea, as briers in the way? Surely a strange *bizarrerie* this in a world not yet, we hope, removed from under the kindly faces of the providences, where all the three parties were really good people and stanch Christians. But can we deny that such cases occur every day? or rather, are we not bound—notwithstanding that the harp of our mind seems strung in pre-accord to the symphony of eternal justice—to admit them, not only as possibilities, but realities, as a sure sign of rewards and retributions awaiting us elsewhere, to equalise the unmerited lots of blind mortals?

But even the fact we have here stated did not terminate the ruck of evils. It has been said that insurance offices, in accepting the lives of married men advanced in years, would do well to examine at the same time the health of the wives.

for the chance of the husbands living depends greatly on the lives of the helpmates. And no doubt it seems to be more common for old men to die soon after their wives, than for wives to succumb to the loss of their partners. We generally attribute the disposing cause to grief, but this is only a general and easy way of explaining a mysterious process of moral dismemberment whereby the physical system comes to be affected even unto death. Whether John Cameron felt consequences similar to those following on separation by death, we cannot take upon us to say. Neither do we know that his strange presentiment had any connexion with a premonitory feeling of eternal decay. Yet certain it is, that at the end of nine months after the fatal separation from his helpmate, our worthy Cameronian was found one morning lying in his bed dead, his countenance bearing no signs of his having suffered pain, nor his body any tokens of muscular struggle—all was placid, as if the spirit, in its ascent to heaven, had reflected back on the inanimate body some of the light which shone before it. Thus, as the brethren said, was taken into the membership of the New Jerusalem a very peculiar man, whose virtues were of that cast which, borrowing their steadfastness from constitutional firmness rather than from an educated and enlightened conviction, are so apt to make exceptional escapades among the weaknesses, if not the vices, of our nature.

As soon as Mrs Cameron heard the intelligence, she revisited her old home, yet, according to her character, firmly and sedately, as one on whom even Death in his assaults had no power to call up regret for conduct wherein she still considered herself justified. Yea, in such mood stood that immoveable being before the clay-coloured face of that man with whom she had lived for thirty years. No tears came,—no response of a sigh to memories which usually move those who, in the ordinary business of life, have shewn no tokens of that sympathy which binds together creatures of the same kind. But the character of no one is known until the end, because the potentialities of his nature have not till then been exhausted by the still recurring evolution of causes.

As yet, Jenny was still under the ban. If the look of the dead body could not move the stern advocate of retribution, it was not likely that she would be affected by the attentions of one who had been the cause of such terrible evils. Yea, she repulsed her as one whose name was on the dark scroll, and therefore far removed from the circle of the sympathies of the elect; and, strange as it may appear, Jenny shewed no inclination to explain, now when John was dead, the unfavourable appearances which so powerfully operated against her; wherein she was as true to her nature as her mistress was to hers, or her master had been to his.

And thus passed the first night in this strange house of misfortune and death. Next day introduced Mrs Cameron to the evils of the former, with, in addition, a stronger conviction of the helpless condition in which she was left. She was a beggar,—John's annuity was ended; and the money which she had laid past by pennies, even for that very day of evil which had now overtaken her, had been stolen from her by the very man (for the examination had proved to her that Jenny was a mere accomplice) who was bound by the laws of heaven and earth to have provided for her in the latter days of her pilgrimage. In this condition of mind she thought she would open John's little cabinet to see if there was anything there to promise relief to her destitution.

Thereupon she took the key out of Mr Cameron's pocket, and proceeded solemnly to the repository; opened it; took out John's policy of annuity, alas! now wrought out by death: and then her hand fell upon the document whereby she had been secured in six hundred pounds. At that moment Mr Henderson called, and explained to her, even when she held the paper in her hand, the fact of her husband having effected it for her benefit; and how he had paid the only premium that time had permitted. Whereupon the woman, with an inquiring, anxious look, put a question.

"Was that premium paid in guineas, Mr Henderson?" inquired she.

"Yes," was the answer; "every shilling of it."

Thereafter, on Mr Henderson's departure, Jenny was called by her mistress. She now admitted all that she knew. Could anything be plainer? Did not the full extent of John Cameron's love and affection for her, Janet, shew itself out of ashes and corruption?

Janet now, in these changed circumstances, looked again on the pale face of the dead Cameronian. The fountains burst by the pressure of a new-born sentiment. Yes; tears fell on the face of the dead. Jenny was present, and witnessed this scene of the triumph of nature over conventional hardness. Then Janet turned to her, and throwing her arms round the neck of her faithful and sorely-tried servant, cried and sobbed in the midst of very pitiful ejaculations. And now, in conclusion, we may state that Mrs Cameron's objection to life policies did not stand in the way of her accepting of the six hundred pounds.

THE END.